LETHAL BEAUTY

June 20, 2005

*For De and Dorothy,
with warm regards,
from Charles*

LETHAL BEAUTY

Charles O'Brien

severn
House

This first world edition published in Great Britain 2005 by
SEVERN HOUSE PUBLISHERS LTD of
9–15 High Street, Sutton, Surrey SM1 1DF.
This first world edition published in the USA 2005 by
SEVERN HOUSE PUBLISHERS INC of
595 Madison Avenue, New York, N.Y. 10022..

British Library Cataloguing in Publication Data

O'Brien, Charles, 1927-
    Lethal beauty
    1.   Cartier, Anne (Fictitious character) - Fiction
    2.   Women teachers - France - Paris - Fiction
    3.   France - History - Louis XVI, 1774-1793 - Fiction
    4.   Detective and mystery stories
    I.   Title
    813.6 [F]

    ISBN 0-7278-6184-0

Typeset by Palimpsest Book Production Ltd.,
Polmont, Stirlingshire, Scotland.
Printed and bound in Great Britain by
MPG Books Ltd., Bodmin, Cornwall.

Acknowledgements

I wish to thank Patricia A. Carlson and Sara O'Neil-Manion, who offered expert advice on equestrian issues. I am also grateful to Andy Shelton for his skill on the Internet, to Virginia Leon for her computer services, to Gudveig Baarli for assisting with the maps, to Jennifer Nelson of Gallaudet University for helpful advice on matters pertaining to deafness, and to the professionals at Severn House who produced this book. My agent Evan Marshall and Arlene Bouras read drafts of the novel and contributed much to its improvement. Finally, my wife Elvy, art historian, deserves special mention for her editorial eye and her unflagging support without which the novel would not have been written.

Cast of Main Characters
In Order of First Mention

Comtesse Virginie de Serre: *wife of the Comte de Serre, equestrienne*

Pierre Fauve: *Comte de Serre's valet, pimp, spymaster*

Anne Cartier: *wife of Paul de Saint-Martin, teacher of deaf children*

Micheline (Michou) du Saint-Esprit: *deaf artist*

Albert Bouchard: *painter, member of the Royal Academy of Painting and Sculpture*

Adrienne: *his wife, portrait painter*

Paul de Saint-Martin: *Provost of the Royal Highway Patrol for the area surrounding Paris*

Joseph Hamel: *painter, senior member of the Royal Academy of Painting and Sculpture*

Marc Latour: *Hamel's studio assistant, Michou's friend*

Comte Richard de Serre: *retired army officer, amateur collector*

Domenico Moretti: *Italian art dealer, gallery owner in Paris*

Georges Charpentier: *the Provost's adjutant*

Jules Gillet: *engraver at the Royal Printing Office*

Cécile Tremblay: *widow, Laure Belora's daughter, the Comtesse de Serre's personal maid*

Laure Belora: *wife of Vincenzo, Château Serre's housekeeper*

Vincenzo Belora: *Comtesse de Serre's groom, Laure's husband*

Victoire Fauve: *flower merchant, mother of Pierre and Thérèse*

Thérèse Fauve: *Pierre's sister and partner, brothel madam*

Benoît Fauve: *Serre's stableboy, Pierre's fourteen-year-old son*

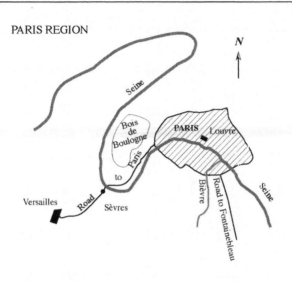

PARIS REGION

Seine

Bois de Boulogne

PARIS Louvre

Seine

N

Versailles

Road

to

Paris

Sèvres

Bièvre

Road to Fontainebleau

Seine

THE LOUVRE DISTRICT
1787

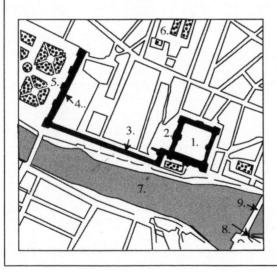

1. Cour Carré
2. Old Louvre
3. Grande Galerie
4. Tuileries Palace
5. Tuileries Garden
6. Palais-Royal
7. River Seine
8. Place Dauphine
9. Pont Neuf

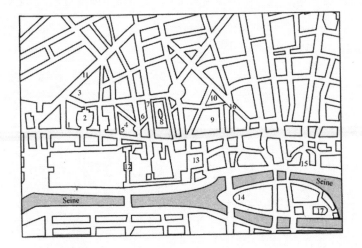

CENTRAL PARIS 1787

1. Residence/office of Paul de Saint-Martin & Anne Cartier,
   Rue Saint-Honoré
2. Place Vendôme
3. Bureau of Criminal Investigation, Rue des Capuchines
4. Abbé de l'Épée's Institute for the Deaf, Rue des Moulins
5. Church of Saint-Roch, Rue Saint-Honoré
6. Comtesse Marie de Beaumont's townhouse,
   Rue Traversine
7. Rue de Richelieu
8. Palais-Royal
9. Central Markets (Les Halles)
10. Church of Saint-Eustache
11. The Boulevard
12. Palace of the Tuileries
13. Louvre
14. Place Dauphine
15. Place de Grève
16. Rue Montmartre
17. Notre Dame

PALAIS-ROYAL 1787

A. Duke's Art Gallery
B. Camp of the Tatars
C. Comédie Française (under construction)
D. Circus (under construction)
E. Café Odéon
F. Café de Foy

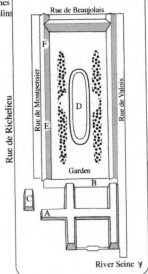

One

Fatal Jump

April 2, 1787

The Comtesse Virginie de Serre rose from her bed in a sweat. A feeling of dread pressed on her chest. She had dreamed of being chained to a post in a dimly lit dungeon. Her husband, the count, had stood stiff and tall, glowering at her, flexing a whip in her face. He raised his arm to strike. Suddenly, a dark-robed figure appeared, thrust a sword through the count's throat. Blood spattered the floor, the walls, her face. She had screamed again and again until the echoes nearly deafened her.

Enough of that! She threw back her head, raked her hands through her hair. The dream lost its power. She thought instead of an invigorating morning ride. It always picked up her spirits. She gazed out the window to the distant wooded hills. The eastern sky had a rosy tint. The weather appeared promising, the air cool and dry. A rising westerly breeze was clearing away the early morning mist that hovered over the ground.

In the dressing room she deliberated, arms akimbo, before a rack of clothes. On this ride she intended to jump her horse over several hurdles. Therefore, she would ride astride instead of sidesaddle. She would be alone, no need to obey fashion's tyranny. She shed her nightdress and put on buff riding breeches and a white shirt.

As she entered her stable, she was greeted by Vincenzo, the groom, in melodic Italian. *'Buon giorno, Contessa.* Your horse is saddled and awaits you in the paddock.' At the far end of the room the stableboy was sweeping the floor. He stopped and stared. Annoyed, she frowned at him until he looked away. She went into the tackle room, put on her boots, black riding coat, and jockey cap.

1

When she emerged from the room, she heard a familiar voice behind her.

'Virginie, would you mind terribly if I rode with you?'

'Domenico!' she whispered. 'We agreed to separate. The count would kill us, if he were to find out.'

'I had to say goodbye this way. It will be our last ride together. I'll return to Paris this afternoon.'

The wild, reckless part of her spirit ached to throw herself into his arms. But the stableboy had turned in their direction again and was watching. He would tell Pierre Fauve, the count's valet. She took a step back. 'Come, if you must. Then Vincenzo shall ride with us.'

Out in the paddock she called to her black hunter, 'Good morning, Blackie.' She petted him, fed him a handful of oats. 'This morning, we shall jump the forest gate. Are you ready?'

The horse whinnied at the prospect of a vigorous run.

The countess climbed into the saddle, urged her mount from the paddock and on to a dirt road to the forest. Domenico followed at a short distance and Vincenzo brought up the rear. They soon left the estate's barns and sheds behind and rode through newly tilled open fields. The smell of fresh earth rose to her nostrils.

She tried vainly to drive Domenico from her mind. The clippety-clip of their horses' hooves worked hypnotically on her and seemed to bring him closer and closer. Soon she could hardly breathe. At first, their days together had been merely an intriguing, frolicsome adventure. Gradually, they had grown fond of each other. Then came secret trysts. These conjured up in her mind rare pleasures she now regretted but would sorely miss. She shivered, though her coat kept out the cool damp morning air.

The forest gate appeared in the distance and helped her focus her mind. To the left and right of the gate extended the rough stone wall. On the far side loomed the forest, spectral in the thin early-morning light. The westerly wind gusted through the trees, stirring their dark rugged mass. To Virginie, still overwrought, the forest seemed alive, and vaguely menacing.

With a powerful conscious effort, she fixed her mind on

2

the gate, urged Blackie to a gallop. The hunter rallied to the challenge, put on an incredible burst of speed. Virginie readied herself.

Suddenly, just as the horse was about to jump, a flock of birds rose from behind the gate in a loud, furious flutter of wings.

Blackie stumbled, struggled to regain his balance, and crashed into the gate with a sickening thud. Virginie felt herself lifted out of the saddle, thrown forward, flying over the gate. In an instant, her head struck a hard, unyielding surface. Sharp pain shot through her body. Then, total darkness.

Two

Michou's Lessons

August 19, 1787

Rain threatened on this warm, gray, cloudy evening. An air of alarm filled the streets of Paris. The police had come out in great numbers, stern-faced, nervous, weapons at the ready. Anne Cartier had just celebrated her twenty-ninth birthday at home and was walking with her deaf friend Michou on Rue Saint-Honoré toward the Louvre palace. Suddenly, Anne heard the clatter of hooves on paving stones. She grabbed her friend and jumped aside. A dozen mounted soldiers rode by, heading toward Pont Neuf.

The two women hurried through the streets to the eastern part of the palace, the Old Louvre. Michou was staying there with an artist, Albert Bouchard, and his wife Adrienne. As the two women approached the palace, Anne's friend seemed to grow preoccupied and anxious.

'Does the tumult at the Palais de Justice bother you?' Anne waved in the direction of the law courts, only a short walk

3

across the river from the Louvre. They were the scene of nightly violent demonstrations.

This was the talk of Paris. The King's ministers insisted that the Parlement of Paris, the kingdom's highest court, had to register reforms and new taxes to ward off royal bankruptcy. The Parlement refused, claiming that only the Estates General, the nation's traditional assembly, could approve new taxes. Thousands of people gathered noisily in support of the magistrates and set fires that could be seen throughout the city's center.

'Since the riots began a week ago,' Michou admitted, signing nervously, 'I've become watchful. I used to enjoy sketching in Place Dauphine behind the Palace of Justice. All kinds of people would pose for me and I met other artists. But now the soldiers chase us away.'

They walked through a passage into the Old Louvre's Cour Carrée. The large square courtyard was enclosed by four tall, connected monumental buildings. During the past century, the Royal Court resided there. When King Louis XIV moved to Versailles, he turned the Louvre over to the Royal Academy of Painting and Sculpture and other royal academies, the royal printers, and many royal favorites and pensioners. It was an island of royal jurisdiction and privilege in the heart of Paris.

'Really, it's not the violence that bothers me most.' Michou's signing became guarded. Two years ago, the Comte d'Angiviller, the royal director of the Louvre, forbade artists to instruct female students in the Louvre. He claimed they distracted the Academy's male students from their work and lowered the serious tone that should distinguish a prestigious academy of art.

Michou pointed to rooms on the first floor of the Louvre's east wing. 'The painters Suvée and David have large studios up there. They ignored the director's order. Their female pupils are young women of good character from respectable families and are instructed apart from the men.' Anne knew that women had lived and worked in the Louvre for decades. Some were even members of the Academy and had studios in the palace. Others were the wives, daughters, and servants of academicians.

4

'Recently,' Michou continued, 'the director, a former army officer, commanded Suvée and David to obey his order. Their protests fell on deaf ears. Today they withdrew all female students.' Michou's eyes began to tear. 'I fear I, too, may be forced to leave.'

'What a pity!' Anne exclaimed.

'Yes, for a painter, it's like being thrown out of heaven. I've been learning so much here.'

Anne and Michou climbed to the first floor of the Old Louvre. The Bouchards' apartment was in the southeast corner. Michou's room off the apartment's entrance hallway was small but comfortable, with a large window overlooking the Seine. The river was dark now, except for boat lights and their reflection on the water.

The room had probably been occupied by a senior servant in the days when the Bouchards could afford one. Only a cook and a maid were left from what had once been a large household. Michou's furniture was shabby and worn but no worse than what Anne had seen elsewhere in the apartment.

In the hallway opposite Michou's room was a door to the painter's studio. Michou signed, 'Shall we go in for a few minutes and look at my latest work? Monsieur Bouchard is away for the evening.' The expression on her face implied that the painter was 'away' most evenings and for no good reason.

Artists' tools and materials littered the room. Canvases of all sizes and degrees of completion were leaning against the walls. On an easel in the middle, a large nearly finished painting depicted a man attempting to kill an enormous sea monster that was about to devour a maiden lashed to a rock.

'Is this new?' Anne hadn't seen it when she visited the studio a few weeks earlier.

'Perseus saving Andromeda,' Michou signed with an assurance born of recent learning. 'In the distance you see people gathered to watch the young woman about to be sacrificed. At the last minute, the heroic young warrior comes with sword and shield, and slays the monster.

'And that's me.' She pointed to the central female figure.

5

'Bouchard began the picture a few years ago, then put it aside. When I came here, we reached an understanding. He would give me lessons if I would pose for him. He can't afford to pay a model. At the beginning, I sat for a portrait study. I sensed he began to like me, then he brought this big picture out of storage and asked me to pose as Andromeda. I put him off at first, wasn't sure of his intentions.'

She smiled wryly, a knowing look in her eye. 'So I approached Madame Bouchard. She encouraged me, said I looked vulnerable like Andromeda, and would fit the role very well. Her husband, she said, finally seemed serious about the painting and would give me the lessons he promised, despite what the director ordered. Madame would sit in the studio while I was posing.'

To encourage her husband, Anne thought, as much as to safeguard Michou's virtue. As Anne gazed at the painting, she felt uneasy. Dark threatening clouds hung over the scene. Through the churning, frothy sea the monster advanced without pity, a huge, long, ugly green-gray winged beast with scaly, armored flanks and a great beaked head. From its nostrils jetted bursts of fire. Its giant claws reached out to seize its prey.

The petite young woman stood helpless on the seashore, her legs and arms tied to the rocky cliff, her naked body arched and twisted in a despairing effort to escape her fate. Surging waves broke at her feet. Anne had no doubt whose body was depicted, but the face was not yet Michou's.

Behind the monster, the slender young Perseus had raised his sword to strike. Anne knew that the myth had a happy ending. Perseus was supposed to kill the monster and marry Andromeda and they would live happily ever after. Yet the painter was telling Anne at least that the monster would brush Perseus aside with a swish of his tail, then devour the young woman.

Anne wondered if this painting opened a window into the painter's soul. He was said to be a troubled man. Did the monster represent the demons that tormented him? Drink, gambling, possibly others. The futility of Perseus's attack could reflect Bouchard's own sense of failure.

6

Fascinated by the artist's remarkable technique, Michou appeared unconcerned about the painting's deeper meaning. She pointed to Perseus. 'That's Jerôme, one of the Academy's servants. He often poses for the students. Bouchard completed Perseus a year ago, then quit painting. But he *is* serious now and may finish.'

'And possibly regain his reputation,' Anne added.

Michou nodded, then led Anne by the hand to a woman's portrait on an easel off to one side. 'I did this.' Michou finger-spelled 'Madame Bouchard' and held an oil lamp for Anne to study the picture.

'A good likeness.' Anne recognized the painter's wife, a plain-featured but intelligent woman her own age, or perhaps a few years older. A furrowed brow, tightly pressed lips, and distressed eyes witnessed to a discontented spirit. Anne knew why. Over the past two months, she had occasionally spoken with Madame Bouchard and sensed that her marriage was in trouble.

'Tell me about her.' Anne pointed to the portrait.

Michou moved it into better light and studied the woman's face for a few moments. 'She's a painter's daughter. Well trained. Does excellent portraits of children and often works on her husband's projects. She has shown me how to prepare a palette and taught me techniques of portraiture.'

'How do you communicate?'

'Awkwardly. We gesture and write notes. She's a tense woman, sometimes impatient with me. I understand, and try to please. The problem is her husband.'

Anne suspected as much, though she hardly knew him.

'He's a little older than us, a talented artist.' Michou explained. 'The son of a great painter, he inherited his father's Louvre apartment and studio. Years ago, he produced large successful historical paintings and was received into the Academy of Painting and Sculpture. His wife told me his future was bright, but he spoiled everything.'

Michou walked over to the unfinished *Andromeda* and inspected it with a critical eye. 'He has worked on it today, added a few highlights to the waves at my feet.'

'What did his wife mean?' Anne persisted. '"Spoiled everything"?'

'She wouldn't tell me and I didn't press her. But early on, I learned that he's poorly disciplined, wastes his talents. He drinks, carries on with other women, and gambles. Fellow artists and patrons distrust him. He passes off his wife's work as his own, doesn't complete paintings that he has promised. His income has declined and he's deep in debt.'

'I understand now why his wife appears unhappy.' Anne met Michou's eye. 'How does he treat *you*?' Anne's gaze shifted to the unfinished but lovely figure of Michou in the painting. Once a poor and neglected orphan, now properly fed and groomed, she had gained poise, and her spare, petite form had filled out. Michou's Andromeda was a fetching victim. Would an irresponsible painter take advantage of her?

'Anne, I know what you're thinking,' Michou replied. 'It's true, he's interested in me, and I look like an easy target. But he's not violent. I can manage him.' Her signing became insistent. 'I also need him.' She explained that she had entered his household in mid-June to expand her skill from miniatures to full-length portraits. Largely self-taught, she was keenly aware of her inability to correctly portray the human form.

She had tried to improve by studying nude figures in the paintings and copies of antiquities in the Duc d'Orléans's collection in the Palais-Royal. To sketch the female nude from life, she had engaged a young maid to pose in Michou's own studio on Rue Traversine.

A good beginning, but she still needed professional training. Bouchard, a member of the Academy, could not take her on officially, but he was willing to instruct her secretly. He didn't have any other students.

To avoid the Comte D'Angiviller's attention, and with the Bouchards' connivance, Michou pretended to be a maid rather than a student. She cleaned brushes, prepared canvases, and did other odd jobs for Bouchard. That trick took her into his studio, sometimes to watch him work, sometimes alone to study his plaster casts of the human form or to paint for herself.

'Thus far,' she concluded, 'the director hasn't noticed me. Most professors and students don't even know I'm here. I just hope it stays that way.' She raised the lantern and looked around the studio. 'Bouchard has made a mess for the maid

8

to clean. I'll start with the brushes.' She picked up one from the floor.

'I'll help,' Anne said, and put on an apron.

As the two women left the studio, Michou turned to Anne and signed, 'You would be surprised how much tension we have here. The Academy has become a dog fight. The artists snarl at one another.'

'I had forgotten,' Anne admitted. 'Now I recall that the Salon of 1787 will open in a week.'

'It's a huge event,' Michou continued. 'Dozens of paintings and sculptures arrive in the great hall every day. Artists quarrel about which pieces will be exhibited and where they will hang on the walls. Students agitate on behalf of their masters.'

'Yes,' Anne remarked, 'I can imagine that many reputations are at stake.'

'Commissions, too,' Michou added. 'Success at the Salon can attract new patrons and make an artist rich.'

'I see,' said Anne. 'Artists must fight for patronage. With so much at stake, tempers will flare up.' She paused to reflect. 'Artists aren't different from other men. A few will try to win by whatever means and at whatever cost.'

Three

The Salon of 1787

August 25

Anne and Michou joined the midmorning crowd that surged up the Louvre's great stairs to the Salon, the most prestigious exhibition of painting and sculpture in the entire kingdom. It opened every two years on the feast of Saint-Louis and lasted for a month. Distinguished living painters and sculptors were

9

displaying their recent works to art critics, art dealers, and the art-loving public.

Michou's face glowed with anticipation. No artist herself, Anne nonetheless caught her friend's enthusiasm. To their left and right they enjoyed a foretaste of the exhibition that had spilled out on to the spacious walls of the stairway.

At the entrance to the hall stood a guard gripping a long halberd with both hands, casually surveying the visitors passing by. Inside the large square lofty room, the sight was overwhelming. Paintings of all sizes covered the walls nearly from floor to ceiling, three or four rows high. Pieces of sculpture stood nearby on green cloth-covered tables.

The two women moved to the middle of the hall, apart from the milling, chattering throng. Paintings in the top row couldn't be appreciated with the naked eye. Anne studied them with her spyglass, sharing it with Michou. While they were reading an entry in the catalogue, a large man approached them.

'Madame Cartier, what a pleasant surprise!' He bowed politely.

'Baron Breteuil! I'm here with my friend Micheline du Saint-Esprit, known to all as Michou. She's a painter and my guide to the exhibition.'

He gave Michou a gracious smile. 'A good guide will be helpful. There is much to see here.' The baron was unusually cordial and expansive today, Anne thought. In the past, he and she had strained relations over her recent marriage to Colonel Paul de Saint-Martin, she a commoner, he an aristocrat. At the time, the baron, who was Paul's relative and patron, had claimed that the marriage would ruin her husband's career. Perhaps in the future—one never knows. For the present, his career depended mostly on the baron's support. And that had not wavered, despite the marriage. Lately, the baron appeared to have mellowed toward Anne.

'Allow me to show you why I am here.' His eyes included Michou in his invitation. He set off across the hall, the two women following him. Anne wondered what could have torn him away from his office. Then she recalled that the Louvre was a royal palace and thus this exhibition fell among his concerns as Minister for Paris and the King's Household.

He stopped in front of a large three-quarter-length portrait of himself. For a few moments they gazed at the painting. Clad in a blue coat and a long cream vest richly embroidered in gold, he stood against a background of the city of Paris that he governed in the King's name. His right hand pointed to his enlightened plan for a hospital, while his left hand touched the sword at his side. His expression was serene and benign.

'Well, what do you think of it?' He addressed Michou without realizing she was deaf.

She easily guessed his meaning and rewarded him with a brilliant smile, then turned to Anne. 'Tell him,' she signed, 'that I would be most proud, were it my work. The technique is masterful. The artist has captured the worth and the dignity of a statesman.'

Just the right thing to say, thought Anne, as she translated to the baron. He gave Michou a thoughtful nod and went on to explain that the painter was Monsieur Menageot, a member of the Royal Academy of Painting and Sculpture. The painter had prudently overlooked his subject's brusque and crafty side.

At that point, several gentlemen approached him with their ladies. Anne winked at Michou. With a bow to the baron, they moved away.

Anne consulted the catalogue again and suggested that they study Jacques-Louis David's *The Death of Socrates*. He was probably the painter most in vogue that year. His painting also was prominently hung at eye level, front and center on the entrance wall.

'Monsieur David has much power here,' Michou signed cautiously, 'and many students. They demand respect for him, shout his praises, claim the best places in the hall for his pictures.'

Politics rules even at an art exhibition, Anne reflected sourly. Then she chided herself for ever thinking it could be otherwise in human affairs.

With her untutored eye she studied the painting closely and agreed that it might deserve its place of honor. As an actress, she was drawn into the picture's theatrical scene.

11

David had depicted the Greek philosopher sitting up on his bed. His right hand reached for the poison he must drink, his left hand pointed to the heavens. The rulers of Athens had condemned him for having dared to lead his fellow citizens in the pursuit of truth. His incessant questioning of received opinions had threatened the interests of powerful men. Many of the common folk hadn't appreciated that he was trying to free them from ignorance. He accepted his fate with noble resignation.

Anne was reminded of a Quaker printer whom she had recently met in Bath. At the risk of his life, he dared to challenge England's commerce in slaves. All those, rich and poor, who benefited from that evil business feared and hated him.

She pointed to the picture and signed to her friend, 'What do you think, Michou?'

'Such beautiful bodies!' she replied, her lips parted in wonder. 'Flesh and blood, frozen in a moment of time.'

To the right of the *Socrates* was a large vacant place on the wall. Anne turned quizzically to her companion. Michou signed that one of the artists, Joseph Hamel, a senior member of the Academy, was usually late hanging his paintings. He was aloof and unapproachable. But she had met him once and had often visited his studio when he was away. 'I've copied the painting that's coming, a beautiful woman's portrait from life. I've also sketched her.' Michou's eyes glittered with a mixture of awe and desire. 'I want to paint like him one day.'

As they watched, the artist Hamel arrived breathlessly. Several paces behind him came a young man about thirty, short and slender, fair-skinned. He and Michou exchanged fleeting glances.

'Marc Latour, Hamel's assistant.' She finger-spelled the names. Latour was nervously leading two porters who carried a large work, covered by a canvas sheet. Another porter followed with an easel.

'A deliberate trick to attract attention,' observed a fashionable, darkly handsome gentleman standing next to Anne. He tapped his gold-headed cane on the floor. 'That's typical of Hamel, an influential academician. No one dares object.' The man smiled, but his remark had a caustic edge that caused

Anne to glance at him. He retreated, apparently embarrassed that he had called attention to himself.

Hamel slowed his pace, engaged the eyes of several patrons and colleagues, bowed to each one in the measure they appeared to deserve. He also took notice of Anne as he passed by and gave her a slight bow. The notoriety of her marriage to Colonel Paul de Saint-Martin had made her more widely known than she cared for.

The painter was a small, energetic middle-aged man. He carried his head high, creating the impression of looking down on people. His bright brown eyes darted like bees flitting from blossom to blossom, quickly sucking in nectar, then moving on. When he wasn't courting a person, he often pursed his lips in an expression of disapproval.

A few months earlier, Anne had met Hamel in his studio and introduced Michou as her consultant in questions of art. Anne was aware that rich women visited the studio when the students weren't working. Hamel wanted to encourage them to commission portraits. Alert to a new prospective commission, Hamel also allowed Michou to visit his studio when it wasn't in use.

His grand entrance completed, Hamel stepped back, chin in hand, examining the empty place on the wall. Impatiently, he ordered his assistant to make sure the picture would fit. Latour dutifully measured the space and nodded to his master. Meanwhile, the picture rested on the easel, guarded by the porters.

By this time, a large, curious crowd had gathered. Before proceeding, the artist turned to a tall, bent, elderly man whom he addressed as the Comte Richard de Serre. From bystanders, Anne learned that he had been a military officer. In his prime, as Anne imagined him, he must have been a commanding figure—thick-browed and hawk-nosed, robust and erect. Now his clothes hung loosely on his spare frame, his eyes sank into dark sockets.

Hamel spoke softly to the count, who nodded gravely. With an elegant gesture, the artist pulled off the picture's cover.

A collective gasp went up, followed by a moment of stunned silence, then by a buzz of agitated voices.

13

'My God!' screamed Hamel, clasping his forehead. He swayed, his knees buckled, and he collapsed in a faint into the arms of his assistant. The count stood stock-still, his mouth half-open in disbelief. Then his eyes narrowed, his right hand gripped the hilt of his sword. 'I'll kill the bastard who did this!'

The painting, Anne quickly learned from Michou, was of the count's late wife, the beautiful woman whom Michou had studied. Anne and Michou drew closer and saw that it had been vandalized. Her head was now a crude, ghastly skull.

'How could this happen?' Anne signed to Michou.

She leaned over the portrait and carefully examined the damaged part. 'I think an enemy has roughly scraped away the original head, or most of it, then painted the skull. It took perhaps ten minutes, and not much skill. He needed only simple tools, a few brushes, and some paint.' She stepped back, for the guard had begun to disperse the crowd.

In the confusion, Baron Breteuil nearly bumped into Anne.

'Someone has defaced Monsieur Hamel's painting,' she told him before he could ask. She repeated Michou's brief explanation.

'Serious business,' he said softly to Anne as he studied the portrait. 'I must speak to your husband.'

'He's at work in his office on Rue Saint-Honoré.'

For a minute the baron continued to stare at the portrait, then cast a glance at Hamel sitting dazed on a bench, and finally gave an order to the assistant Latour. He threw the cover over the painting and the porters carried it away.

The baron turned to Anne. 'I may speak to you later about this.' He bowed to her and strode out of the hall.

In the corner of her eye, Anne caught a flash of gold. The gentleman with the cane had been eavesdropping. He hurried away and was lost in the crowd. 'Did you notice him?' Anne asked Michou.

She nodded. 'He's Monsieur Moretti, an art dealer and connoisseur. Madame Bouchard would know him.'

Anne and Michou moved to the other side of the room. Anne looked back at the blank place on the wall and commented on the obvious fact that the painter must not have

14

checked the picture that morning before bringing it to the exhibition.

'He was busy with several other paintings for the Salon,' Michou explained. 'In his haste, he simply assumed the portrait was in good condition.' It had been ready when she saw it a few days earlier. The painter had kept it in the studio, should he wish to add a few light touches. Michou's face glowed as she described the painting—subtle, complex, truthful, highly finished. She had copied the original head during several visits to Hamel's studio.

'How did you manage to make the copy, Michou? You were only supposed to visit the studio, not to work there. I'd imagine the Comte d'Angiviller would disapprove, if he ever found out.'

'But he won't, unless you tell him.' She flashed a teasing smile, then explained that she had approached her acquaintance Marc Latour. Fortunately, he knew signing—his older sister was deaf. Michou had offered to pose for him if he would let her sketch and copy in the studio while Hamel and the students were away. She wanted to study works about to be exhibited, especially the countess's portrait.

The assistant agreed, persuaded by Michou's great green eyes and innocent, heart-shaped face. 'Perfect model for a portrait à la Greuze,' he had said. 'The studio is empty at Hamel's dinnertime, two to four in the afternoon. Or on Sunday. Come then.'

On several occasions, with Marc looking the other way, Michou took the portrait from its rack, set it on an easel, and copied it for an hour or more. Then she carefully returned it to the rack.

'Could Hamel do the head over again?' Anne asked.

'No,' Michou replied. 'He would need the countess to pose. But she died in a riding accident months ago, shortly after the last sitting. The finished portrait was supposed to be a memorial. Her husband hasn't paid for it yet. Hamel painted the face from life and has no sketch to fall back on. I doubt that he can do it over quite as well from memory. His impressions of her have faded and have bled into other images in his mind. The Serre portrait was one of his finest achievements. He had hoped it would earn him great fame and large commissions.'

While they were discussing the artist, he appeared to have recovered from his faint and had risen on shaky feet. A few well-wishers gathered around him.

Anne beckoned Michou to follow her. 'I want to hear what he has to say.'

Hamel was sipping from a flask of brandy.

'Who do you think did this dastardly thing?' asked someone. Anne translated for Michou, who stared intently at Hamel.

The artist blinked, taking in the question, then flushed with anger. 'Bouchard, of course. Who else?'

Michou started. She had read the artist's lips. Her face grew pale and taut.

'What's the matter, Michou?'

'I need to think about it.' She shook her head. 'Bouchard's a fool!' Without looking back, she rushed from the hall.

Four

Recriminations

August 25–26

Michou's sudden departure left Anne stunned. This was so unlike her friend. Something was seriously wrong. Was she caught up in Bouchard's trouble? To deface the countess's portrait was no prank. If Bouchard did it, he would soon feel the iron fist of the law. Or worse. Anne's eyes were drawn to Hamel, now in a rage, his mouth spraying spittle, as he cursed his enemy.

In need of relief, Anne moved away from the circle of Hamel's sympathizers. When she recovered her calm, she thought of what must be done. Michou would take the extraordinary news from the Salon to the Bouchards and warn them. Monsieur Hamel had publicly accused Monsieur

Bouchard of causing the outrage to the Serre portrait.

Paul also needed to know precisely what had happened. Breteuil seemed certain to have already consulted him. Anne gazed once more at the portrait's empty place on the wall. Unbidden, the Comte de Serre's face surged into her mind, grotesque, twisted by anger. He was staring at his wife's violated image. His menacing oath echoed in her mind. 'I'll kill the bastard who did this.'

He meant what he said. As Anne wandered through the exhibition hall, she overheard remarks about him. He was easily offended and prone to wrath. As an army officer, he had been notoriously jealous of his honor and had ordered severe flogging, the gauntlet, and other harsh punishments, even for minor infractions or for impertinence.

At noon, Anne left the Salon and walked home on Rue Saint-Honoré. Nearing the entrance gate, she pushed the count out of her mind and hastened across the courtyard. She imagined Paul at the desk in his office, watching out the window for her, waiting to hear her account of the scandalous events at the exhibition.

He rose to greet her and they embraced. She stepped back to admire his new uniform, blue coat with red lapels and cuffs, buff breeches. He was meticulous about his appearance. In French society, he claimed, it mattered. What pleased her most were his eyes, a limpid blue, frank and honest, kindly, intelligent. But, she conceded, she was newly wed and still living on a cloud.

He pulled up a chair for Anne, then sat at his desk across from her. 'Baron Breteuil has been here, told me about the defaced portrait at the Salon. I've seldom seen him so distressed. He takes a personal interest in the Academy. This incident puts the institution in a bad light.' He glanced at the pile of papers on his desk. 'As if keeping peace in the countryside between peasants and landlords isn't enough, the baron has put this new case in my hands.'

Anne was not surprised. The Louvre, a royal palace, lay outside the jurisdiction of the Paris police. Paul's ordinary responsibility was for public order in the region surrounding the city. But the baron had previously used him for other

17

cases requiring tact and sound judgment. Paul excelled in both qualities.

And they were needed in this case. A senior member of the Royal Academy of Painting and Sculpture had accused another academician of defacing his work. This was scandalous. And the vandalizing of an expensive work of art was also a serious crime.

'Is there any way to calculate the damage?' she asked.

'Hamel's price for the portrait was six thousand livres,' he replied.

She tried to imagine the sum, almost ten times what a simple artisan could earn in a year.

'Since you were at the scene,' he went on, 'could you add to the baron's observations?'

Anne related Michou's remark. 'She seems to further implicate Bouchard in the crime.'

'She's well placed to know him,' Paul remarked. 'I've sent Georges to take statements from him and everyone else involved.'

'And to secure the damaged painting?'

'For the present, I'll leave it with Hamel. It may eventually reveal its secret, even lead us to the culprit.'

The following morning was clear and sunny, but a cool breeze blew from the north. Anne was glad of the scarf over her shoulders. This was Sunday, when the city lived in a more relaxed rhythm. Fewer carts and wagons. Less shouting and crying. Men and women put on their best clothes and strolled in the streets and gardens. Church bells called the faithful to worship.

Anne walked briskly to the Louvre, concerned about Michou's cryptic remarks as she left the exhibition. What did she mean by calling Bouchard a fool? Had she reason to suspect him?

Crossing the Cour Carrée, Anne saw the familiar figure of a sturdy, older man in a trooper's blue and red coat, Georges Charpentier, her husband's adjutant. Since they first met two years ago, she and Georges had often worked together on investigations.

18

'There you are, Madame Cartier. I was just about to call on you. I need your help.' They withdrew to a quiet corner of the courtyard.

He explained that he had completed the preliminary investigation, with particular attention to Messieurs Hamel and Bouchard. He was pleased to learn that she was on her way to Bouchard's apartment in the Old Louvre. 'You can translate for me and Michou. I also have to question the Bouchards again and madame is shy with me.'

'I know her rather well,' Anne remarked. 'What do you hope to learn from her?'

'Her husband's movements early yesterday morning. Monsieur Hamel has accused him of destroying a painting.'

'I know. Michou and I were at the exhibition when he uncovered it. He made his accusation shortly afterward for all to hear.' Anne cocked her head. 'Why should he suspect Bouchard?'

'Hamel claims they've had disputes in the past and had competed for the Comte de Serre's commission. When Bouchard lost, he became impertinent, called his competitor a snake, a cheat, a puffed-up sheep's bladder. Hamel, on the other hand, had earlier declared publicly that Bouchard's work was far beneath what the Academy expects of its members.'

Anne nodded. 'Then I can understand that Bouchard would be provoked. When could he have taken his revenge?'

'After returning from a gambling den on the Left Bank. A watchman thought he saw someone of Bouchard's size and shape leaving Hamel's studio early in the morning, but couldn't be sure. The studio was open and unguarded from midnight to dawn.'

'Bouchard has denied the accusation, I suppose.'

'Of course.'

They entered the building and climbed a flight of stairs to the apartment. Bouchard himself opened the door and showed them in. He was in his shirtsleeves and paint-stained breeches, his hair a thicket of black tangled curls.

He stared at Georges's uniform, then at Anne. 'Have you joined the Royal Highway Patrol, madame?' He snickered at his witty allusion to her recent marriage.

19

'I have indeed, as you well know, Monsieur Bouchard. By chance, I met Monsieur Charpentier in the Cour Carrée.'

Georges put an end to the exchange. 'Madame Cartier will help me speak first with your wife and then with your maid.'

'Madame Bouchard is at her easel in the studio.' Bouchard left the visitors to fend for themselves in a modest parlor, while he sauntered off to fetch his wife.

She arrived in a paint-spattered smock, a kerchief protecting her hair. 'My husband said, come right away. I don't usually receive visitors like this.' She gestured to her garb, tucked a stray lock of hair under the kerchief. 'What can I do for you?'

'Where was your husband early yesterday morning?' Georges asked gently.

A moment passed while she shifted her weight from one foot to the other. Her eyes were downcast, studying the floor. 'My husband came home from his gambling den a little before midnight and went directly to bed with me.'

'Are you sure he didn't slip out later?'

'No, he didn't leave the apartment until well past dawn. I sleep lightly. He would have awakened me.'

The woman was a poor liar, Anne thought. Her response seemed rehearsed, unconvinced, and she avoided Georges's eyes. Anne felt sorry for her, a wife forced to protect her husband.

Georges kept his opinions to himself. 'That's all for the time being, madame. You may go back to the studio. Please send Michou.'

A few minutes later, Michou arrived, having removed her smock. Anne noticed paint on her hands. Working on Sunday? She used to go to church and visit the Palais-Royal. Painting appeared to have become her obsession.

Georges posed his questions to her in a gentle, matter-of-fact way, Anne translating. Nonetheless, Michou became disconcerted and wary, reluctant to communicate. She indicated only that she had gone to bed early and couldn't be of help.

Anne was surprised. Then she realized that Michou's old fear of the police had surfaced. Almost two years ago, a police inspector had frightened her so badly that she retreated into herself. It seemed she had done it again, though she knew Georges well. He had always been considerate of her feelings.

Her remarks brought a doubtful expression to Georges's face. Anne, too, sensed that Michou was holding something back and resolved to question her friend further when Georges wasn't present.

'What have you learned thus far?' asked Anne, as she and Georges stood in the Cour Carrée, about to go their separate ways. He would not normally discuss a case with a layperson, but he regarded her as a promising apprentice and enjoyed training her in techniques of criminal investigation. She seemed to have an aptitude.

'I've established the basic facts,' he replied without hesitation. He had learned that Hamel's studio was often left unlocked. During the day, he or his assistant Latour were in charge, the students were working there, or servants were cleaning up. At night, a few students usually slept on the studio floor.

But the opening of the Salon traditionally called for celebration. On the previous evening, artists and their patrons gathered for wine in the garden of the Tuileries, the nearby royal palace to the west of the Louvre. This year, the party continued into the early hours of the morning. Hamel stayed to the end, then went to bed and slept late. The Academy's students spent the night carousing in neighborhood wine shops and cafés until dawn. The studio was left unwatched for several hours. The watchmen celebrated too, and couldn't be relied upon to do their duty.

'I shall look into the possibility that one or more of Hamel's students, either drunk or sober, could have taken the opportunity to punish his master. He's reputed to be harsh and demanding toward them.'

'An angry student could be provoked to violence,' Anne agreed. 'But why would he scrape away the woman's face, paint a skull, and leave the rest of the portrait undamaged? I would expect him to slash the canvas to shreds. The vandal seems to have meant to affront someone in a personal

21

relationship with the countess—her husband, for example.'

'I'll ponder your question, madame. If you find the answer, let me know.' He bowed politely to Anne with a teasing twinkle in his eye. 'Good day, madame. Tell your husband I'll see him later.'

Michou knew exactly when Bouchard had come home, as Anne discovered when she found her friend at work in his studio. They sat facing each other on wooden benches, Michou in her painter's smock, dispirited. She regretted her reaction to Georges's questions. They had evoked not only bad memories but also a recent dilemma.

With Anne prompting, Michou explained what she hadn't wished to tell Georges. At two o'clock in the morning of the Salon, Bouchard had entered her room. His clothes reeked of tobacco, a foul product that his wife forbade in the apartment and in the studio. He must have come from the gambling den or from somewhere other than his wife's bed. By the light of a lamp, he gestured plainly enough his passion for Michou. He spoke in the same vein, expecting her to read his lips. She gathered that he was praising her beauty, her charm, her talents.

She had put on her fiercest face and pointed him to the door. He had shuffled out with a sheepish look.

Then what mischief did he commit? Anne wondered. Why would Michou cover his tracks?

Michou appeared to read her mind. 'I worry that a police investigation of Bouchard would expose what I'm doing here— studying art, not serving as a maid. The director would order me out and I would lose this rare chance to become a true painter. Madame Bouchard would also be evicted. What could she do? She would have no home, no studio, no place to work. That would be a great pity.'

Anne leaned forward and held Michou's hands. 'The investigation will go forward whether we like it or not. We shall try to lessen the harm it does to innocent bystanders.'

Five

Questions

August 27

Early the next morning, Anne and Georges met in the Cour Carrée to visit the Bouchards again. Anne had persuaded a reluctant Michou to reveal the painter's visit to her room. Georges couldn't realistically carry out his investigation unless he knew that Bouchard was out and about at two o'clock that morning.

'You look tired, Georges,' Anne observed with concern. His face was lined with fatigue.

'I spent most of yesterday until past midnight checking alibis of Hamel's students. Most of them hardly knew where they had been during the early morning hours of August 25. Too much drink had fogged their brains. So far, I've detected one or two who might hate their master enough to spoil his work. I'll need to investigate them further. One of them is Marc Latour, Hamel's assistant.'

'And Michou's friend,' Anne added, then hesitated and spoke tentatively. 'She wants to see you again about Bouchard's movements.'

Georges merely nodded; he didn't seem surprised or annoyed. Anne felt relieved. She hoped that Michou would be more at ease under questioning than she was last time, even though she might have to implicate her master. And might suffer retaliation. Anne hoped not.

His wife would also have to change her story in light of what Michou would say. She could no longer vouch for her husband's whereabouts in the early hours of August 25. At the end of the day, he was likely to remain the chief suspect.

Madame Bouchard opened for them this time. 'Come in.

23

I've been expecting you.' She seated them in the parlor.

Her eyes were red. Lack of sleep? Guilt? Anne wondered. 'I'll fetch my husband.'

'Let him wait,' Georges said. 'I'll speak with you first.'

She knew what was on his mind, and spoke up before Georges could question her. 'I really didn't expect you to believe what I told you earlier, Monsieur Charpentier. In fact, my husband didn't return home until nearly dawn. And he didn't tell me where he had been. He'll have to explain for himself.'

'That's all I really need from you, madame. I'll speak to your husband now.'

As she walked to the door to the studio, Georges stopped her with a wave of his hand. 'By the way, did you ever hear him threaten to deface Monsieur Hamel's painting?'

'No, sir,' she replied evenly.

Bouchard entered the parlor with a resigned expression on his face. He obviously realized that his wife had taken away his alibi.

'What do you have to say for yourself?' asked Georges, his tone of voice insinuating that he knew all.

Bouchard hesitated for a moment, apparently calculating how much he could withhold.

'Where did you go after leaving the gambling den?' Georges's eyes fixed the painter in an iron grip. 'You weren't with your wife.'

'I roamed through the Louvre, looking for a woman to bed with me.' He fell into an embarrassed silence.

'Yes? Go on.'

'I found a maid I knew and spent the hours till dawn with her.'

Anne held her breath, fearing that he was about to incriminate Michou. For a moment she feared that her friend had not ejected him from her room.

'Where?' asked Georges.

'Near the passage to the Quai du Louvre. She works for the concierge there.'

Anne and Georges exchanged quick glances. The passage

24

was a minute or two away from Hamel's studio. Georges would find the woman. Anne breathed easier. Michou's honor was secure, and she was spared the trauma of an interrogation.

That afternoon, Anne and Michou met Paul at the Salon. He especially wanted Michou for her artistic eye. The two women reenacted for him the incident of the Serre portrait. Its space on the entrance wall was still empty. In a few minutes, according to Marc Latour's message to Michou, Hamel would put another portrait there. Paul wanted to speak to him.

In the meantime, they studied the large painting of Marie Antoinette and her three surviving children that hung directly above Hamel's space. The artist, Madame Vigée Le Brun, had placed an empty cradle at the Queen's side to represent her daughter Sophie, who had died two months earlier. Anne watched Paul, his eyes riveted on the little boy Duc de Normandie on his mother's lap. Searching his features for a paternal likeness, Anne thought. The Queen's enemies claimed the boy's father might be someone other than the King. A likely candidate was Paul's friend the Swedish Comte Axel von Fersen.

A commotion at the entrance distracted them. Hamel was arriving, followed by porters carrying a covered picture. A crowd gathered to watch, and Anne and Paul joined them. Hamel uncovered the painting without a flourish and hung it. His enthusiasm for the exhibition had obviously diminished.

'She's an actress, the wife of a prominent tax farmer,' Paul remarked, pointing to the richly gowned, jewel-bedecked woman in the picture. He turned to Michou and signed, 'What do you think of it?'

She studied the portrait, the concentration creasing her brow. 'Excellent technique, as usual. Dull. Skin-deep. No life in the character.' Though she had signed her reply, she still cast an apprehensive glance over her shoulder. Hamel stood nearby.

The crowd quickly dispersed. Paul took the opportunity to introduce himself and converse with the painter. Anne and Michou joined him in expressing regrets for the Serre portrait's misfortune.

Paul suggested that they move to Hamel's studio, a few

minutes' walk away. The artist agreed with a shrug, then led them through the building into a hallway, paused at an open door to his studio, and looked in. His glance was hasty, pre-occupied, probably a habitual mindless gesture. Due to the Salon, students were away on a short holiday. Their abandoned easels were scattered about the room, empty and forlorn.

Marc Latour, who was painting at a nearby easel, sensed the visitors' presence and looked up. His eyes avoided his master and fixed brightly on Michou. She returned his gaze with a ravishing smile.

Hamel appeared not to notice—he was already moving on. But Anne lingered for a moment and observed the scene. She had noticed Marc and Michou together before, and had concluded they were friends. Now she sensed with a frisson of concern that they were in love. Latour was largely unknown to her. Would he take advantage of her deaf friend? Michou longed for professional training; he was well placed either to help or to abuse her.

At the end of the hallway was Hamel's private office, a large, well-lighted room, tastefully furnished in the style of the reigning monarch. Hamel sat down at a highly polished brown mahogany writing table, while his visitors took seats facing him.

Paul began. 'Has anyone besides the Comte de Serre recently shown *unusual* interest in the portrait of the countess while it was in your studio?'

At first, Hamel couldn't grasp the drift of the question. Many visitors to the studio must have expressed *polite* interest. He seemed to puzzle over what might be considered *unusual*. Finally, he shrugged a shoulder. 'Most visitors came once, looked at the picture for a few minutes, declared it to be beautiful, and left. But Monsieur Moretti studied the painting several times, and asked if it was for sale. I said no, the count wanted it for himself as a memorial to his wife.'

Saint-Martin raised an eyebrow.

Hamel cautioned, 'You should know that Monsieur Moretti, an art dealer, has often visited the Academy's other studios as well as mine.'

'Yours more often than others?'

Hamel took a moment to reflect. 'Why, yes, I suppose he has. Come to think of it, he came to the Serre château several months ago to examine the count's art collection. He watched while I painted the countess's portrait.' Hamel frowned. 'You don't suspect Moretti, do you? He moved here from Italy about a year ago. Knows Italian art better than anyone in Paris. Perfect gentleman. He and I have a good business relationship. And he has no reason to dislike either of the Serres.' Hamel's eyes narrowed in anger. 'That rascal Bouchard is your man.'

'Right, we have him in our sights,' Saint-Martin granted. 'Before we leave, I'd like to study the defaced portrait.'

The artist grimaced at the request. But he went around the table to a picture leaning against the wall. He lifted it on to an easel. 'Here it is. I can barely force myself to look at it.'

When it was displayed in the exhibition hall, Anne had focused only on the damaged head. Now she studied the painting as a whole. The artist had depicted the Comtesse de Serre in a red riding dress and matching tricorn hat, standing before a fence. In the background was a rural scene of horses grazing in a meadow. Her right hand gripped a riding crop. She faced the viewer with hollow eyes. Her ghoulish skull had a sinister aspect. Anne averted her gaze.

At Paul's request, Michou had brought along her copy of the countess's head, a remarkable character study. She had dark brown eyes and creamy skin. Her thick black hair was tied back in a chignon. The mouth was wide, the lips full, the chin firm. This was an energetic, impulsive, and headstrong woman, who could master a powerful horse—or a man.

Hamel had been standing off to one side, ignoring the painting. As Michou placed her work alongside the damaged original picture, Hamel's curiosity got the better of him, and he reluctantly joined the group in front of the easel. His initial reaction, virtually automatic, was to shake his head dismissively. But he finally studied Michou's painting. Slowly his gaze shifted inward to his memory of the defaced original. His eyes widened in amazement.

27

'This is an excellent copy,' he murmured to Saint-Martin, then turned to Michou. 'Did *you* do it?'

She read his lips effortlessly, as it was what she expected him to ask. She grew tense, nodded yes.

Confusion clouded his eyes, then came a frown of displeasure, and finally, a flash of anger. 'I gave you permission to visit my studio, not to copy my work.' He reached for Michou's painting. 'Every piece produced here belongs to me, unless I say otherwise.'

Saint-Martin seized the artist's arm and firmly lowered it. 'Her copy is evidence in a criminal investigation, as is your damaged portrait. I may need them for further study. For the present, you may keep the portrait here. I shall take the copy to my office on Rue Saint-Honoré. Its owner will be determined later. And, by the way, Mademoiselle du Saint-Esprit is working for me on this case. As you have just indicated, she has an excellent grasp of portrait painting, at least the face. I expect you to assist her where you can.'

Hamel stared at the colonel, mouth half open, as if struck dumb. Anne strove to hide her satisfaction, pleased also to notice that Michou hid hers as well. Did Hamel think that he could use Michou's copy to repair the damaged portrait? If so, Michou could bargain for a portion of Hamel's commission.

'We shall leave now,' Saint-Martin announced, then addressed Hamel. 'I would like to speak with Monsieur Moretti. Where might I find him?'

'Just across the river. He lives above his gallery on Place Dauphine.'

The police were still numerous on Place Dauphine. But the rioters had left. Quiet had returned to the area at least in the daytime. Anne and Paul had inquired about Moretti before making this visit. Last summer, he had leased a tall, narrow, old building facing south on the square and opened a gallery on the ground floor. He lived in several well-appointed rooms upstairs. Forty years old and a rich widower, Domenico Moretti was born and raised in Florence, where he also owned a gallery. He traveled often to France and spoke fluent French.

By now, it was late in the afternoon. His gallery was open. A clerk went upstairs to announce his visitors. For ten minutes Anne, Michou, and Paul gazed at prints on display, mostly excellent Italian engravings from the previous century.

The clerk returned and led them up to Moretti's apartment. He greeted them at the door with a courtly bow.

Anne started. He was the gentleman with the gold-headed cane she had seen at the exhibition. His features were even more handsome—and sensual—than she had remembered. He had a fencer's body, lithe and supple. His hair was thick, black, and glossy, his facial features strong and clean-cut. In his dark, smoky brown eyes, Anne sensed powerful, disciplined passion. With a sweeping glance he examined her, his eyes dancing with pleasure. It annoyed her that she felt flattered.

He led them into a large parlor. On its walls were oil paintings and drawings of Italian landscape and urban scenes. Michou's eyes widened with delight.

'These are all for sale,' Moretti remarked, observing the effect they had on his visitors. 'I show them only to clients with good taste and sufficient resources.'

He directed his visitors into a drawing room with a view of Place Dauphine and seated them at a fine tea table. A servant came with tea and fruit tarts, then withdrew. Moretti motioned to a vitrine of exquisite Sèvres porcelain that had caught Anne's attention. 'My late wife's collection.' He smiled sadly. 'Not for sale.' He turned to Saint-Martin. 'And now, Colonel, how may I help you?'

'I understand, sir, that you have made yourself more familiar than most laymen with the Louvre studios, especially Monsieur Hamel's, and with the defaced Serre portrait. You have even watched it being painted.' He paused for the art dealer to object if he wished. Moretti merely tilted his head slightly in a gesture of interest.

'Could you suggest a reason why someone would attack the painting and particularly the face? Why paint a skull?'

Moretti took a few moments to reflect. 'I see your point, Colonel. I can only conjecture, as you surely realize. The vandal might have wished to insult the Comte de Serre by attacking the image of a person he honored and loved. Monsieur

29

Hamel has accused the painter Bouchard of the deed, a reasonable accusation, given his intemperate reaction to losing the commission.'

Saint-Martin acknowledged the art dealer's opinion with a nod, then went on, 'You often met the countess while she resided in the Louvre. You observed her also at her country estate while the portrait was being painted. In its finished state, you asked if it was for sale. Why such interest?'

'The countess was an extraordinary human being, not only the most beautiful woman I've ever seen, but also wild, passionate, fascinating. I never tired of her company and took every opportunity to be with her.' He paused, met Saint-Martin's eye. 'And, yes, I remained on friendly terms with her to the end. The Comte de Serre and I have continued a cordial business relationship to this day.'

'Then could you tell me, was the face painted by Hamel a true likeness?'

The shadow of a frown flitted across Moretti's face. He apparently didn't clearly see the direction of the colonel's questions.

'A likeness, certainly. But I hesitate to speak of the countess's character. She kept much of herself hidden. It's true that Hamel captured a person behind the face. That's what really distinguished the Serre portrait from others he has done. How true Hamel's countess is to the woman herself, I'd rather not judge.'

Saint-Martin nodded again. He reached into the portfolio at his side and pulled out Michou's painting. 'What kind of person do you see here?'

Moretti glanced at the picture, then reared back in his chair. 'An extraordinary copy! Where did this come from?'

Saint-Martin pointed to Michou. She was studying Moretti with intense concentration. Anne signed the question to her. She gazed thoughtfully at the countess's features, then signed back, 'I painted it from the original and my own sketches. Last winter, I often sketched the countess in the garden of the Palais-Royal, and sometimes in the Church of Saint-Roch. And I sketched her when she came once to a presentation by students from the Institute for the Deaf. She reminded me of a beautiful actress I knew in the Théatre des Italiens. Headstrong and reckless. She also died in a riding accident.'

For an instant, as Anne translated Michou's signs, Moretti dropped his mask and uttered a sound that Anne thought might have been a groan of pain or regret.

After they left Moretti's gallery, Anne stood with Paul on the Pont Neuf in the shadow of Henri IV's bronze equestrian statue, watching Michou's small figure returning to the Louvre and the Bouchard apartment. When she disappeared into the riverside passageway, they turned their gaze to life on the river. On its surface, boatmen were scampering about, like overgrown water bugs. Beneath them, the river held its dark secrets and flowed inexorably on to the sea.

Anne turned to her husband. 'Moretti knew the countess better than he cared to admit.'

'Yes, Georges has picked up credible rumors of a brief, intimate relationship between her and Moretti, beginning late last autumn.'

'In the few months before her death?'

'Right.'

'Then he could have a motive to deface her image—if she jilted him.'

Six

A Noble Grief

August 28

The next morning, Anne, Michou, and Paul climbed the stairs to the second floor of the Old Louvre to visit the Comte de Serre in his apartment. Paul had asked Anne to join him. She had been reluctant. Of what use could she be? The count would ignore her. Paul had explained that he wanted Michou to show her portrait of the late countess to her husband. Anne would be needed to translate for Michou and to give her moral support. The count's haughty manner might intimidate her. 'Also,' Paul had said, 'I value your power of observation. Study the count closely while I question him.'

They paused on the landing outside the count's door. 'Why is he living here?' Anne asked. 'Does he belong to one of the royal academies?'

'No, the King's "grace and favor", as they say, allows him the use of the apartment.' Paul explained that the count was one of several royal favorites who enjoyed pensions and free lodgings in this ancient palace in the heart of Paris. The count came from a distinguished line of army officers and had served the Crown well during the Seven Years' War. He was known for his skillful use of evasive tactics and deception to outwit the enemy. After leaving military service ten years ago, he pursued a serious interest in art and became an amateur collector. Like the other privileged lodgers, Serre also had a home in the country.

Paul knocked on the door. A liveried servant in buff and silver opened, bowed to Paul, then to the two women. 'The Comte de Serre is in his study,' declared the servant and beckoned them to follow him.

The count stood at a window to the Cour Carrée, his black silk dressing robe hanging loosely from his shoulders. He turned around, a preoccupied expression on his face, as if they had surprised him while deep in thought.

'Have we disturbed you, sir?' asked Paul apologetically.

'Yes, but I am thankful that you did.' He stepped forward to greet them. 'That outrage to my wife's portrait occupies my mind more than is healthy. I have thought of little else since it happened three days ago.'

He probably had not slept well, Anne surmised. Lines of fatigue creased his face. Nonetheless, he remained aware of a host's duties. He seated his visitors at a table and ordered tea.

'Colonel, before we begin, I should mention that I knew your father, the general of cavalry. We were together at Minden in fifty-nine in the thick of the battle with the British. I came through without a scratch, more fortunate than he.'

Anne noticed her husband's jaw tighten. The memory of his father's death from wounds still pained him.

'He was a brave man,' the count continued, 'and a shrewd commander. We couldn't afford to lose him.'

Nor could Paul, added Anne to herself, who knew well her husband's history. The death of his father and his mother's subsequent depression had deprived him of parental guidance and love and had darkened his youth. Hidden beneath his stoic exterior, he still bore the scars. Opening up to others, even to her, took an effort.

Tea arrived and was served. Carried back to his days of military glory, the count related tales of Minden and other battles of the Seven Years' War. Paul showed polite interest but contributed little. When the count paused to drink his tea, Paul seized the opportunity to change the conversation to less personally painful topics.

'Sir,' he began, 'what do you think of current plans to transform the Louvre? The royal academies, the printing office, and worthy royal servants, such as yourself, would be moved to other, more suitable quarters. Then this building could be fitted out to display the King's collections to the public throughout the year.'

'A good idea, no doubt,' the count agreed. 'The Comte d'Angiviller has already put artists to work drawing plans for the Grande Galerie. But the project would be costly and the royal treasury is empty. It will be a long time before I'll have to move.'

Throughout this conversation, Anne detected in the count more physical strength and nervous energy than she would have expected in such a sickly, elderly man. The lift of his head, the curl of his lips suggested pride of class and a heightened sense of honor. From the cool blue of his eyes, she suspected he would be aloof, indifferent to others' pain, and contemptuous toward anyone outside his class or circle of friends and acquaintances. He ignored the servant who poured the tea.

Over the rim of her teacup Anne quickly scanned the study. On the shelves were miniature plaster copies of antique sculpture, copies of antique vases, and the like. Engravings of gigantic Roman ruins hung on the walls.

The count followed her gaze. 'My wife and I made a grand tour of Italy two years ago, from top to toe. These are a few of the souvenirs. There's more at the château. It was a memorable experience.'

'Which is your favorite Italian city?' Paul asked politely.

'Rome, for its ruins.' He passed around sketches he had made in the Roman Forum, the Baths of Caracalla, and other ancient sites. Michou nodded with approval at their accomplished technique. The memories of that trip brought a sad smile to the count's face. 'Occasionally, the countess accompanied me to the ruins. But they really were not to her taste. She preferred to ride into the countryside to a picturesque village, take in the fresh air and the view. Sometimes she went alone, despite the bandits. She was a fearless woman and, perhaps, also a little foolish.'

Anne understood that the count was referring to the countess's accidental death. 'How did it happen?' she asked hesitantly, reluctant to open a festering wound. Yet she sensed that the accident could prove significant. And the count's answer might be revealing.

'Riding her favorite horse, an English hunter, an excellent jumper.' He spoke readily but in a monotone from which any feeling had been pressed out. 'At our château south of Paris. She went out riding early in the morning to jump over various hurdles. Did it regularly, almost daily. Never had a problem. But this time, birds startled her horse, and it crashed into a gate. My wife was thrown out of the saddle and broke her neck. A strange coincidence. I could never understand it. The horse had to be put down.' The count stared into the distance, his voice trailed off into a deep silence.

Anne felt momentarily at a loss for words and increasingly ill at ease as the count's silence persisted.

Finally, Paul remarked, 'You must miss her greatly.' The count looked up and nodded. Paul went on to express regret for her death and sympathy for the count. Anne remained quiet, appearing sympathetic, but mindful of her task to observe. At first glance, the count's grief appeared genuine, even profound. Still, she wasn't sure. That sentiment, somehow, seemed out of character. Could an egotist, such as the count, love any woman sufficiently to deeply feel a sense of loss at her death?

After lighter conversation, Paul explained that this visit had to do with the late countess's portrait. Then he introduced Michou. The count seemed confused, as if wondering why she had come.

Paul directed the unspoken question to Michou. Through Anne, she explained to the count that she had copied his wife's head from Hamel's portrait in its undamaged state. She signed to Paul, who took the painting out of his portfolio and placed it on the table in front of the count.

He casually glanced at it. Then, for a moment, he looked stunned, emotionally gripped by the image of his wife. When his feelings threatened to overwhelm him, he forced his eyes away from the picture.

'How did you do it?' he asked Michou.

With Anne speaking for her, Michou described her copy work in Hamel's studio. 'He's unhappy about it, angry with me,' she added.

'Hamel be damned! I like it.' He turned again to the picture, stared intensely at it. 'Incredible! This copy is a true likeness of my wife, even though it's not quite the same as Hamel's. Here she's more enigmatic, mysterious, complicated.' He pointed to the eyes. They seemed slightly hooded, opaque. 'She's hiding something of herself.' He hesitated, unable to say more.

He gazed astonished at Michou. 'But you've never met her, have you?' Anne translated for him.

'I never met her, sir, but I observed her often, sometimes closely and in unguarded moments. At Mass in Saint-Roch, for example, she was like a different person, no longer bright and lively, but turned inward, sad. I filled a sketchbook with her likeness, especially her face. She fascinated me, she was so beautiful—and unusual. While copying her portrait, I asked questions where I suspected Monsieur Hamel was guessing. When she hid her mind or refused to reply, I sometimes found the answer in my sketchbook, or learned about her at the Institute for the Deaf and in Hamel's studio. Then, too, I know women like her.'

35

'Extraordinary!' the count murmured, still incredulous.

'You should know, sir,' Anne explained, 'that Michou has a rare ability to read faces. She has sketched people and painted miniature portraits for years. She observes others much more closely than hearing people do, and reads eyes, chin, brows, as well as lips. And, of course, posture and gestures.'

Paul retrieved the painting, adding it was needed in the investigation.

Displeasure flashed in the count's eyes. 'Hamel should use it to repair the portrait I have commissioned.'

Paul nodded. 'I'm sure we can work out an arrangement that will satisfy everyone.'

Michou would receive some benefit from her work, Anne thought. Neither Hamel nor the count appeared inclined to acknowledge or compensate her, as if she were beneath their notice.

'Sir,' continued Paul, 'who else besides the painter Bouchard would have wanted to deface the portrait?' He carefully replaced Michou's copy in his portfolio.

The count seemed surprised by the question. 'I don't know, Colonel. Could there be anyone else?'

'At the beginning of an investigation, it's prudent to cast as wide a net as possible. Bouchard had a motive for the deed and my adjutant is looking into the question of his opportunity. We have not yet found evidence of his guilt. Until we are certain, we must look for other possible suspects among those who may also have had motive or opportunity.' He paused for a moment. 'Monsieur Moretti has shown much interest in the portrait. What do you know about him?'

The count shrugged. 'He's an art dealer, a connoisseur.' He met Paul's eye and blinked. 'Of course, I heard the gossip months ago about an affair behind my back between him and the countess. Rubbish. He flattered her with his attention. She played games with him. I can't see him in the role of a rejected lover who destroyed her portrait in a fit of anger. Even if she had sent him away, he's the kind of man who would blow her a farewell kiss and find another woman.'

Paul's eyes narrowed but he didn't comment. Anne shared

his doubt. Neither the count nor Moretti could be fully trusted to tell the truth. Both men were personally involved with the countess.

'Given your interest in collecting art,' Paul asked, 'did you ever cross paths with him when you were in Italy? He's from Florence and has a gallery there.'

'No, I heard of him, but we never met. There are many art dealers in Florence and I didn't visit them all.' He stared with exasperation at Saint-Martin. 'Colonel, I think you're missing the point. Bouchard didn't attack my wife. She's dead and can no longer feel pain. By destroying her image he meant to attack me, to hold me up to ridicule, because I didn't give him the commission. Such a man is a base coward. This is a point of honor for me. A duel is out of the question. I could never bring myself to challenge a vile painter. But I shall not be satisfied until he is suitably punished.'

Seven

A Painter's Fate

August 28–September 1

After the Serre visit, Anne and Michou returned to the Salon, while Saint-Martin and Georges went to Bouchard's apartment. He was at work in the studio, his wife said. They were to wait in the parlor. She would tell him that they had come. A few minutes later, the artist arrived, his shirtsleeves and hands spotted with paint, his hair a tangled, curly black mess. On his face was a smirk.

Bouchard's insolence irritated Saint-Martin. But he told himself to keep an open mind and an even temper. 'Monsieur,' he began, 'the maid whom you visited in the early morning of August 25 has admitted to being with you for about an hour. You left her room a little after three o'clock, at least a

37

couple of hours before dawn. That allowed you time enough to enter Hamel's studio and deface the portrait. Please explain.'

The painter looked away, fumbling for a reply.

'Your story has come apart,' said the colonel, trying to catch the artist's shifty eye. 'You had better tell us the truth.'

'Yes, of course.' He began haltingly. 'I was afraid that if I told the truth, I would be blamed for attacking Monsieur Hamel's picture. You must know that there's bad blood between us. He stole a large commission from me and insulted me for good measure. I may have responded rudely.'

His eyes darted from one man to the other. They didn't speak. Finally, he sighed, as if capitulating, and began to explain. 'After leaving the maid, I walked past Hamel's studio. The door was ajar. Strange, I thought. It's usually unlocked but closed. Someone's always in the room—students, or a watchman. I pushed the door open and looked inside. No one there. Then I remembered the Salon party at the Tuileries. The students were out celebrating. The watchmen, too. I became curious. Hamel would display the Serre portrait in the exhibition hall that day. He had often bragged about how great it was. His best work, he claimed. Worthy of Titian. I *had* to look at it.

'I searched the room in vain. It was dark, except for rays of moonlight coming through the windows. I wasn't familiar with the studio. He would never let me in. Suddenly, someone entered the room. I hid behind a canvas and watched. A hooded person with a small lantern went directly to a rack of covered canvases, picked one out, and put it on an easel. His back was toward me but I could see him prepare a palette. He scraped the surface of the canvas, then quickly brushed paint on it.

'All this took maybe ten or fifteen minutes. He covered the painting, returned it to its place in the rack, and stole out of the room. I left my hiding place and slipped off the cover. He had painted a skull where the head had been. I was shocked, thought of raising an alarm. Instead, I just replaced the cover and left. Hamel would have declared I was the culprit.'

Saint-Martin thought to himself, this was probably the best story Bouchard could invent under the circumstances. If the story was true, he must have silently applauded the vandalism and looked forward happily to Hamel's public embarrassment later that morning. 'Are you sure that you didn't recognize the vandal?'

'Yes, his back was to me all the time.'

'I'm not through with you,' said Saint-Martin, sensing strongly that he hadn't heard the whole truth. 'You shall remain in Paris and be available for further questioning.'

A day passed with little movement in the case. Then on Thursday Madame Bouchard claimed she didn't feel well and asked Anne to sit in the studio while Michou posed. Anne agreed gladly—with an ulterior motive. After interrogating Bouchard, Paul had told her and Michou to keep an eye on him. He remained the principal suspect.

With a nod and a word to Bouchard at the easel, Anne sat off to one side. Michou removed her robe and stood against the rocky cliff.

'I'm happy you've come, Madame Cartier,' he said, an irritable edge on his voice. 'Working with Michou can be difficult. You will translate when I ask for a certain expression on her face—terror at the approaching sea monster, or resignation to her fate, or trust in Perseus to save her.'

While posing as Andromeda, Michou had noticed a marked change in Bouchard's attitude and told Anne about it. Previously, he focused on the project before him. He had carefully arranged her position, tilting her head slightly this way, then that way. Recently, however, he had become easily distracted and gave Michou confusing instructions. Like Michou, Anne sensed that a hidden anxiety was disturbing the painter's concentration.

After the session and throughout the rest of the day, Anne kept an eye on the painter. In the evening he left the apartment without saying a word. She hastily threw a dark brown cape over her shoulders and followed him out of the Louvre and across the river into Place Dauphine. The square was lit mostly by light from adjacent buildings. It was also empty, as far as Anne could see. The rioters and the soldiers had left, but people didn't feel safe there yet.

A hooded figure stepped out of the darkness into the circle of dim light cast by a single street lantern. Bouchard approached him . . . or her. A conversation ensued. From behind a tree Anne peered through her spyglass. The hooded figure shook a fist at Bouchard. The painter took a step back, raised his hands in protest, the hooded person returned to the darkness. Anne followed the painter back to the Louvre, convinced that he had attempted to transact some kind of dangerous or illicit business.

Late in the afternoon of the next day, Anne and Michou took their places in the studio for another session of painting *Andromeda*. Even more preoccupied than before, Bouchard dropped his brush again and again, and dripped paint on the floor. Earlier in the day, his wife had complained loudly that he had taken money she had just received for a portrait. He would waste it on gambling, she claimed. Why didn't he stay home and finish his work instead? He had cursed her for nagging, threatened to beat her, and declared he would do as he pleased.

Now, as he stood at the easel, he impatiently ordered Michou to lean this way and that. He couldn't make up his mind. Soon the brush began to tremble in his hand. Finally, halfway through the hour, he abruptly turned to Anne. 'Tell Michou to dress and to clean up the studio. I'm not feeling well. Perhaps I'll paint tomorrow.'

He didn't appear ill, but he had a wild look on his face. Anne followed him again across Pont Neuf to a gambling den on the Left Bank. He was likely to be there for hours and return to the apartment drunk and without his money. There didn't seem to be any sense in waiting for him. She walked back to the Louvre and shared her experience with Michou, then returned home, troubled by a vague uneasiness.

At dawn, Michou left the Louvre with her sketchbook for a promenade on the riverbank. Boats at anchor engaged her eye. She sketched a few. A fisherman waved to her, someone she recognized from previous visits to the water. She waved back, sat down on a wooden cask, and sketched him.

Returning to the Bouchard apartment, as she approached

40

the long passage from the Quai du Louvre to the Cour Carrée, she saw a man sitting on the tile floor in the early-morning shadows. His head bent forward, his back leaned against the wall, a wine bottle stood at his side.

A man walking ahead of her passed him with only a cursory glance. Michou might have done the same, but something about the man caught her eye. It was the hair, the thick black curly hair! She drew closer and recognized him. Monsieur Bouchard.

She had seen him before when he lay drunk on the floor of the studio. But now he was too still. Her heart began to pound. She touched his shoulder. He didn't stir. From her bag she drew the knife she always carried and held the steel blade to his parted lips. No moisture gathered on the smooth surface. He must be dead. She glanced at the bottle. Had the drink killed him this time? Then she noticed the large dark spot on his shirt over his heart. He had been murdered!

Eight

Investigation

Saturday, September 1

Michou waved frantically to a young man walking through the passage toward her. He appeared to notice her distress. Hesitantly, he came closer. She recognized him, Monsieur Gillet, one of the engravers at the Royal Printing Office in the Louvre. His eyes darted between her and the dead painter.

She pointed to the bloody spot on Bouchard's shirt, then drew a card from her pocket. She had written a message for when she needed help. Now she showed it to the young man.

I am Micheline du Saint-Esprit and I am deaf. In case of an emergency, please contact Colonel Paul

41

de Saint-Martin or his wife, Anne Cartier, at the residence of the Provost of the Royal Highway Patrol on Rue Saint-Honoré.

Gillet nodded that he had understood. He faced Michou and said he would first fetch a nearby watchman and then go to the colonel.

By the time the watchman arrived, a small crowd of the curious had gathered and were gaping at the scene. He dispersed them and approached Michou. She pulled out her sketchbook and wrote down her name and pointed to herself, then the dead man's name, and pointed to him.

The watchman took her book and wrote that help would arrive shortly. In the meantime, she should remain where she was.

She had been standing next to the dead Bouchard all this time, her mind occupied with the engraver from the printing office, the gaping onlookers, and the watchman. Only now did the enormity of what had happened to the painter begin to sink into her consciousness.

Her first reaction was a sudden weakness in her knees, a lightness in her head. She feared she might faint. The watchman glanced at her with concern. She leaned back against the passage wall for support, drew deep breaths of air. A wave of sorrow swept over her. Bouchard had been a weak, troublesome man in many ways. But he had been kind and had begun to teach her. He was also a talented artist. As his model for Andromeda, she had taken pride in his work and had built up hope in its promised perfection.

She glanced down at his lifeless body. Someone must take the news to his wife, now a debt-burdened widow. It was sad to think that her final memory of him was their quarrel the night before and his threat to beat her. Nearly overwhelmed by the misery crowding into her mind, Michou felt the onset of panic. Would Anne come soon?

After what seemed like hours, Anne finally arrived with her husband and his adjutant. She embraced Michou, held her tightly. Michou's panic subsided. She grew calm enough to sign to Anne and the two men what had happened. The colonel smiled gently and signed that the two women should leave now and do what they could for Madame Bouchard.

Colonel Saint-Martin and his adjutant, Georges Charpentier, heard the watchman's report, and ordered him to keep the passage clear of the gawking crowd. For a half hour, they had the passage to themselves. Finally, Inspecteur Quidor arrived with a pair of his agents and a cart. The Louvre lay within his district. As a royal palace, it was exempt from his authority. But murder was an exception and he had been called.

'What do we have here?' he asked, gazing down at Bouchard's corpse.

Saint-Martin nodded the question to Georges, who often worked with the inspector.

'To judge from the small wound, I'd say the killer pierced the painter's heart with a poniard. Time of death, maybe one or two this morning. His jaw and neck have begun to stiffen.'

Quidor knelt down, examined the wine bottle at Bouchard's side. 'A common cheap variety. Half full. I smell it on his clothes. Was he drinking at the time of his death?'

'Perhaps the autopsy will tell us,' Georges replied. 'After stabbing Bouchard in the passage, the killer must have arranged his body in a sitting position, poured wine on him, and set the bottle upright next to him. If Bouchard were carrying it when he was stabbed, it would have fallen to the tile floor of the passage and shattered. The killer had a special reason for what he did. Otherwise, he could have thrown the body in the river.'

Saint-Martin glanced at Bouchard with a feeling of pity. 'That's hardly a dignified position for a member of the Royal Academy of Painting and Sculpture. I believe that the killer intended to insult the victim.'

'I agree,' said Quidor. 'This murder was planned, rather than impromptu.'

Georges nodded. 'Also, the killer and his victim may have known each other. I see no bruises or cuts on the victim's face or hands. His clothes have not been torn. There were no other signs of a struggle. The killer apparently confronted his victim in the early hours of the morning when the passage was dark and deserted. Rain had fallen off and on. The passage was dry and could have served as a rendezvous for the killer and his victim.'

'Robbery?' asked Quidor.

'Possibly,' Georges replied. 'I searched the dead man's pockets. If he had any money or keys or a watch, they're gone.'

Quidor beckoned his agents to come forward with the cart, then turned to Saint-Martin. 'We've seen enough, Colonel. My men will remove the body to the Châtelet for an autopsy.'

'Keep me informed,' Saint-Martin said. 'In the meantime, I'll report to Lieutenant-General DeCrosne that the central figure in a public scandal has been murdered. A royal academy might be tainted. He'll want to determine how this investigation should go forward.'

Anne and Michou left the passage and went upstairs to the Bouchard apartment. Madame Bouchard sat in the kitchen, looking out the window. She rose when they entered, a concerned expression on her face.

'What's going on in the Cour Carrée?' she asked Anne. 'I saw your husband and his adjutant, and a watchman, and a crowd of people. Is there trouble?'

'I'm afraid there is, madame.' Anne drew close and spoke kindly. 'Your husband is dead.'

Madame Bouchard flinched as if struck and took a step back, then shook her head. 'How did it happen?'

'He was stabbed in the heart. Death was quick. Sometime during the early-morning hours. Michou found him in the passageway to the river. The police don't know who killed him.'

The woman turned pale and began to sway. Anne moved quickly to her side and lowered her into a chair. Michou came with a cool, damp cloth and applied it to her forehead.

When the woman appeared to have recovered, she asked if she could see her husband's body. 'Not at this time,' Anne replied. 'The police will take the body to the Châtelet for examination. Later, when you are feeling stronger, I'm sure you may see him.'

'What's the point? We've long since ceased to care much for each other. Still, I'll miss him.' She didn't cry, just sat very still for a minute, staring at the floor. Then, without looking up, she rose, went into the bedroom, and closed the door.

'I'll wait here in the kitchen,' Anne said and glanced toward the bedroom, 'in case she may want help.'

Michou reflected for a few moments. There wasn't anything she could do now for the grieving widow. 'I'll be in the studio if you need me.'

The room seemed more still than usual. Not that Michou could hear anything. But she was very sensitive to movement and to touch. She could feel even the slight vibrations of sound. She often sensed Bouchard's presence before she saw him. She realized now that he was gone forever.

The *Andromeda* stood in front of her. She stared at it. A profound sadness came over her. The painting was cut short, like its creator's life.

She studied the painting closely, a dramatic story of salvation told in vivid, striking colors. The great, ugly sea monster, the valiant Perseus, the seashore and the cliff—they were perfect. In the young Andromeda chained to the cliff, Michou recognized her own slender body. Only the face was incomplete, though it was already heart-shaped, and its eyes were large and wide like hers.

Michou started to cry, then thought better of it. She tore herself away from the painting, walked across the studio, stopped before a finished portrait on display. It depicted a beautiful lady sitting in a chair, holding a cat in her lap. The lady's long, full gown, her creamy skin and shining eyes—everything about the painting spoke of perfection, down to the cat's whiskers.

An idea began to dawn in Michou's mind. She recalled that Bouchard had begun the portrait, but his wife—as so often—had completed it. She was as well-trained, as capable as her husband, especially where the face of a portrait was concerned. *She* could finish *Andromeda*!

Michou's mood began to improve. She felt optimistic. After Madame Bouchard had grieved sufficiently, she would also see the advantage of completing the painting. It would give her something useful to do and could earn her money that she sorely needed.

Feeling better by the minute, Michou wandered about the studio as if it were hers. She opened a storage closet and threw a swift glance at its contents. The paints, the brushes, the canvases, and other supplies seemed in good order. She started to close the door, then stopped abruptly. Things were in order, yes, but not exactly where she had left them late the night before.

Since then, neither Bouchard nor his wife had been in the studio. He had gone to the gambling den. She was in bed. Someone else had a key to the studio and had entered it secretly. Michou looked about the room now with fresh, inquisitive eyes and noticed that it had been thoroughly searched. There were traces of the intruder's presence everywhere.

'He or she spent much time and effort trying to conceal the search,' remarked Anne. She had joined Michou in taking an inventory of the studio. They agreed that nothing was missing. So what exactly had the intruder been looking for? Had he found it?

Anne conjectured that the intruder was after something valuable that Bouchard had hidden away. If he hadn't found it last night, he might come back and search again. That was a very disturbing thought!

She mentioned her concern to Georges when he came to the apartment after examining the murder site. She and Michou took him through the studio and gave him the gist of their findings.

His expression turned grim. 'This intrusion could be related to Bouchard's murder. His keys, as well as his money and watch, are missing. For a start, we shall change the locks to the studio and the apartment.'

He paused with an afterthought. 'Have you learned anything else of use?'

'Yes, it didn't seem important at the time but does now. Last night, I followed Bouchard to the gambling den on the Quai des Augustins and left him there. Didn't observe anything out of the ordinary, so I haven't mentioned it before.' She paused. 'Bouchard gambled habitually and usually in the same place. And I'd wager that he always walked there and back the same way. If enemies wanted to kill him at night, they could easily find him.'

'You've raised a good point, madame. I'll suggest to the colonel that we pay a visit to the gambling den and try to retrace Bouchard's movements.'

'And I'll stay here with Michou and Madame Bouchard, at least until the locksmith does his work.'

'For safety's sake, take this.' He handed her his service pistol. 'It's loaded. You know how to use it. If the intruder were to return, he might be more . . . forceful.'

Nine

Gambler's Luck

September 1

As evening approached on Rue Saint-Honoré, Saint-Martin and Georges put on civilian clothes, equipped themselves with false papers. Saint-Martin was to be an army officer on leave, and Georges, his friend, a rich businessman from Rouen in Normandy, a disguise he often used. His Norman accent was authentic. They were going to follow Bouchard's tracks. Anne had placed him at a Left Bank gambling den in the hours before his death.

Lieutenant-General DeCrosne had ordered them to add the murder investigation to the Serre portrait case. The two crimes could well be related. The victim Bouchard was strongly suspected of defacing the portrait.

Late that evening, the two men set out. On the Quai des Augustins, a street lantern marked the entrance to the den. A clandestine business, it was otherwise indistinguishable from other buildings in the neighborhood. They walked through a noisy crowded café and up a stairway to a parlor overlooking an enclosed courtyard.

A servant at a desk asked who they were and looked closely at their attire. He turned with a glance toward two muscular, unsmiling men standing guard near the door. One of them gave the newcomers a gimlet-eyed look, paused, then nodded slightly. The servant turned back to Saint-Martin and Georges, apparently assured that they had money and would not rob the house. 'You may enter.' They wandered through several simply furnished, busy rooms, observing different games of chance and hazard—faro and lotto among many others. The players at the tables were a mixed group. Some were coarse, sinister-looking men who would cut the throat of anyone who tried to cheat them. Others were young prodigals, bent on squandering their fathers' money. A few were poorly dressed, probably artisans. Saint-Martin wondered where they found the money to gamble.

'Let's watch this,' Georges whispered. He and the colonel had stopped at a table where a game of hazard, called biribi, was being played. A green cloth with seventy numbered squares covered the table. A slim, callow young man placed ten louis d'or on one of the squares, and drew a numbered chip from a velvet bag.

A crowd gathered around him. He slowly raised the chip, stared at its number, then groaned softly. His chip failed to match his square. The banker collected his money.

Georges leaned toward Saint-Martin. 'Had the young man won, he would have received sixty-four times his wager, six hundred and forty louis. With that much money, sir, a gentleman like yourself could live very nicely for a year.'

The colonel humored his adjutant with a thin, ironic smile. He understood well enough what had happened, though he wagered seldom and only on horses. Games of hazard particularly offended his sense of what was reasonable. They required of the player no skill whatsoever. The odds heavily favored the banker.

Eventually, they came to a tearoom. A buffet table with light fare stood to one side, opposite a bar. Several men sat at tables, eating and drinking. Saint-Martin bought brandy for himself and Georges and nodded toward the last empty table. 'Let's try to eavesdrop.'

As he suspected, the surrounding conversation dealt with Bouchard's murder. The painter usually had bad luck, but last night, he had won more than a thousand louis, a princely sum. He had ordered several drinks to celebrate. Then, late at night, he left alone, with a large purse full of money, and walked out into the dark in the direction of the Louvre. That was the last anyone saw of him alive.

Georges managed to strike up a conversation with a middle-aged, verbose man who invited himself to sit at their table and talk about the murder.

'How well did you know the painter Bouchard?'

'As well as anyone here.'

'Who was the next person to leave after him?'

The talker wrinkled his brow, trying to recall, then grew wary. 'Police?'

Georges nodded. 'Routine question. You won't be involved.'

'Him.' The talker furtively pointed to a slender, tense young man who was just entering the room. 'He's Jules Gillet, an engraver. Works in the Royal Printing Office in the Louvre. He left shortly after the painter. They seemed to be acquainted, often placed bets together.'

'I recognize him,' Saint-Martin whispered to Georges. 'He's the man Michou sent to tell us of Bouchard's murder.'

Georges's face lit up with interest. 'We must become better acquainted.'

For the rest of the evening, they observed Gillet at the gaming tables. He was probably about thirty-five. Stooped from years of bending over the engraver's work, he also had the strong hands and long slender fingers of his craft. Fair-haired, fine-boned, he looked frail. His forehead was high and furrowed. His face, long and pale. His small thin mouth was petulant, his pale blue eyes, sullen. In short, thought Saint-Martin, this appeared to be a very intelligent but troubled man, probably from a cultivated family.

He moved quickly from table to table, trying his luck at

several games. His concentration was intense, his expression humorless, as if winning was a matter of life or death. It was near midnight by the time he was ready to quit. He had won a few louis but didn't look happy.

Saint-Martin and Georges followed him from the den over the same route usually taken by the murdered painter. At the Old Louvre, Gillet entered the Cour Carrée by the eastern passage. The two policemen continued to follow him to his room in the north wing.

As he was opening his door, they confronted him, showed him police identification. 'Monsieur Gillet,' the colonel said, 'we need to talk to you.'

For a moment he was speechless, and he fumbled with the key. 'What do you want from me?' he asked, as he let them in.

He lived alone in a single small simple room. A few prints hung on the walls. As an engraver, he earned a decent wage, but gambling kept him poor. He brought forward plain wooden chairs and they sat down.

'It's late, so we'll be brief,' Georges began. 'Where were you early in the morning when the painter Bouchard was murdered?'

'Here, in bed,' he too quickly replied.

'Really? We know that you followed him to the Louvre. Did you meet him?'

'No, I went directly to my room.'

'Why were you at the passage when his body was discovered?'

'I was on my way to the Quai du Louvre for a morning walk.'

They briefly searched his room without finding Bouchard's missing keys, watch, or money. Nor were there any signs of sudden wealth. They learned that Gillet and Bouchard had once discussed engraving one of the painter's works. Otherwise they had had little contact with each other, except at the gambling den. There had been no bad blood between them.

On the way home in a cabriolet through darkened streets, Saint-Martin asked, 'What do you think, Georges?'

'Gillet is poor. Bouchard's purse would have sorely tempted

50

him. He could have caught the painter by surprise, stabbed and robbed him. Later, like many other criminals, he was drawn back to the scene of his crime, curious to learn what the police had discovered.'

'Why would he so deliberately arrange the body and the bottle to look like an insult?'

'To lead our conjecture astray, perhaps.'

'And if he stole Bouchard's keys, why would he search his studio and take nothing?'

'He may have looked only for more money and found none. He wouldn't pilfer art supplies. Not enough value, considering the risks involved in trying to fence them.'

At the residence on Rue Saint-Honoré, Saint-Martin opened the door. 'We have our first serious suspect but no evidence yet that he's a murderer.'

'I'll ask a police agent to follow him for a few days,' Georges said. 'He may have hid the missing money outside his room. And I'll visit the printing office. I expect to find that he has not told the truth.'

Ten

Serre

September 2

Early Sunday morning, under a misty blue sky, Colonel Paul de Saint-Martin strolled in his garden among the flower beds, enjoying their fragrance. He stooped and picked a bouquet of pink damask roses for the breakfast table. He was snipping off the thorns when a servant came with a tray of bread, butter, marmalade, and coffee and set places for two.

'Madame has arrived,' the servant announced, offering a vase for the flowers. 'She will be here shortly.' After a final, solicitous glance over the table, he bowed and left. Paul arranged the roses in the vase and placed it on the table.

A few minutes later, Paul heard her footsteps on the tiles of the adjacent garden room. His heart beat a little faster in anticipation of her coming.

'How charming,' she cried, standing framed in the doorway. Her eyes glowed with delight in the flowers. Paul cherished moments like this, gazing at his wife, a vision of loveliness, even in gray street dress. Her cheeks shined pink with exertion. She had just walked from the Bouchard apartment. 'I trust you and Michou slept well.' Paul embraced Anne. Late last night, hoping to frustrate the intruder should he try again, she had supervised a locksmith while he changed locks in the studio and apartment. She had stayed on to reassure Michou and to assist Madame Bouchard, who had not yet come out of her deep depression.

While eating breakfast, Paul related what he and Georges had learned at the gambling den. 'Bouchard left the gaming tables with a thousand louis d'or in his purse. Foolish man. He had been drinking. An engraver named Gillet followed him to the Louvre. Gillet claims they didn't meet. We think they did. What happened then is still a mystery.' He glanced at Anne over the rim of his cup, inviting her comment.

'Since the money has disappeared, I suppose that Monsieur Gillet took it. But there's no evidence yet. Right?'

Paul nodded. 'Georges will investigate Gillet. I shall question one of the other suspects.'

'Which one?'

'The only person who openly threatened to harm Bouchard . . . the Comte de Serre.'

Anne finished her coffee. 'And today Michou and I shall search the apartment and the studio in case the intruder may not have found what he was looking for.'

After Anne left for the Bouchard apartment, Paul sent a note to the count, asking to speak to him today about the recent violent incidents at the Louvre. The count replied by return courier that he would expect the colonel in the early afternoon. Promptly at one o'clock, Saint-Martin presented himself at the count's Louvre apartment. They sat in the study again.

After the opening civilities, Serre met Saint-Martin's eye.
'What do you need to know, Colonel?'

'Where were you, sir, early yesterday morning between
midnight and first light?'

Serre raised an eyebrow a fraction. 'I dined late at the
Comte d'Angiviller's home and returned to this apartment
near midnight. I went to bed shortly afterward and didn't rise
until eight in the morning.'

'Can anyone attest to those facts?'

'My host, of course, for the dinner engagement. As for the
early-morning hours, I slept alone, if that's what you are curious
about. My valet sleeps soundly, as do the cook and the maid,
in rooms of their own. I could have slipped out of the apartment without their noticing and stabbed the painter Bouchard.
I would have liked to have killed him, but not *that* way. My
valet informed me of the murder. He was in the crowd that
gathered in the passage and saw the victim. What he couldn't
see for himself, he heard from the watchman.'

Saint-Martin reflected. Like the engraver Gillet, the valet
was promptly on the murder scene. Merely a coincidence?
Too bad the watchman was so talkative. Certain details of a
crime were often better kept secret. Knowledge of them might
incriminate a suspect.

'Poniard. Wine bottle. No, Colonel, that truly is not my
style.'

Saint-Martin was inclined to agree. But he reserved judgment. Serre could be one of those nobles for whom the word
'honor' came easily to the lips, casting a veil over base deeds.
Expediency governed their lives. The count might not have
plunged the poniard into Bouchard's heart, but he could have
hired or incited someone else to do it.

'Sir, we are still investigating the defacing of your late wife's
portrait. Tell me about the servants who used to attend her.
They could perhaps lead us to a clue.'

'She had a personal maid, a woman named Cécile, as well
as a housekeeper and a groom. After she died, I let the maid
go. Laure, the housekeeper, and Vincenzo, her husband the
groom, still work at the château. They live together. I believe
they are married.'

At the mention of the groom, Saint-Martin cocked his head with surprise.

'Yes, Colonel, she had her own stable. The groom looked after her carriages and her horses with all their gear. Drove her anywhere she wanted to go, to Paris, even to Italy. She kept him busy.'

'And where might I find your valet? I'll need to speak to him.'

'Somewhere in the Palais-Royal, I suppose. Sunday is his day off. Perhaps the cook could tell you. They appear to be on friendly terms. If you miss him, come back tomorrow. He and I shall still be here. Later in the week we shall move to the country for the vacation season.' He paused, as if to mull over an idea. 'Would you and Madame Cartier be my guests in the country for a few days in the following week? My château is only a couple of hours from Paris on the road to Fontainebleau. You would enjoy hunting grouse in the estate's woodland and meadows. I understand that your wife, like yourself, loves horses and rides expertly.' He paused again, lowered his voice. 'I would like you to meet several landowners in my neighborhood, who are as concerned as I am about the dangers of rural unrest. They would enjoy speaking informally with a provost of the Royal Highway Patrol.'

For a moment, the colonel silently considered the count's invitation. On the personal level he was reluctant to accept. He didn't care for the count, a haughty, insufferable bore. The prospect of several days in his company didn't promise to be pleasurable. Finally, he didn't really enjoy hunting, an unequal contest between a frightened bird or beast and a horde of excited horsemen and their dogs. On the other hand, the visit could be worthwhile. He and Anne *did* enjoy riding in the country. And there were other reasons, having less to do with pleasure. The count was among those landowners whose peasants had become restive in recent years. Saint-Martin had often heard their complaints. This visit could offer opportunities to study the situation at firsthand as well as to hear the landowners' point of view.

Finally, there was the question of the countess's death in a riding accident. It occurred within Saint-Martin's jurisdiction.

But, at the time, he and Georges were on a mission to Bath in England. The junior officer who investigated the incident failed to uncover any evidence of wrongdoing. A flock of grouse had startled her horse as it was about to jump over a closed gate. The countess was thrown against a tree, badly injured, and died shortly afterward.

An unlikely coincidence, the officer had added privately to his report. Odd things do happen, Saint-Martin told himself. But in view of the recent attack upon her portrait and Bouchard's murder, it might be worthwhile to examine more closely the circumstances of her death. There just might be a connection.

'Yes, monsieur, I can speak for my wife and myself; we accept your invitation gladly. May I bring my adjutant, Monsieur Charpentier?'

'Of course. And bring the little portrait painter with her picture of my wife. I shall invite Monsieur Moretti, as well. We have business to discuss.'

Saint-Martin and Georges surveyed the rollicking crowd in the garden of the Palais-Royal. It was only midafternoon, and many young men were already listing to port or starboard. A few lay wrecked on distant benches where burly waiters had deposited them. Serre's cook had assured the colonel, 'On a sunny afternoon like today, you'll find Pierre at a garden table in front of Café de Foy.' She had also described him, a square-faced man with coarse but handsome features, erect as a sergeant major in the royal army. For that he had once been, before becoming the count's valet. A quiet man who kept his own counsel, the cook had said.

'That must be him.' Georges pointed discreetly to a table where a man and a woman sat side by side. They had finished their drinks and appeared to be discussing an issue on which they disagreed.

From a table nearby, Saint-Martin studied the valet. True to the cook's description, a handsome man, indeed, but for a complexion pitted by the smallpox. The woman appeared to be a courtesan, to judge from her precious gestures and her gaudy, stylish clothes. Her hat was a fantastic, wide-brimmed concoction of peacock feathers.

'The count must pay him well,' said Saint-Martin. 'His companion would normally cost more than a valet could afford.'

'Pierre may have another source of income,' offered Georges.

This wasn't the time to pursue that point, thought the colonel, but he would keep it in mind.

After a few minutes of apparent negotiation, the woman shrugged her shoulders, rose from the table, and sauntered away. Pierre appeared indifferent to her departure, and remained at the table idly fingering his empty glass.

'Let's join him, Georges.'

Pierre seemed unabashed by the arrival of two policemen. Saint-Martin ordered iced fruit drinks for the three of them.

'Where were you, monsieur, early yesterday morning?' asked the colonel, after introducing himself and Georges.

'In bed.' He taunted the policemen with a smirk.

'Where?' Saint-Martin met his eye sternly.

Pierre looked away. 'At a brothel near the Palais-Royal.' He waved in a southerly direction and gave an address.

The colonel glanced at his adjutant, who shrugged. 'I'll find it.'

Saint-Martin continued, 'And how did you happen upon the murder scene just at the moment it was discovered?'

'By coincidence. I was on my way to buy bread for the cook.'

'How well did you know Bouchard?'

'A passing acquaintance. Saw him occasionally in the Louvre.'

Saint-Martin was struck by the valet's nonchalance. His gaze was steady. An enigmatic smile masked his feelings. 'Can you think of anyone other than Bouchard who might have disliked the count or the countess enough to have defaced her portrait?'

The valet gave the question a long moment of silent reflection. 'Your troopers know that the count's peasants have already resorted to violence. Many of their relatives live in Paris. A few even work in the Louvre.'

'We shall look them up.'

Georges took over. 'What can you tell us about Laure, the late Comtesse de Serre's housekeeper, and Vincenzo, her groom?'

The valet hesitated for just a second before replying. 'Laure fancies herself a lady. Whenever she comes to Paris, she stays with her daughter Cécile. She also used to work at the château and now has a room and a shop on Rue Sainte-Anne, close to the Louvre. Laure was here for the Salon but has returned to the château ahead of us.' He paused, frowned, apparently recalling the groom. 'Vincenzo should be at the château looking after the stables.'

During this exchange, Saint-Martin studied Pierre. His eyes were cold and unfriendly. A steward, presumably, as well as a valet, he wielded authority over other servants and probably not in a kindly manner.

The men finished their drinks, observing the passing crowd. Little more was said until Pierre rose from the table and sauntered toward an attractive young woman leaning against a tree. A few words were exchanged. The couple locked arms and disappeared into the bustling Montpensier Arcade.

Georges slapped his thigh. 'There goes a man willing and able to do the count's dirty work.'

Saint-Martin and Georges made their way a short distance west to Rue Sainte-Anne to a café that was open for business. The two policemen entered and inquired after Laure's daughter. One of the patrons knew her by name, Cécile Tremblay, a seamstress. He pointed to the building across the street. She had a room upstairs and a shop on the ground floor. He believed her to be about forty, a withdrawn, well-mannered widow. The patron shook his head. 'I think a visit from two strange policemen would scare the wits out of her.'

Saint-Martin reflected. Anne might be able to disarm the woman's anxieties. He and Georges made a few more inquiries in the neighborhood and gained a sense of Cécile's routine. She went regularly to the market and to Mass at Saint-Roch a few blocks away. Anne might chance to make her acquaintance and find a way to speak about her late mistress. Her life

57

and death might somehow be related to the murder of the painter Bouchard.

Eleven

The Grip of Vice

September 3

Early the next morning at the Royal Printing Office in the Louvre, the presses were already hammering out royal ordinances and other expressions of the King's will. A worker directed Georges to the steward of the engraving department, a thickset, forthright man. He drew Georges into a small storeroom to escape the noise.

Georges identified himself and inquired after Gillet.

'He hasn't come in yet,' replied the steward in an irritated tone.

'Oh?' Georges raised an eyebrow, feigned surprise.

'He's a skillful engraver,' the steward granted. 'To be honest, he's the best man in the shop when he applies himself. But his behavior is erratic. He often arrives late, looking like he's been up the entire night. I'm concerned. A tired man is apt to make mistakes, and he's dangerous near the presses, might hurt himself or others.'

'What's his problem?'

'Gambling. Everyone knows it. He's always short of money. Tries to borrow from others, but he's slow to repay. The men here won't lend to him anymore. He must work at extra jobs to earn more money, but I don't know where, nor does anyone else in the shop.' Georges also learned that Gillet was a secretive fellow. That in itself seemed suspicious. Perhaps he was a thief.

Georges's next stop was the Criminal Investigation Department on Rue des Capucines. Inspecteur Quidor was at his desk. Georges pulled up a chair. 'Have you heard of an engraver named Gillet?'

'Yes, he has come to our attention,' replied the inspector, opening a small silver box. He offered it to Georges. 'Snuff?'

Georges shook his head.

Quidor took a pinch and returned the box to his pocket, then leaned back. 'I suspect Gillet's hand in some of the nasty, antigovernment broadsheets coming out of the Palais-Royal, paid for by the Duc d'Orléans. Gillet probably engraves them for the money, not out of conviction. If he didn't, someone else would. One of these days, when I find more evidence, I might threaten him with arrest, offer him a little money, use him as a spy.'

'Could he have murdered Bouchard for the money he was carrying?'

'You know as well as I, Georges, that there's not a man alive who wouldn't kill, given sufficient provocation and the right circumstances.'

Georges continued to the gambling den on Quai des Augustins. It was late afternoon, and business was slow. The banker agreed to shut down his table and talk. Yes, he knew both Bouchard and Gillet. They appeared to be friends, or at least familiar. The banker had noticed that they occasionally cleared each other's debts.

'Did Gillet come here yesterday with a large sum of money?'

The banker frowned, answered reluctantly. 'Why, yes, he did. Paid off the debt he owed the house. He had lost heavily during the past week. We give our regular customers a few days of grace before we go after them.'

The banker's eyes were pitiless. Clandestine gambling was illegal in France, even if the law winked at it. Bankers, such as this one, could not go to court for redress, but had to collect debts privately, by force, if necessary.

Upon entering the den, Georges had noticed a pair of the house's 'debt collectors', stout, hard-faced ruffians, who could press money out of stones. Gillet had good reason to pay promptly. Georges was confident that the engraver's money had come from Bouchard's purse. But how?

*   *   *

It was dark outside when Saint-Martin and Georges made their way to the engraver's room in the Louvre. Gillet was at the point of leaving for a night of clandestine engraving at the Palais-Royal or gambling at his customary place on the Left Bank.

'Where are you going?' asked Georges, as he strode into the room, forcing Gillet to step back.

'To the Quai des Augustins,' replied the engraver, his eyes shifting from his visitors to the open door. Saint-Martin shut it, then nodded to Georges to lead the interrogation. They sat around a table. An expression akin to terror began to spread over Gillet's face.

Georges stared him down. 'Tell me where you found the money you used to pay your gambling debt last night.'

For a moment, Gillet seemed tongue-tied. Finally, he stammered, 'My friend the painter Bouchard gave it to me.'

'Really?'

'He had won a thousand louis d'or—enough for a lifetime of leisure—and then sneaked out ahead of me. We were supposed to help each other. When I caught up with him, he claimed he had to pay his creditors, who threatened him with prison. I said that the banker had told me, "Pay up or be beaten." Bouchard and I argued all the way to the Louvre. At the passageway by the river, he finally gave me the money.'

'And you gave him a receipt?' Saint-Martin cocked his head, sensing that he hadn't heard the whole truth.

'That wasn't our custom. We shook hands on the agreement.'

'Sounds to me that it may have been a loan. Have you told his widow?'

'No, the money isn't hers. Bouchard and I had agreed to cover each other's losses, share our winnings.'

'You must have been angry that he tried to trick you.'

Gillet flinched at the colonel's insinuation. 'I didn't kill him, sir. He was alive when I left.'

'Any witnesses?'

'I'm afraid not.' Gillet's eyes wavered.

The colonel's doubts persisted. 'Stand off to one side, monsieur. Your room will now be searched.'

*   *   *

60

For half an hour, Georges lifted floorboards, tapped walls, and looked in all the likely places where a person might hide valuables. Finally, he discovered a secret cache under a windowsill. He spread its contents on the table—an account book, a journal, a package of letters, several drawings and sketches.

Gillet moaned, hung his head. Saint-Martin told him to sit down at the table. Georges joined them.

The account book revealed the engraver's financial history. He had carefully entered his wins and losses, the latter greatly in excess of the former. His wages from the printing office failed to balance his accounts. That was achieved only by the considerable sums received from the Palais-Royal, no names mentioned.

Saint-Martin closely studied the drawings and sketches and concluded that they had artistic merit. But were they original? They were unsigned.

He held them up for Gillet to see. 'Are they yours?'

The engraver hesitated before tentatively nodding.

Georges whispered to the colonel, 'These were intended for the duke's antigovernment broadsheets. I recognize this one.' He pointed to an obscene sketch of the queen together with her friend the Princesse de Lamballe. 'Inspecteur Quidor would dearly like to see that one.'

Among the letters were several from Gillet's father in Paris, a master engraver, reproaching his son for gambling. In the last one, three years ago, the father repudiated him.

The colonel swept the cache into his portfolio and turned to the engraver. 'I shall study these things more carefully. In the meantime, you shall remain in Paris under Inspecteur Quidor's eye. You are suspected of the murder of the painter Bouchard.'

Late in the evening, Anne returned home, eager to meet her husband. With her so often at the Bouchard apartment, they had seen little of each other yesterday or today. He warmly embraced her at the door—had noticed her crossing the courtyard.

He led her by the hand into his office. 'How is Madame Bouchard?' he asked.

'Still depressed. Silent. Stays in her room. Michou keeps trying to draw her out.'

As she sat down, he remarked, 'We've spoken before about the engraver Gillet, and you've met him once.' He briefly reported on the investigation of the engraver. 'Can you comment on him?'

While untying her bonnet, Anne gathered her impressions. 'I observed him closely when he brought us Michou's message and the news of Bouchard's death. His long, sad, pale face is imprinted on my memory. At the time, I sensed that he was no ordinary messenger. A tense, anxious man, he seemed more personally involved in what had happened—and better informed than I would have expected.'

'I had a similar impression of him. Please study these items and I'll ask you some questions.' He handed her the books and letters from the engraver's room.

When she had examined them, Paul asked, 'Do you think that Gillet is guilty of Bouchard's murder?'

'Possibly. He had an excellent opportunity and a strong motive for the crime.'

'But where is the poniard? He denied having had one, and none of his acquaintances have ever seen him with one. When we searched his room, we couldn't uncover it.'

'It's in the river, I suppose.' Anne paused. 'The more difficult problem for me is the premeditated nature of the crime, apparently staged to dishonor the victim. I think that Gillet would have acted on impulse. He might have carried the poniard for protection, and didn't know in advance that Bouchard would win so much. On the way home, Gillet would have simply seized the opportunity to kill the painter and steal his money. Neither man was carrying a wine bottle when they left the gambling den. After killing Bouchard, Gillet would hardly have gone to the trouble of finding a bottle, drinking half of its contents, and placing it next to the seated corpse.'

'I agree entirely,' Paul granted with a smile, then pointed to the items on the desk. 'These indicate that Gillet and Bouchard were only limited partners. According to Gillet's account book, their previous exchanges of money had been small and erratic. Gillet paid most of his gambling debts from extra income at the Palais-Royal.'

Anne added, 'I know Bouchard to have been a self-centered

and greedy man. It seems to me out of character for him to yield to the engraver's entreaties and generously hand over his purse in the middle of the night. He would more likely have said, "I'll think it over and see what I can do for you.'"

'Yes,' Paul conceded, 'if he were to yield, he would do so only under threat of violence, literally at dagger's point.'

'What shall we conclude?' Anne asked.

'That Gillet never did catch up with Bouchard, but found him dead sitting in the passage, the bottle at his side, the money still in his pocket. Gillet fabricated a story about gambling partners that would justify his theft of the money.'

'What a foolish risk he has taken! He could be convicted of murder and cruelly executed.'

'But I am not entirely surprised. His addiction to gambling is like a sickness that robs him of reason. The prospect of winning a fortune with Bouchard's money makes him willing to risk life itself.'

'If he didn't kill Bouchard, might he have observed the murder?'

'Possibly—he was near the scene at the time that it happened.'

'If the killer saw Gillet, he is in great jeopardy. What will you do with him?'

'Put him under close surveillance. Prohibit him from gambling. Attach his wages at the printing office and force him to pay back to Madame Bouchard the money he stole from her husband.'

'And if he were to refuse to cooperate?'

'I'd bring him before a magistrate and charge him with the theft of one thousand louis d'or. There's sufficient circumstantial evidence to convict him. The magistrate would imprison him for a later trial. Meanwhile the investigation of the murder would continue.' Paul moved Gillet's materials into a file box and put it on a shelf.

'Apropos of another matter,' Anne began. 'I spent much of today observing Cécile Tremblay, the Comtesse de Serre's former maid, now living near the Louvre and working as a seamstress. From a café across the street from her shop, I watched customers going in and coming out. Some with small items, kerchiefs and the like. Others with heavy woolen gowns. One person stood out, the old lady who sells flowers from the steps of Saint-Roch.'

'Nothing unusual there,' Paul observed, lines of puzzlement gathering on his forehead. 'Why shouldn't she try to sell Cécile a flower?'

'Flowers aren't her real business,' Anne replied. 'A few minutes later, she came out, crossed the street, and entered my café. Took a seat at a table facing me. I pretended to read a newspaper. Cécile soon left her shop—didn't lock the door, probably left a shop girl there to serve customers. She hurried across the street and joined the flower lady. I couldn't see Cécile's face. Her back was to me. She was shaking, her shoulders hunched forward.

'"You have four days to find the money," said the old lady. "Or Pierre will pay you a visit. You know what that means." She got up, glared at Cécile, and left.

'Cécile stayed at the table, began sobbing. She wiped her face with a kerchief, then returned to the shop.'

'Did you smell extortion?' Paul's interest picked up.

'Yes. And my impression was strengthened when I left the café. The old lady was still in sight. So, I followed her. Guess where she led me? To the garden of the Palais-Royal, where she spoke to Pierre, the Comte de Serre's valet. He looked displeased.'

'A remarkable coincidence! Why would the count want money from his former maid?' Paul reflected for a moment on his own question. 'Perhaps Pierre is operating independently, raising extra income.'

'I thought so. I continued to watch him for a while. Several persons approached him in a similar way, as if he were a kind of spymaster. I must avoid his spies when I have a conversation with Cécile. Someone has an unhealthy interest in her.'

Twelve

Healing

Under a clear blue early-morning sky, Anne set off for the Bouchard apartment, wishing she could bring the painter's widow out into the fine weather. Was she well enough yet to discuss her husband's business?

Anne's visits to the apartment had become irregular, since she began keeping track of Cécile Tremblay. There had been little Anne could do for Madame Bouchard. Her depression lingered. She continued to seclude herself in her room. Michou prepared her meals, looked after the apartment, and otherwise occupied herself in the studio.

Anne let herself in with her key to the new lock. The apartment was quiet at first, but as she neared the kitchen, the hissing of a kettle greeted her. She was mentally preparing to sign a greeting to Michou, when she recognized Madame Bouchard at the stove. Michou was nowhere in sight. But breakfast for two lay on the table in the middle of the room.

Madame Bouchard sensed Anne's presence, may have heard her steps, and turned around. The hint of a smile appeared on her haggard face. 'Madame Cartier, if I'd known that you might come, I'd have set another place.' With an inquiring side-glance at Anne, she started for the dish cabinet.

'I'm happy to join you. Where's Michou?'

'In the studio. Would you kindly call her? Everything is ready.'

Anne found her friend in a thin dressing gown, standing before the *Andromeda*. A palette and brushes lay in front of the easel. A good light was coming through the windows. Anne was puzzled. 'Are *you* preparing to work on this

65

painting?' Then she noticed that Michou was removing the pins from her hair. It fell in an auburn cascade down her back. She was ready to model, to step into the role of the sacrificial young woman.

When she saw Anne, she grinned. 'Madame Bouchard will begin painting after breakfast.' Michou slipped out of her gown and struck her pose, as if tied to the cliff depicted behind her, twisting to escape from the monster's clutches, a mixture of terror and despair on her face. After a few moments, she smiled mischievously and left her pose.

When she had covered herself, she went on signing. 'Last night, Adrienne—that's what she wants me to call her now—left her room for the first time in almost four days. "I need to get back to work," she wrote to me. For an hour, we discussed with pen and paper what she might do, a child's portrait, for example. I encouraged her to talk, didn't think it wise to push her. But when none of the ideas appealed to her, I mentioned *Andromeda* and offered to pose. Gradually she warmed up to the project, gained self-confidence.'

'How does she feel about her late husband?' asked Anne.

'She now recalls his better side—he could be charming, like a talented boy who wouldn't grow up. She misses him. Will bury him tomorrow morning at Saint-Roch. Will you join us?'

Anne nodded. She would find someone to keep an eye on Cécile.

Michou gazed thoughtfully at the painting. 'She sees it as his memorial, probably his best work. She wants to complete it, and I'm sure she can.'

Anne wondered how Bouchard's peers would receive the finished painting. Could they judge it without prejudice? He was estranged from most members of the Academy of Painting and Sculpture. The investigation into his death would probably confirm his reputation in their minds as a rascal. But, for now, that didn't really matter. Work on the painting would improve Madame Bouchard's health and possibly her finances. Michou would benefit as well by helping her new friend.

At breakfast, Anne brought up the issue of the intruder's mysterious search of the studio and the apartment a few days earlier. 'What could he have been looking for?' she cautiously asked Adrienne, hoping that the topic wouldn't distress her.

'The intruder, like everyone else in the Louvre, would know that we have no money nor any items worth stealing, except for certain paintings. And these he didn't touch.' She grew still, unnaturally quiet for a moment. 'My husband sometimes hid things from me—bottles of brandy, for example.' A frown gathered on her face. Her throat tightened. It looked like she might break down. But she breathed deeply and went on. 'He may have hidden something special that the intruder desperately wanted.' She paused again, searching her memory. 'I know a few of his hiding places.'

She finished her coffee and rose from the table. 'Come with me.'

In the studio Anne and Michou watched while Adrienne opened secret panels to reveal a half-empty bottle of brandy, another of laudanum, and a package of tobacco, nothing the intruder would want, even if he could find them. 'My husband also kept records and carried on correspondence about certain secret business deals. Here.' She raised a ladder to rest against a high shelf, climbed up, and handed Anne a plaster cast of a statue of Mercury standing on a low pedestal. She set it on a table.

Adrienne rested the statue on its side, removed a piece of heavy paper glued lightly to its base, and pulled out a small package tied with string. 'I can't bear to go through this,' she said in a taut voice. 'Here, Anne, you search for whatever may have cost my husband his life.'

Anne's hands trembled as she took the package. She stared at it for a moment, steeling her nerves, then spread the contents out on a table and began reading. There were many notes written in minuscule script on odd scraps of paper. The name Gillet appeared occasionally on signed receipts for loans. Anne quickly calculated that the engraver owed Bouchard several hundred livres, strong reason to search for the receipts and remove his debt.

One item, written in Latin, stood out. Anne couldn't read the language, but she recognized Monsieur Hamel's name. She put the note aside. Paul could study it.

She picked up a small, official-looking envelope, its seal broken. Inside was an invitation addressed to Monsieur Moretti, requesting him to attend the evening party in the garden of the Tuileries for the opening of the Salon of 1787. That's odd, Anne thought. Where did Bouchard find it and why did he hide it?

Also in the envelope was a note in Bouchard's hand. It read: *August 30 ... 10 louis ... Place Dauphine ... September 1.*

August 30 was the evening she had followed the painter into Place Dauphine and he had met a mysterious cloaked figure. Moretti? This note smelled of extortion. Bouchard would exchange the invitation for ten pieces of gold, the price of an engraving or two. September 1 was perhaps the deadline for the payment in Place Dauphine. It was also the day he was murdered. Anne held up the note in one hand and the invitation in the other, stared at them. What could they mean?

Paul arrived at noon and sat at the studio table next to Anne. She put the newly discovered notes and the invitation in front of him. He began with the Latin note, soon struggled with it. Finally, he tapped the note. 'This doesn't make sense, must be written in code. I give up. Perhaps the Comte de Savarin can figure it out. Aunt Marie will take it to him.'

A pleasant memory brought a smile to Anne's lips. Her friend Comtesse Marie de Beaumont had recently become close to the count, she a widow, he a widower. A brilliant man, archivist at Versailles, he also deciphered secret correspondence for the Ministry of Foreign Affairs. Anne wondered when he would find time for the note.

Paul sifted through Bouchard's financial papers. In a few minutes he had finished and set them aside. 'Gillet could be the intruder. The receipts also show that Gillet had to return whatever he borrowed. In my view, he should repay the money he most likely took from the dead man's pocket.' Paul acknowledged the doubt rising in Anne's face. 'Madame Bouchard shouldn't expect much from him. At the moment, he's penniless.'

Paul then picked up the invitation, fingered the broken seal, assessed the high quality of the paper. 'Moretti had it with him at the garden party. Bouchard was never there. For him to find it, Moretti must have lost it after leaving the party. According to Bouchard's own account, he did not leave the Louvre that night. Therefore, Moretti must have gone to the Louvre after the party and lost the invitation in a place where Bouchard could find it.'

Anne nodded. 'That puts Moretti in a position to enter Hamel's studio. We know Bouchard was also in the studio. He may have observed Moretti from hiding and seen him deface the Serre portrait. I would guess that Bouchard also saw the invitation slip out of Moretti's pocket. Later, he met Moretti in Place Dauphine and threatened to tell all unless he was paid.'

Paul lifted a cautionary hand. 'Moretti, of course, could claim he never entered the Louvre—no one, except perhaps Bouchard, has claimed to have seen him in the building. He could have lost the invitation elsewhere. By chance, Bouchard found it and concocted his story.'

Anne pointed to the invitation and shook her head. 'Just think of the odds. In the dark of night in an area as vast as the Tuileries and the Louvre, would Bouchard have chanced upon this small envelope? Moretti would have returned home from the party by way of a passage through the Galerie du Louvre into the Quai du Louvre, on to Pont Neuf, thence to Place Dauphine. He would probably never have crossed Bouchard's path. It seems to me that Moretti *must* have entered the Louvre and Hamel's gallery and there lost the invitation.'

'You may be right, Anne. But all this is conjecture. We lack convincing evidence.' Paul thought for a moment. 'Nor do we know why Moretti might have entered the studio. And why would he deface the portrait that he admired and wanted to buy?'

Late in the afternoon, after a few inquiries, Paul and Anne found Moretti in the Salon's exhibition hall. He arrived nearly every day after an early dinner and systematically studied the collection, beginning with the most important pieces. He could often be seen leaning on his gold-headed cane in ardent discussion with art critics and serious amateurs.

Today, he stood before one of Hubert Robert's large paintings of ancient Roman ruins, *The Pont du Gard*, depicting the Roman aqueduct that used to carry water to Nîmes in southern France. In the painting's foreground small human figures were washing and fishing in the river that ran beneath the aqueduct's great arches. The monumental stone structure, still remarkably intact, stretched majestically across the picture's middle ground against a cloudy sky.

Anne and Paul waited until Moretti was momentarily alone. 'Monsieur, may we join you?' Paul asked.

The art dealer replied with a tentative smile. 'I would be honored.'

After a brief exchange about the merits of the painting, Paul said evenly, 'I have a few questions. Please follow me.'

Moretti's eyes darkened. 'Police business?'

'Yes.'

Paul led the way to an empty room. The two men took seats at a table opposite each other. Anne sat off to one side with pen and paper. Paul had coached her on the art of taking notes. She could be helpful when Georges was busy.

Moretti tried vainly to appear nonchalant, but he had begun to perspire. 'Would you tell me, Colonel, the reason for this mysterious procedure?'

Ignoring the question, Paul took the garden party invitation from his portfolio and showed it to Moretti. 'Do you recognize this?'

'Yes.'

'Where do you suppose I found it?'

'How should I know? After the party it was of no use. I dropped it, or threw it away somewhere. You can't expect me to recall such a trifle.'

Paul put ice in his voice. 'Did you enter the Louvre after the party?'

Moretti's eyes wavered. 'I went directly home to Place Dauphine.'

'Then how did Monsieur Bouchard find this invitation? I can account for his movements that night. He did not leave the Louvre.'

'I should think the answer to your question is obvious, Colonel. I must have dropped the invitation on the grounds of the Tuileries or on my way home. Someone may have seen it fall. For whatever reason, he picked it up and left it in the Louvre.'

'Far-fetched, monsieur. Did Monsieur Bouchard use this invitation in an attempt to blackmail you?'

Beads of perspiration now covered Moretti's brow. 'No, he did not, though I'd be surprised if the idea hadn't crossed his mind.'

Paul raised his hands. 'I must contradict you. Six days ago, Thursday evening, August 30, an informant working for me followed Bouchard to Place Dauphine. A hooded figure came out from your gallery and met him. Tell me, what took place between you?'

Moretti looked away, his fingers gripped the gold head of his cane, his lips tightened. Finally, he sighed, frowned at Anne, whose pen was poised in anticipation of his next word.

She shivered. He might have guessed that she had observed the meeting.

He turned to Paul. 'Colonel, I feel uncomfortable trying to mislead you. And, in any case, I am doing it badly.'

'Then, monsieur, let's begin again. Did you visit the Louvre after the garden party?'

'Yes, I did. At the party, I learned that Hamel had touched up the portrait since I had last seen it. That made me curious. Later, as I drove away alone from the Tuileries, I suddenly thought of the picture. On an impulse I parked and went to his studio. It was dark, but for the moonlight. I unshuttered my lamp, studied a few changes in the portrait, then left. The invitation must have slipped out of my pocket. Bouchard found it.

'A few days later, he approached me. In the meantime, someone had defaced the portrait. Bouchard said he had seen me entering Hamel's studio and had found the invitation there. Bouchard warned that others might think I was the culprit. He promised that he would say nothing and would return the invitation to me, Thursday evening, in Place Dauphine. "Bring ten louis d'or for my trouble," he told me.

'I should have caned him on the spot for the rogue that he

71

was. But he was also a hotheaded, malicious fellow. He would malign my gallery, blacken my reputation, insinuate that I had damaged the portrait. The public might believe him. I'm a newcomer and a foreigner. So I agreed to pay him—ten louis wasn't a great sum. By Thursday evening, however, I had come to my senses. When we met, I told him to go to the devil.'

'My informant told me that you also threatened him. Shook your fist at him.'

'He was impertinent, insulted my Italian heritage. I warned him that if he tried to cause me harm, I'd beat him to within an inch of his life.'

'I would like to think that you showed him that much restraint.' Paul leaned forward, arms resting on the table. 'That will be all for now. Thank you for your cooperation.'

Moretti rose from the table and walked to the door.

Paul raised a hand. 'One last thing, monsieur.'

Moretti stopped, his hand reaching for the door handle. He turned with a look of annoyance. 'Yes?'

'Where were you in the early hours of September first when Bouchard was murdered?'

'I entertained several gentlemen and courtesans until midnight, then went to bed with one of the women, called Louise, address unknown, and slept late into the morning.' He opened the door. 'Any more questions, Colonel?'

Paul shook his head.

Moretti walked out and closed the door with exaggerated care.

Paul leaned back in the chair, arms crossed on his chest. 'Monsieur Moretti may have raised a few more questions than he answered. What do you think, Anne?'

She took Moretti's place at the table, glanced at her notes. 'He looked uncomfortable trying to explain that lost invitation. His drive home alone from the party was planned so that he could slip into Hamel's studio unobserved. He couldn't know that Bouchard would be there. I would suspect that he defaced the Serre portrait, if I knew *why* he would do that.'

'Look at it this way, Anne. Perhaps Moretti simply went

into Hamel's studio to study the portrait by himself and lost the invitation there. Bouchard found it while he was vandalizing the head, then figured he could shift the blame to Moretti and extort a few gold pieces from him. Angered, his reputation threatened, Moretti stabbed Bouchard to death.'

'That's consistent with the facts, Paul. We can't trust Moretti, he has lied to us before. Unfortunately, he sounded confident that the courtesan Louise would verify his alibi for September first. But, of course, he could hire an assassin, equip him with a poniard, and stage Bouchard's death.' Anne threw up her hands. 'I've had enough speculation. Let's have supper.'

Thirteen

A Poniard

September 6

Michou had completed a morning of work with Madame Bouchard and was now eager for a change. She set out for Hamel's studio. On the way, she pondered Anne's report yesterday that Moretti had admitted being secretly there on the eve of the Salon. Strange as it might seem, he could have vandalized the Serre portrait. He might even have arranged Bouchard's assassination.

As she approached the studio, Moretti vanished from her mind. Her pace quickened. It was two in the afternoon. Hamel would have left for dinner by then. Her friend, Marc Latour, the painter's assistant, would be there alone. Michou peered through a half-opened door into the studio. Marc looked up from his easel and stretched. She caught his eye. He beckoned her in.

'Where have you been?' he signed, his brow creased with concern.

'Looking after Bouchard's widow, working in his studio.'
She took a seat next to him.

'Hamel wants to see you.' He smiled, having noticed the look of surprise on her face. 'Yes, he changed his mind when he realized that with your help he could complete the Serre portrait and earn six thousand livres. He'll be back in a couple of hours. In the meantime, I'm happy you're here.' He gazed at her for a moment with a persuasive smile. 'Would you pose for a half hour?' He gestured toward his canvas.

She studied the partially-finished frontal sketch of herself. Her face had a pensive look, touched by sadness. Her lips were slightly parted, as if about to speak. A sudden, sharp inner pain served as a reminder that God had denied her the power to hear or to utter words. It seemed cruel, and she had sometimes reproached Him. But He had given her the ability to express her feelings, her needs, with signs and gestures. He had also endowed her with an artist's eye that brought her great pleasure.

In a mood of general satisfaction she acquiesced with a nod to Marc's request, then moved her chair into position in front of him and struck her pose.

While she sat motionless facing the artist, she reflected on him. A kind, gentle person, he had an honest and generous smile. She thought of him as Marc, though she still addressed him as Monsieur Latour. He and she were alike in many ways—both of them short and slender, about the same age. They seemed to get along well together. She enjoyed their walks on the Quai du Louvre, tea and biscuits at a café in the Palais-Royal.

It helped greatly that he could sign, for he had lived many years with a deaf sister. He could also reach into the souls of deaf people and understand the different ways they experienced life. With him she felt normal; with most hearing people she felt odd, a stranger.

At the end of the session, the artist put down his brush, leaned back, and gazed at the picture. His eyes glowed with pleasure. Michou stepped behind him, laid her hands on his shoulder, examined what he had done. She was delighted. He had given her the hint of a smile. She leaned forward and kissed his cheek. He raised his hand and caressed the spot.

She signed that she'd like to look at what Hamel and his

students were doing. Marc left his easel and led her through the studio, stopping at a variety of pictures. She found his comments helpful. Finally, they came to a large, highly finished oil painting of a woman in ancient garb stabbing herself—as accomplished a work as many she had seen in the Salon. 'I like it,' she signed. 'Excellent composition, honest pathos. Who painted it?'

He raised his hand. 'I did,' he signed modestly. 'Just finished it.' He finger-spelled the title of the work, *Lucretia's Suicide*.

'Why haven't I seen it earlier?'

'I didn't want to show it to you before it was ready. I've displayed it in the studio since Monday. Hamel, of course, has watched me paint it.'

'Does he like it?'

'He shakes his head, quarrels with details. Doesn't offer helpful criticism.'

Michou drew near to the painting, studied it closely, then stepped back, frowning. 'Why did she kill herself?'

He related the ancient tale of Lucretia, the Roman matron, so proud of her virtue that when a tyrant's son violated it, she took her own life, preferring to die rather than to live with dishonor.

Michou shook her head with disapproval. 'My life,' she signed, 'is more precious to me than what others think about my virtue. Lucretia didn't lead the man on. He forced himself upon her. Why in heaven's name should she kill herself?'

In the course of this discussion Michou's eyes fastened upon the weapon in the woman's hand. 'What's that?'

'A long, thin knife.' Marc handed her a magnifying glass.

'Have you used a real knife for this detail?'

He nodded hesitantly. 'It's in the storeroom.'

'I'd like to see it.' Michou's heart began to race. They left the studio, crossed a hallway, and entered a room with shelves of supplies on one wall and cabinets on the other. One of the cabinets was full of swords, spears, pieces of armor, shields, and helmets—a virtual ancient armory. Marc opened a wooden case to reveal an assortment of knives.

The one she suspected, a poniard, was there. She carried it to the light and borrowed his magnifying glass again. On either

75

side of the blade were long, deep, narrow grooves. Her hand began to tremble. She gripped the glass with both hands, steadied it, and searched. A few moments later, as she suspected, she saw brown flecks in the grooves and more flecks at the weapon's hilt. This knife had drawn blood.

She glanced up at her companion, looked into his eyes, and felt an almost overpowering rush of fear. He, too, had realized the significance of her discovery. Someone might have used this knife to murder the painter Bouchard. The killer suddenly seemed very close.

For a long moment Michou and Marc stared at each other, silently, frantically, each considering what to do.

'We must wipe it clean and return it to the box,' urged Marc, pointing to the knife. 'It can't be the murder weapon, but it will draw suspicion to Hamel or to someone in his studio. The police will turn this place upside down, completely disrupt our work. Hamel will be furious and blame me—I'm responsible for this cabinet.'

Marc reached for the knife. But Michou raised a warning hand and signed, 'The colonel should determine how this knife has been used. He's fair and will protect us.' At least, she thought, he would do all that he could. 'I must take it to him.'

'What can it prove?' Marc insisted. 'Someone may have used it to stick a pig or stir a pail of paint. There's no murderer in this studio.' He glanced nervously toward the door, then signed with caution, 'I dislike Hamel. He's arrogant, pompous, and selfish. But he wouldn't kill anybody. Nor would any of his students. Nor would I.' He paused for a reaction from Michou.

She stood stolidly in front of him, trying to conceal the growing turmoil in her mind. She sensed that this issue was separating her from a man she had grown fond of. And she was of two minds. Perhaps the colonel didn't need to study the knife. It might not help determine who killed the painter Bouchard. So why cause a lot of trouble for innocent bystanders? Was she being stubborn and proud? On the other hand, a quiet inner voice insisted that the colonel be allowed to judge the knife's usefulness.

Michou signed with all the conviction she could muster,

'The colonel is a reasonable man. He won't disturb the studio any more than necessary.'

Marc pleaded, 'Michou, let me return the knife to the box.' He reached out his hand to her.

She shook her head, then backed away from him. Tears threatened to burst from her eyes. She turned abruptly and left the room, and didn't look back.

She hurried to the provost's office on Rue Saint-Honoré, looking neither right nor left, stumbling, bumping into people. A great sadness filled her heart. She realized with a sudden, blinding clarity that she had longed all her life for a good man to love her. Deaf, an orphan from birth, poor and without patrons, she had almost despaired. But recently, God seemed to have relented and given her friends like the colonel and Anne. God had even guided her toward Marc, a kind man who had accepted her limitations, understood her need for friendship, and even seemed inclined to love her. 'So, God,' she muttered inwardly to herself, 'why have you placed this obstacle between us? It isn't fair!'

Late at night, Colonel Saint-Martin sat at his desk, magnifying glass in his right hand. Michou had brought the knife to him several hours earlier, pointing out the brown flecks. A chemist had tested them and had agreed that they were, indeed, blood and rather fresh. The surgeon who had examined Bouchard's body reported that the knife matched the victim's wound.

Anne joined him. Michou had also related to her what had happened in the studio. 'What's to be done?' she asked her husband. 'Michou is nearly heartbroken. I couldn't console her. She has gone back to the Bouchard apartment.'

'We shall proceed with care, Anne, and cause the least possible pain to the guiltless.' He paused, then laid the magnifying glass on the desk. 'I regret Michou's predicament. Still, Georges and I must ask Hamel and the students, has anyone recently used the knife to slaughter an animal? And so on. But I do believe we have the murder weapon.'

'Why would the killer use that particular weapon?' Anne asked. 'Outside the Louvre, he could have easily found many knives to choose from. And, having used it, why didn't he throw it into the river?'

'That's how a common killer might reason,' Paul replied. 'But we've already noticed peculiarities in the murder of Bouchard—the seated arrangement of his body, the wine bottle at his side, and the vandalized Serre portrait.'

'This knife,' Anne said, pointing to the weapon lying between them on the desk, 'might have been associated in the killer's mind with the story of Lucretia. In her hands, the knife was the instrument for restoring a family's honor. The murderer might have reasoned, as Michou did, that he should kill the man who violated his honor rather than kill himself.'

'True. We may be dealing with a person inclined to artistic images and ways of thinking that distinguish him from more common killers.' He paused to weigh a new thought. 'Or he might be an unprincipled schemer within Hamel's studio, or having access to it, who is pointing us away from himself to someone else.'

Less inclined to conjecture than her husband, Anne simply concluded that, next to Moretti, Hamel was the most likely killer. He was already a prime suspect because of his open hatred for the man he believed had violated the Serre portrait, his masterpiece. He also had easy access to the weapons cabinet and hadn't offered an alibi. Or, she wondered, could the villain be a disgruntled student? Marc Latour, for example, though it was hard for her to imagine such a gentle man killing anyone.

Fourteen

A Desperate Man

September 7

Early the next morning, after seeing Anne off to the Bouchard apartment to comfort Michou, Saint-Martin and Georges made

78

their way to Hamel's studio. They paused at the open door to his office. He sat at his writing table, studying a sketch, a sour expression on his face. Probably a student's work, Saint-Martin thought. He cleared his throat.

Hamel looked up. Their grim appearance in uniform startled him. He dropped the sketch and lurched to his feet. 'What do you want, gentlemen?'

The colonel ignored the question. 'Do you recognize this?' He laid the newly found knife on the table in front of the painter.

'Yes,' Hamel replied after a moment's hesitation. 'It's mine.' He motioned the colonel to a chair and sat down. Georges sat off to one side with paper and pen. Hamel appeared puzzled, glanced again at the knife. 'Why do you ask?'

'It has recent bloodstains, sir. Can you explain why?' He pointed out the brownish flecks on the long, thin blade.

'No. I've had nothing to do with it. Haven't used it in years. Ask my assistant, Marc Latour. He's painting the Lucretia story.'

'I shall. But before then, I must ask, where were you on the night the painter Bouchard was killed?'

For a moment, Hamel stared aghast at Saint-Martin, as if unable to imagine that anyone could suspect him of murder. 'Colonel, how dare you insinuate that I might have had anything to do with the painter's death?'

Saint-Martin received Hamel's protest calmly, accustomed as he was to theatrical outrage while questioning high-and-mighty suspects of serious crime. 'A bloody knife has been discovered in the room next to your office. You and the victim had harsh words for each other over the Serre portrait. I would be remiss in my duty if I failed to ask an obvious question. So, tell me, where were you that night?'

Hamel looked away, chewed on his lower lip. His tongue seemed paralyzed. 'I was . . .' he stammered.

'Yes? Get on with it, man. Won't your wife vouch for you?'

'My wife has moved to our country estate. I was with Jerôme, the Academy's servant.'

Georges caught Saint-Martin's eye with a knowing glance. The adjutant had interviewed the servant along with Hamel's students in connection with the defaced portrait. Michou had also mentioned him. Jerôme Duby was the academy's principal male model.

'Where were the two of you and what were you doing?' The colonel tried to banish from his voice the satisfaction he felt while pricking Hamel's bloated pride. This senior member of the Academy loudly presented himself to society as a respectable married man in contrast to lewd, irresponsible artists like Bouchard.

'We were together in his room.' His voice had fallen to barely a whisper. Sweat gathered on his brow. He cleared his throat and struggled to regain some of his lost dignity. 'I know what you must be thinking, Colonel. But it isn't true. We merely discussed artistic matters.'

The colonel was silent for a long moment, gazing skeptically at Hamel. Though flustered, the man had sufficient presence of mind to avoid confessing to sodomy, still a capital offense in France. At midcentury, two men convicted of the crime had been burned at the stake on Place de Grève. Since then, the offense had not been prosecuted to the full extent of the law. But the police could arrest Hamel, exposing him to public ridicule and scorn. Magistrates might hold him in prison for a week or two and banish him from Paris.

'Colonel, all this is confidential, is it not? Your discretion is well known.'

'Monsieur Hamel, this is an interrogation into serious criminal matters, not a polite conversation. My discretion, as you call it, will depend greatly on the degree of your cooperation. Do not attempt to intimidate those students and other persons under your authority whose testimony I shall seek.'

Saint-Martin picked up the knife and told Georges it was time to leave. The adjutant finished writing, then confronted Hamel with his statement.

'You will sign it,' ordered Saint-Martin.

Eyes narrowed and dark, Hamel glared at the colonel, then glanced at the paper. He seemed paralyzed again.

'Those are your words, monsieur. If you were to renege, you would have no alibi. I would take you to prison for further questioning as our prime suspect in the murder of the painter Bouchard.'

Georges took a step toward Hamel. That was enough. The man dipped his pen into ink, readied his hand for a moment, and signed.

Out in the hallway, Georges remarked softly, 'The hypocrite! He resents having been exposed and will cause trouble for us if he can.'

Saint-Martin nodded. 'He remains a prime suspect until his friend gives him a credible alibi. Pity him, Georges. He is faced with a dilemma. Without the alibi he may be charged with murder, even though his friend could have done the actual killing. With the alibi he has exposed himself to a scandalous legal prosecution and the ruin of his reputation.'

'Where can we find Jerôme?' Saint-Martin asked a student in the hallway outside Hamel's office.

'At *work*, in the studio,' he replied, the hint of a leer in his eyes.

Mindful of the need for caution, the colonel opened the door slowly, quietly. He and Georges stepped into the room.

Jerôme lay on his side in the center of the studio, nude, resting on his right elbow, portraying a wounded warrior. A rope from the ceiling held his left arm high, imploring heaven's aid. A dozen students in a drawing exercise sat on chairs in a semicircle around him. A blazing candelabra hung above the reclining figure, adding to the diffused light from the windows and threatening him with dripping hot wax.

A slender young man approached the policemen. 'I'm Marc Latour, in charge of this drawing exercise. How may I help you?'

Saint-Martin identified himself and Georges, noting that the young man suddenly grew anxious. 'We want to speak with Monsieur Duby privately when he has dressed. In the meantime, if you are free, we shall ask you a few questions.'

'The students can work on their own for a while. I'm at your disposal.'

'Then show us the storage room.'

Latour led them across the hall and opened the door. In reply to their questions, he explained that, as far as he knew, only he and Monsieur Hamel had keys to the room. It was kept locked. A bother, to be sure. But there were items valuable enough to tempt a student to steal.

While Georges carefully examined the room, Saint-Martin lifted the knife from his portfolio.

'Has anyone recently shown interest in this knife?'

A shock of recognition came over the young man's face.

'A few weeks ago,' he replied through tightened lips, 'I was working on the story of Lucretia's suicide and used the knife while painting a detail. Monsieur Hamel, fellow students, and a few visitors have studied the picture.' He paused. 'I can't recall any of them showing particular interest in the knife.' The young man's voice had become uncertain.

'Who were the visitors?'

'Monsieur Moretti, the Comte de Serre, and Michou du Saint-Esprit.'

Saint-Martin met the young man's eye. 'Why do my questions appear to distress you, sir?'

'Monsieur Hamel has told me and the other students to refer questions about the Academy to him.'

'He cannot mean to obstruct the work of the police, I'm sure. Now, please answer my questions.' Saint-Martin held the knife in both hands before Latour. 'Tell me, who could have taken it and plunged it into the painter Bouchard's heart?'

Latour stared at the weapon silently. His expression was guarded. Saint-Martin detected a strong scent of fear. If the young man were to implicate Hamel or any other powerful man in the murder of Bouchard, or in any way sully the reputation of the Royal Academy of Painting and Sculpture, he would seriously risk losing his position in the studio, as well as his lodging. The Academy would offer him no prospect of future employment. No one would recommend that his paintings be exhibited or that he become a member. What must he think of Michou, who brought him into this situation?

'I'm sorry, Colonel, I have no idea who might have taken the knife.'

'Then tell me, who has recently borrowed the key and entered the cabinet and could have taken the knife while you were not watching?'

Latour was silent for a moment reflecting. He finally replied, waving toward the studio. 'Most of our students. And our recent visitors.' He went on to list several men and women while Georges wrote down their names. Among them, the colonel noted again Monsieur Moretti and the Comte de Serre, neither of whom was likely to have used the knife himself. The former had a courtesan's alibi, the latter would not have wielded an assassin's weapon.

'However, the knife was always in its place when I locked the cabinet at the end of the day.'

'In that case, the murderer must have been someone who had a key to the cabinet and took the knife after you checked the contents and returned it before you checked again the next day. Is that correct?'

A look of dismay came over the young man's face. He realized he had implicated either himself or his master in the crime. 'It must be correct, sir. I can think of no other answer.'

The colonel pressed him further. 'Where were you, monsieur, the night that Bouchard was killed?'

Latour appeared to shudder. Ever since his quarrel with Michou, he must have dreaded hearing that question. 'I was alone in my room in the attic above the Hamel apartment.'

'Did you know the painter Bouchard? Had you any dealings with him?'

'I knew him by sight and carried messages between Hamel and him in the course of their quarrel over the Serre portrait commission. He and I had no reason to be friends—or enemies.'

'That will be all, monsieur. You are not under suspicion. But I would like you to be available in case I have more questions. We'll wait for Monsieur Duby inside the studio until his work is finished.'

He glanced at Georges, who signaled that he had completed his study of the storage room. As they left, Saint-Martin turned to Latour and remarked casually, 'It cost Michou a great deal to bring the knife to me. She thinks highly of you. But she did the right thing. I take seriously my duty to protect persons who help me investigate this crime. Tell me if Hamel tries to punish you.'

Latour said nothing. His expression was full of doubt.

For the last few minutes of the drawing session, Saint-Martin and Georges waited in the shadows just inside the studio door.

'This is a drafty room,' the colonel whispered. 'How must Monsieur Duby feel in the winter?'

'Chilled! They offered me the job, said I had the body.' He patted his stout torso and winked. 'But I'm too shy. I turned them down.'

'What a pity!' exclaimed the colonel in a tone of mock regret. 'French art has lost its Hercules.'

The rope holding Duby's arm was lowered. The model rose to his feet with only a trace of stiffness and put on a robe. Marc Latour approached him and they exchanged words. Duby tied a cord around his waist, slipped his feet into a pair of clogs, and sauntered up to the waiting policemen.

His manner was neither impertinent nor insolent. Yet Saint-Martin gathered that this was an intelligent man with a mind of his own, rather like the Comte de Serre's valet, Pierre. Both men appeared outwardly deferential to persons in authority but inwardly contemptuous of them.

Duby was fully aware of the beauty of his body, and expected others to admire its classical proportions, its perfectly developed musculature. Sensuality seemed to ooze from his pores. About thirty years old, he appeared to be in the prime of life. His hair was black and wavy, his beard short, and also black. He moved with an effortless grace.

The colonel again identified himself and Georges. 'We want to ask you a few questions. May we go to your room?' Saint-Martin had learned that the model lodged in the Louvre.

'Follow me,' the man replied without hesitation.

On the way, Duby explained that he grew up in the Louvre. An orphan from birth, in his youth he had been a servant in various artists' households. Ten years ago, Hamel had hired him for odd jobs in his studio and, soon after, asked him to model for the Academy. The artists kept him busy.

Throughout these remarks, Saint-Martin noticed that the model spoke like an academician, though with traces of Parisian argot and occasional lapses in grammar. A self-educated man with an ear for language and a retentive memory.

He lived on the ground floor off the Quai du Louvre, directly below Hamel's studio. His room was a spacious square with the bed in a curtained alcove. Engravings of ancient sculpture

84

and shelves of plaster models covered one wall. Fine brown mahogany chairs and a table formed a group on the opposite side of the room. Three upholstered chairs and a round tea table stood by the fireplace. Heavy crimson velvet drapes covered the windows. All the furnishings were worn but of high quality. To judge from appearances, Duby was a privileged servant.

'What can you tell us about the murder of the painter Bouchard?' asked Saint-Martin.

'No more than what I've heard. I don't know who did it.' He went on to say that he had regularly modeled for Bouchard during his productive years. Recently, he had posed for the Perseus in the painter's *Andromeda*. Bouchard was demanding, easily distracted, and tried to avoid paying the model's small stipend. But their relationship had remained civil.

At a nod from the colonel, Georges asked, 'What were you doing early in the morning when Bouchard was killed?'

'I was here in bed.'

'Can anyone vouch for that?'

He hesitated a fraction. 'No, I was alone.'

'A certain person claims that he was in bed with you.'

Duby didn't flinch. 'I was trying to shield him. Yes, he was with me.'

'In bed?' Georges persisted.

'No,' the model replied evenly, seeing a trap.

Georges nodded to Saint-Martin and stepped back to write down the model's statement.

'Do you realize that you have nearly confessed to a crime?' asked the colonel.

Duby shrugged. 'One that is rarely prosecuted in these enlightened times.'

Saint-Martin acknowledged the comment with a thin smile, then remarked, 'The murder weapon has been found in the studio.'

'Oh?' Duby's surprise seemed genuine. 'I hadn't heard. You shouldn't suspect Monsieur Hamel. He had a reason to kill the painter, but he didn't do it. Nor did any of the students. I can't speak for our visitors.'

*   *   *

85

'A canny servant, Monsieur Duby,' said the colonel, as he and his adjutant walked on the Quai du Louvre. 'He gave Hamel the best alibi he could under the circumstances. Hamel holds both him and Latour on a short leash.'

'We must find a way, sir, to cut that leash and hear the truth from them.'

The two men left the quai and descended to the water's edge. For several seconds, Georges gazed silently over the river, then spoke to no one in particular. 'I detect in Hamel an Achilles' heel. I don't mean his relationship with Duby. That man is a decent fellow and will not betray his master. He's as close to a loyal friend as a self-centered person like Hamel could ever find. But I suspect that Hamel is not loyal to Duby.'

Georges reached down for a stone, and threw it skipping over the water. 'I need to talk to my friend Quidor at the Criminal Investigation Department. He has access to a secret archive of police reports that might cast a revealing light upon Hamel's activities.'

'The Lieutenant-General of Police holds the key to that archive, Georges. It's secret, because it bears witness to the follies and crimes of this country's most rich and powerful men and women. The lieutenant-general uses it rarely and with great care.'

Anne was preparing a late-afternoon tea in the kitchen of the Bouchard apartment. Michou and Adrienne were at work in the studio. There was a knock on the door. She opened to her husband. Paul breathed deeply and inhaled the scent of tea and fresh baking.

'May I join you?'

'Of course, I'll set one more place on the table. What have you learned this morning?'

While Anne brought cups and plates, Paul related to her the gist of the interrogation of Hamel, Latour, and Duby. 'Hamel had easy access to the knife, but his friend Duby has given him an alibi and tried to divert suspicion to visitors like Moretti and Serre.'

'Duby?' It took her a few moments to recall. 'Oh, Jerôme, the "Adonis of the Louvre", as Michou calls him. She has disguised herself more than once as a boy servant, and observed him in a studio modeling the mythical lover of Venus.' Anne paused with a concern. 'Is he a credible witness?'

'I think so, but he won't tell us anything that might implicate his patron Hamel in murder and threaten the comfort he enjoys. Marc Latour won't help us, either. Hamel must have warned his studio that we were dangerous.'

At that moment, Michou and Adrienne entered the kitchen. Tea was poured and sweet cakes served. Anne repeated to Michou what Paul had told her concerning Marc Latour. Michou attended calmly to Anne's narrative with little show of emotion, except for sadness in her eyes and the downward turn of her mouth.

'Do you believe that Monsieur Latour told you all he knew?' Michou signed to Paul.

'No, he's withholding something. His master has a powerful hold on him. He seems unwilling to cause trouble for himself. I can sympathize with him, but we need to learn more. At the moment, he is too frightened to be of use to us.'

Anne raised a hand. 'Would it help if I spoke with him?'

'Perhaps.' Paul gave her a warm smile. 'You, more than anyone else I know, might find a way to calm his fears.'

Fifteen

A Gentle Touch

September 7

It was early evening when Anne said goodbye to her husband. He needed to return to his office on Rue Saint-Honoré. Piles of unfinished business for the Royal Highway Patrol awaited him. Reports from troopers throughout the countryside were worrisome. The harvest looked poor, aggravating bad feelings between landlords and peasants. In the coming months, there could be violence over rents and fees.

Shortly after Paul's departure, Michou rose from the table also, expressing a desire for fresh air and exercise. Outside, it was warm and fair, perfect late-summer weather. Anne suggested to her friend that she take over the task of following the Comtesse de Serre's former maid Cécile Tremblay. At this time of day she would be at evening prayer in Saint-Roch.

Michou welcomed the suggestion. Yes, she would look out for spies and anything unusual in the woman's behavior or in her surroundings.

Anne wanted to be alone in the kitchen with Adrienne. The widow had made a remarkable recovery since coming out of her depression. Still pale, her eyes dulled by sorrow, she went about her chores quickly, purposefully.

As was her custom, Anne helped her companion. They worked well together, quietly and efficiently, with occasional conversation.

'How is the painting of *Andromeda* progressing?' asked Anne as she cleaned the teapot.

'Better than I could ever have hoped,' was the reply. 'Michou is an unusually good model, lives in the role of Andromeda. It's as if the sea monster is truly coming at her. She reacts with genuine fear and despair.'

Anne understood. Michou had learned to act while sewing costumes or painting sets in theaters. She had watched famous actresses in productions ranging from tragedies to comedies. Her favorite entertainments were farces and marionette shows. From her many years as a poor, deaf orphan, she also knew what it meant to be a victim. And she had met predatory evil, firsthand, embodied in human moral monsters. Two years ago, she had witnessed the brutal double murder of Anne's stepfather and his mistress. The experience deeply shocked her.

'Unfortunately, now she has new cause for sorrow.' Anne described the disagreement between Michou and Marc over the knife suspected of being the murder weapon.

Adrienne nodded. 'I realized something had gone wrong last night, when she came home looking sad and red-eyed. She didn't want to discuss it. I was sorry for her. She and Monsieur Latour seem to fit well together in so many ways. He's a good man and an excellent painter. I suspect that she loves him.'

Adrienne had known Marc Latour since he first came to the Academy as a young student. 'His father and mother are poor and sickly and depend on what little support he and his sister Josephine can give them. He has little hope for advancement, other than under Hamel's patronage. But Hamel treats him like a slave, refuses to promote him. I don't know why.'

Anne left the Bouchard apartment reassured that Adrienne shared her own impression of Marc's situation. The next step was to find out how Marc felt. She would approach him indirectly. His deaf sister might have influence over him. She worked as a seamstress in a dressmaker's shop in the Palais-Royal's Montpensier Arcade. Anne had met her before while teaching at Abbé de l'Épée's Institute for the Deaf.

The shop was about to close when Anne reached the door. She was told that Mademoiselle Latour was still at her workplace in the rear of the building. Anne waited a few minutes until she emerged. A small, slim, energetic woman a few years older than her brother, she bore a distinct resemblance to him. A long day's work had etched lines of fatigue on her face. She recognized Anne with a wan smile and signed a greeting.

'Would you join me for supper?' Anne intended to treat her to a modest meal in a quiet corner in the Café Odéon. 'I'd like to speak with you about your brother Marc and his friend Michou.'

For a long moment, Josephine searched Anne's face. 'Gladly,' she replied, with edgy, determined gestures, 'at my home.'

This forthright reaction took Anne aback, but she signed with a smile, 'I'd be most pleased to meet your parents.' On the way, she learned that Josephine's father had been a master mason and had earned enough to educate his daughter at the abbé's institute. In recent years, however, Monsieur Latour's health had declined. He lost his job and had to move the family into cheaper quarters.

Home was a small two-room apartment on the top floor of an old building on Rue Richelieu. In the parlor sat a pale, hollow-faced man. Josephine embraced him and signed, 'Father, I'd like you to meet Madame Cartier, Mademoiselle Michou's friend.'

He greeted Anne with a feeble smile and doubtful eyes. 'We've heard about you, madame,' he said in a wheezy voice, then nodded her to a nearby wooden chair. Josephine joined her mother in the kitchen.

Anne experienced a frisson of anxiety, similar in small measure to what Daniel felt in the lion's den. The family knew her much better than she knew them. She wondered what she could hope to achieve during this visit.

After a brief polite conversation, supper was served. A guest hadn't been expected. Nonetheless, Madame Latour produced a tasty cheese omelet. Anne discovered that she also was deaf. Her husband, like her son, had learned to sign. As the meal drew to a close, the table conversation died down to a tense moment with everyone's eyes fixed on Anne.

The sister began. 'So, can you tell us anything about Marc?'

'Disturbing news, I'm afraid. He appears to have become involved in the murder investigation at the Louvre, not as a suspect, I must add, but as a witness. A bloodstained knife that was used in the crime was found in Hamel's studio in a storage cabinet for which Marc is responsible. The police believe that he is withholding certain vital information out of fear of reprisal from Monsieur Hamel and even from other members of the Academy who want no more scandal. Marc's situation is difficult, I grant. But until the killer is arrested, Marc and others remain in grave danger. If you have any influence over him, you must persuade him to cooperate with the investigation.'

Anne's report seemed to surprise the family. They glanced at one another with concern. Marc apparently hadn't confided in them. The parents turned to their daughter to reply to Anne. 'We will raise the issue with him tomorrow if he joins us for supper. He might not listen to our best advice. He goes his own way. That's why he's working like a slave in Hamel's studio, trying to become a great painter, instead of taking up a trade and earning money to help his family.' She stopped signing for a moment and met Anne's eye. 'Now tell us about your friend Michou.'

'She's fond of Marc and believes he feels the same about her. Yesterday, they quarreled over the knife. He wanted to conceal it from the police. She opposed him and took the knife to my husband, Colonel Paul de Saint-Martin. Michou and Marc haven't seen each other since then.' Anne paused, considered the earnest faces fixed on her. It was best to be direct. She signed to Josephine, 'Do you know how he feels about her?'

'She has bewitched him,' was the quick reply. 'Did they quarrel? Then that's why he's not here tonight. He has often described her lovely auburn hair, her deep green eyes, and her wise, gentle nature. She's his muse, stirs his creative powers. He told us that he would like to marry her when he becomes an established painter.' She rolled her eyes. 'That could mean never. In the meantime, he's too busy at the studio, too distracted by Michou, to meet young women of good families whose wealth could establish him in a useful business or trade. Michou can do nothing to advance his prospects and shouldn't encourage his affection.'

Anne realized the futility of arguing with Mademoiselle Latour. Considering the family's situation, her point had merit. The economic outlook for Marc and Michou was poor. The family would encourage Marc's present alienation from Michou. Anne sighed inwardly. There wasn't much more that she could do here. She thanked Madame Latour for supper, repeated her wish that the family would persuade Marc to cooperate with the police, and left for the Bouchard apartment. Her heart ached for Michou.

Sixteen

A Terrible Secret

September 7

Evening prayer in Saint-Roch was about to begin when Michou arrived. From the rear of the church, she surveyed the small

91

scattered congregation. Most Parisians were outside in the streets or at the Palais-Royal enjoying the mild late-summer weather. Cécile Tremblay sat near the front and was easy to recognize. Michou had seen her once before, on a visit with Anne to the central market. A slim, proper lady, Cécile carried herself with a certain dignity, held her head high, sat erect, moved gracefully. Her clothes were a somber gray but well fitted. After all, she was a seamstress.

A thin, soft declining light sifted through the windows. The sexton had lit the candles on the altar. Michou searched for the flower woman, or other spies with an interest in Cécile. None were visible. With eyes fixed on Cécile, Michou allowed her mind to wander through the past several days. Until the defacing of the portrait and the murder of Bouchard were solved, she could not feel safe in the Louvre. The perpetrator of these crimes might also have invaded the Bouchard apartment and studio.

Still, what disturbed her more than the threat of violence was her painful separation from Marc. She had not tried to reach him since it happened and had not heard from him. She sensed that this wasn't merely a lovers' spat that she could easily resolve with a few penitent gestures. He was somehow entangled in the web of suspicion surrounding Bouchard's murder. Michou was sure of his innocence, of course, but he might have knowledge that would implicate the murderer. If Marc spoke up, he could suffer grievous harm.

Suddenly, she saw Marc in her mind's eye, in a dark place, his back to a rough stone wall, terror-stricken, facing an assassin's long, slender knife. Michou wanted to cry out a warning. Then the vision passed.

The strength of her feeling for him prompted her to reflect. She really didn't know him well. Had never met his family. What must they think? Had he ever spoken to them about her? A deaf female painter, dependent upon the goodwill and generosity of her patrons. No social standing or money to her name. What could she bring to a marriage, if it ever came to that?

She had begun to feel sorry for herself, when the prayers

ended. The priest left the sanctuary and the congregation moved toward the door.

Instantly alert, Michou scanned the church for someone following Cécile. During the service, no one had aroused her suspicion. As Cécile drew near, Michou studied her face— thin, pale, and tense.

Suddenly, from behind a pillar on the opposite side of the church, a man stepped out of the shadows and swiftly joined the crowd at the door. He wormed his way to Cécile, took her by the elbow, and led her into a side chapel. She had stiffened at his touch, but appeared to go with him without resistance.

Sheltered by a pillar, Michou approached to within a dozen paces of the chapel and looked around to see if anyone was watching. The church was now empty, except for the sexton, who was carrying books into the sacristy. His back was to her. She cautiously peeked around the pillar. Cécile stood at an angle, her face in profile. Even with the spyglass that Michou had borrowed from Anne, she still couldn't read Cécile's lips. But she had a full frontal view of the stranger. He looked familiar. She had seen him in the Louvre.

Light from a rack of burning votive candles in the chapel shined on his face. His lips moved slowly, articulated clearly.

'You are being followed, Cécile. The police are interested in you. Tell them nothing. You know what will happen to your mother.' He snapped an imaginary twig in his hands.

Cécile flinched, took a step back but said nothing.

Michou's heart pounded so hard, she feared that the strange man would hear it.

He and Cécile turned to leave.

Michou hastily ducked behind the pillar. As they passed by, she scrunched down between two chairs. When the church door closed behind them, she rose from her hiding place and looked around. The sexton had reappeared at the altar and was frowning at her. Did he think she meant to hide in the church overnight, sleep there or even desecrate the altar?

She pressed her hands together as if she had been lost in prayer, smiled as sweetly as she could.

He shook a finger at her and impatiently waved her out.

She hastened from the church and walked rapidly east on

Rue Saint-Honoré until she caught sight of Cécile. The stranger was a few steps behind her. Michou followed them at a safe distance. Several times, Cécile glanced nervously over her shoulder. When she reached her residence on Rue Sainte-Anne, the man deftly slipped into the crowd and disappeared.

Pierre sat at a table in front of Café de Foy, sipping from a glass of brandy. The warm, dry summer evening had enticed a huge throng to the arcades and the garden of the Palais-Royal. He had been fortunate to find an unoccupied table. A row of tall potted plants sheltered him from the crowd's view. A few of his spies had already stopped to report. Nothing noteworthy thus far.

He was lifting his glass when the sexton of Saint-Roch came toward him with the urgent step of one who thinks he has something exciting to say. Pierre lowered his glass and sat up, nodded the man to the seat facing him.

'What do you have to tell me?'

'The little deaf painter spied on you and Madame Tremblay in the church. Snuck up close to you.'

'What does it matter? She's deaf.'

'If she's close enough and the light is right, she can read lips. From what I saw, I believe she knows what you said.'

Pierre received the report with a nonchalance that he didn't feel. He murmured, 'Well done,' gave the sexton a few small coins and sent him off.

Stroking his chin, Pierre took a moment to reflect on what he had just heard. It had stung him. He prided himself on his skills as a spy. And here a little deaf woman had succeeded in spying on him. She would pay dearly for that trick, he resolved. She undoubtedly worked for the police and would report that he had threatened Cécile and her mother with harm. The police would wonder why. They might investigate him and expose his network of spies—and much more serious matters. He shifted uneasily in his chair.

Still, the police would first question Cécile. She would declare that the deaf woman misunderstood what was said in the chapel. There had been no threats. Why should the police doubt her?

He emptied his glass, stood up, stretched. For a few minutes, he surveyed the women offering themselves in the nearby arcade, a wide variety, from blooming beauties to toothless hags, all of them garnished with ribbons, feathers, and bows. None were to his taste this evening. He set off in the direction of the Louvre. The Comte de Serre might have something useful for him to do.

In the Bouchard apartment, Adrienne had retired to her room. Anne was alone at the kitchen table preparing an herbal tea for herself, eager to learn what Michou might have discovered while following Cécile. Anxiety for her friend's safety had begun to creep into her mind, along with guilt for having sent her.

When Michou finally arrived, Anne felt relieved, fetched another cup, and poured for both of them.

'I have interesting news to report from Saint-Roch,' Michou signed. She described the strange man who had accosted Cécile.

'He's Pierre Fauve, Comte de Serre's valet,' Anne remarked.

'I could have guessed.' Michou went on to relate what had transpired in the chapel.

Anne leaned forward, intently reading Michou's signs, then commented, 'The mother and daughter appear to share a terrible secret that Pierre—and whoever pays him—must protect. I need to find a way to talk with Cécile soon.' Anne paused awkwardly, shifted in her chair. 'While you were at Saint-Roch, I met Marc Latour's sister at her shop. I'm trying to approach him through his family.'

Michou looked at Anne over the rim of her cup. 'What did you learn from Josephine?'

'She took me to supper with her parents on Rue Richelieu,' Anne replied evasively. 'They didn't know about the knife. Hadn't heard from Marc.'

'He was probably alone in his room in the Louvre.' She stared at Anne, wretchedness lining her face. 'What did they say about me and Marc?'

Anne could tell from Michou's expression that she already knew they were displeased, but she wanted confirmation. It was time for the truth. 'They think he's infatuated and would like to marry you. That's foolish, they claim. Instead he should seek a rich bride who would bring money into the family.'

'And what do you think, Anne?'

'The family's misfortune has warped their judgment. If Marc were forced to marry for money, he would be a very unhappy husband. Though you two have known each other for only a few months, you have become friends. I'm not the only one to notice that your character and your interests are well matched with his.'

Michou merely nodded. The hopelessness of her situation was starkly clear, free from any misconception. But her heart was deeply given to Marc. She could not be consoled.

When Anne entered the courtyard off Rue Saint-Honoré, an oil lamp was burning in Paul's ground-floor office. This was comforting for it was late at night. She had walked home alone through dark streets, sensing someone following her. His footsteps had echoed off the stone walls, almost in tandem with hers. And when she stopped, he stopped too. When she turned to look, no one was there. She wondered if it had been wise to send Michou out as a spy, even if to a church.

Anne heard voices through Paul's open door. Georges was sitting opposite him. They both stood and smiled as she joined them and pulled up a chair. When they were seated, Paul pushed aside a stack of papers and leaned toward her. 'What brings you home at this late hour, my dear?'

'Michou,' she replied. 'I'm concerned.' She went on to describe Michou in Saint-Roch, observing Pierre's intimidating conversation with Cécile.

'The Comte de Serre appears to have a hidden reason to keep close watch on his female servants, past and present,' Georges observed. 'How shall we find it out?'

'We have a way,' Paul remarked, 'Cécile's secret is shared by her mother, Laure, at the count's château. We should question her. The count will move to the château this weekend for the vacation season. I'll arrange for us to join him in a few days. While we enjoy the pleasures of the French countryside, we may chance upon evidence of the person responsible for

Bouchard's death. The count himself is a suspect, despite his protestations of honor.'

'How did Michou manage to get close enough to read Pierre's lips?' asked Georges. 'That was risky. Did anyone observe her?'

'Yes,' Anne replied. 'The sexton waved a warning finger at her.'

Georges frowned. 'He's a notorious peddler of gossip. By now, he must have passed this bit of news on to Pierre. Michou had better be careful, give up spying, stick to painting.'

'We need to know Pierre better,' Paul remarked, turning to his adjutant. 'Consult your friend Quidor at the Criminal Investigation Department. Anne, would you visit Cécile, preferably without a spy listening in? And try to pry loose from Marc Latour the information that he seems afraid to part with. I'd like to be as well prepared as possible for what we may find at the Comte de Serre's château.'

Seventeen

The Power of Persuasion

September 10

On this Monday morning, Anne walked up Rue Sainte-Anne, hardly noticing the blue sky above or the pleasant weather. She nimbly dodged oncoming wagons, ignored the insistent pleas of peddlers. Her mind was fixed on the course of action she was about to take. There was little margin for chance or error. Her plan could easily fail.

She had spent much of the weekend studying Cécile Tremblay, the seamstress, and thinking of the best way to approach her. The Comtesse de Beaumont's town house on Rue Traversine offered an intriguing opportunity. It was only a few minutes' walk from Cécile's little shop on Rue

Sainte-Anne, not far from the Louvre. And once inside the house, Cécile could be made to feel secure. She might speak freely, believing that whatever she said would remain in the house. There would be less reason for her to fear retaliation.

The town house was almost vacant. The countess and most of her entourage had moved back to Beaumont, her country estate. Since becoming involved with the Bouchards, Michou hardly ever used her studio on the second floor. Only a pair of maids and the porter remained to keep the house clean and safe. The countess had left her friend Anne in charge.

Saturday morning, two days ago, while inspecting the countess's wardrobe, Anne had discovered several gowns in need of repair. She assumed permission to use them in her plan. That afternoon, having carefully chosen an hour when the flower woman, Pierre's spy, customarily visited a wine tavern, Anne had gone to Cécile's shop with one of the countess's torn gowns, a rose silk costume, embroidered in silver.

As Anne had spread the gown on a table, Cécile's eyes widened in amazement. She could recognize high quality in material and workmanship, but she didn't often see either in the clothing brought to her shop.

'Could you repair this gown over the weekend?' Anne had asked. 'If necessary, I'll pay a premium for rushing you.'

Cécile had examined the gown, then replied with assurance that it would be ready Monday morning. The repair was minor. There would be no extra charge.

Now, as Anne came within sight of Cécile's shop, she noticed the flower woman pretending to sell her wares across the street. Anne had anticipated this problem and, with Georges's help, had devised a solution. She signaled one of Inspecteur Quidor's agents a few paces behind her. He nodded, then walked briskly up to the lady and politely asked to see her license to sell on the street. She had none, of course, so he told her to go with him to the district's magistrate. When her protests threatened to become shrill, he warned her sternly to be quiet or he would arrest her for disturbing the peace. That worked. She went away with him, muttering under her breath.

The police would hold the spy overnight. The way was clear to carry out Anne's plan. When she walked into the shop, Cécile was expecting her. The gown hung prominently behind the counter where customers could admire it. Anne examined the repairs carefully and found them nearly perfect.

'The Comtesse de Beaumont will be most pleased,' she remarked, grateful that she could honestly compliment Cécile's skill.

In the conversation that followed, the two women grew comfortable with each other and chatted easily. Cécile was a bright, good-hearted woman. She smiled readily whenever Anne managed to divert her mind from Pierre's hold on her, or whatever else distressed her.

'It's nearly time for lunch,' Anne observed. 'Could you go with me to the countess's town house on Rue Traversine? It's only a few steps from here. I'd like your opinion on the condition of her wardrobe. I can offer you a simple noon meal and perhaps more work on her gowns.'

Cécile agreed readily, although this was near the hour when she usually went to the market. She packed up the gown, ordered a young shop girl to carry it, and walked with Anne toward the town house.

From time to time, Cécile glanced nervously over her shoulder. 'I'm relieved,' she remarked, having noticed the question in Anne's eyes. 'A woman often follows me, but I don't see her today.'

'Odd things can happen in Paris. How long has this been going on?' The traffic on the street had become dense. Anne pushed through a slowly moving crowd, dodging animals and carts. Cécile came close behind her.

'For weeks,' she replied, distracted, dodging a pail of slop tossed from an upstairs window. She glanced back, a look of horror on her face. Had the slop landed on the countess's gown? 'Thanks be to God!' she murmured. The gown was safe. The shop girl had foreseen the danger.

'Perhaps a would-be suitor has hired her to take your measure.' Anne spoke with a smile in her voice, sensing that Cécile wouldn't mind. 'A persistent fellow. Still, a man can't be too careful when choosing a partner for life.'

Cécile's forehead furrowed with the effort of grasping Anne's suggestion. 'And a woman should be at least as careful.' She gave Anne a tentative, nervous smile.

That remark made Anne curious. Cécile wasn't thinking of a woman's enormous legal disadvantage in a marriage contract, nor of marriage at all. There were no men in her life. Except Pierre. He was reputed to be a lecher, quite likely the predatory kind. Did he have designs on Cécile?

With that possibility in mind, Anne studied Cécile more closely. At least ten years older than Anne, to judge from thin streaks of gray in her dark brown hair, she was still a comely woman, with soft brown eyes, a pleasing oval face, a slender shapely body. And she was also a widow, though with few resources, other than her shop. A yielding person, she could be influenced or intimidated, but she was no fool. She wouldn't even consider marrying Pierre.

Still, another kind of partnership might be possible. Anne wondered about Cécile's shop. Georges had learned that she and her late husband had purchased the business from an elderly seamstress and paid in cash. Where did they find the money? The Comte de Serre did not pay servants well, Anne suspected. Could Cécile be in debt to Pierre? In that scene Michou observed in Saint-Roch, Cécile and Pierre acted like uneasy partners.

In what kind of enterprise? A small inner voice warned Anne, 'Proceed with caution.'

She held back her questions about Pierre until later.

In the course of this conversation, Cécile appeared to grow inquisitive about Anne. 'Your accent isn't typically Parisian. Are you English?' she asked. 'While in Italy with the Comtesse de Serre, I often observed the wives and daughters of English travelers. Their manner was so free and straightforward.'

'I was raised in England,' Anne confessed, willing to be 'straightforward' for the moment, and cautious. The seamstress was proving to be mentally alert. 'But my family came from Normandy.'

'My usual customers are calculating and cynical—so French,' Cécile remarked with distaste. 'So what brought you to Paris, may I ask?'

100

'A great loss in my life,' Anne replied. She spoke openly of the murder of her stepfather and her coming to Paris to investigate. 'I had the good fortune to receive help from Colonel Paul de Saint-Martin, a prince of a man. We recently married.'

At the mention of murder, Cécile raised an eyebrow. The reference to marriage brought a smile to her face. 'I'm happy for you. A loving marriage is a true blessing.' There was a tone of regret in her voice, a hint of loneliness. 'I lost my husband three months ago and now live alone.'

At the town house, the porter opened the gate. The women crossed the cobbled courtyard and knocked on the door. A maid welcomed them. Anne gave orders for lunch in an hour. Cécile sent the shop girl back with instructions to say only that she had been called to a customer's home.

While waiting for the meal, the two women went to the countess's dressing room to study the contents of a large wardrobe. Anne removed a dozen gowns one at a time and hung them on a rack. Carefully inspecting each in turn, occasionally laying one out on a table, Cécile pointed out tears and worn spots in need of repair and estimated the cost. Anne wrote down her observations, intending to pass them on to the countess.

Cécile was most impressed with a formal gown, some twenty years old, designed to be worn at Court or at the opera. It had a wide, pale green top skirt of the finest silk designed to fit over a petticoat stiffened with horsehair. A master dressmaker had richly embroidered it with intricate silver floral patterns.

For several moments, Cécile gazed at the garment with rapt wonder, her fingers caressing the cloth, tracing the intertwined lines of metallic flowers. 'The Comtesse de Serre owned a similar gown, and looked like a queen when she wore it. But it was not nearly so fine as this one.' Upon closer inspection, Cécile pointed out tears at the hemline. 'I would feel deeply honored if I were allowed to repair them.'

As they returned the gowns to the wardrobe, Cécile asked, 'Why would the countess want to repair these gowns? She hasn't worn them in several years.'

'True, not since she retired from the Court and from fash-

101

ionable society ten years ago, at the time her husband died. However, she has recently found a new friend, the Comte de Savarin, archivist at Versailles. Now she's thinking ahead to entering society again and attending the theater and the concert hall. She may use these gowns—they will require little alteration, for her figure has hardly changed over the past decade. And neither she nor the count feels the need to follow the latest fashion.'

A bell rang. Anne shut the door to the wardrobe. 'Our meal is ready.'

Lunch was served in the countess's intimate private dining room. A chandelier's smooth crystal pendants refracted light from the windows, giving a lively warm tone to the pale green-paneled walls, graced by gilded garlands. Anne and Cécile sat at a small round table covered with fine linen. A spinach soufflé was served together with a fine white wine. Anne had instructed the maid to keep Cécile's glass filled, hoping to encourage her to speak freely. Fortunately, she took to the wine like an old friend. As a servant in the Serre household, she would have found ways to share in the costly food and drink enjoyed by her master and mistress.

Anne opened the conversation with her forthcoming visit to Serre's château. 'You have mentioned the countess. How well did you know her?'

'I knew her better than anyone. My husband was the estate's steward, kept her accounts, looked after her property, until her death.'

'What were your duties at the château?'

'Personal maid to the countess.' Cécile's chin lifted with pride. 'For ten years. I went with her everywhere, even to Italy.'

'Tell me about her. I've heard that she was a remarkable person.'

'Indeed!' Cécile replied.

As she went on to describe the countess, Anne thought of the woman she knew from Michou's copy of the Serre portrait—a headstrong, impulsive, and high-spirited woman, with thick black hair, dark brown eyes, a strong chin and wide mouth, full lips, and, above all, an indomitable fire in her eyes.

Nature itself had designed her for the horses she rode—large, powerful and spirited. She would bend them to her will. Cécile clearly admired her mistress, stood in awe of her. The countess in turn had been generous toward Cécile and a few other servants. Or so it seemed. From Cécile's account, Anne deduced that the gifts were small, probably given out of her exuberance and according to her mood at the moment, more than from love or affection.

'Truly, an extraordinary woman,' Anne remarked honestly. 'Did anything interest her, apart from horses?'

'Men,' replied Cécile, 'especially vigorous intelligent men. She could dance for hours, debate with them, flirt.'

'And the count?'

'Much older than she. He stood aside, let her do whatever she wished—within reason of course,' Cécile quickly added. 'The countess treated him with respect, performed her wifely duties—so far as I know.'

'Did she have a favorite?' Anne hesitated to ask, for fear that Cécile might balk. But the wine had lowered her inhibitions, transported her back to the brilliant, exciting life she had witnessed, even if from a servant's distance, at the Serre château.

'Monsieur Moretti, without a doubt. They were fascinating to watch, both of them darkly handsome, she reckless and impulsive, he guarded and calculating, though as powerful in his way as she was in hers. They complemented each other. The count seemed to enjoy watching them ride, dance, play together.' Cécile paused, stared at Anne with a puzzled expression. 'That does seem strange, doesn't it? I hardly thought so at the time, but I do now.'

'What has caused you to reconsider?'

'The defacing of her portrait. The count's harsh reaction makes me wonder if, all along, he had been more genuinely concerned about his honor than I had thought.'

'And less indifferent to his wife's behavior than he had seemed,' Anne added. 'Perhaps he merely pretended to approve her dalliance with Moretti.'

Cécile nodded with a distracted expression, as if slipping further into a murky past. 'Yes, the countess and Moretti, a curious pair. I've come to sense something sinister in their relationship.' She paused, drank deeply from her glass.

'Oh? In what way "sinister"?' Anne encouraged her companion with an intrigued tilt of the head.

'I mean, on Monsieur Moretti's part, not hers. He was always amiable when anyone was watching. But I recall the first time he visited her. At one point, she had her back to him, and he must have thought they were alone. He stared at her, eyes narrow and cold. I sensed that he loathed her. For her part, she sometimes spoke roughly to him, went out of her way to challenge him, but that was all sport.' Cécile emptied her glass, and smiled up at the maid, who promptly refilled it.

'Really?' Anne asked. 'How observant of you. Did you see further signs of ill will on his part? His attitude might have changed. He could have grown to like her—after all, he wanted to buy her portrait.'

Anne's remark seemed to confuse Cécile. She struggled for a reply. 'Well, I suppose he did.' Her gaze, fixed on a distant place, seemed troubled.

It was time to take a different tack. 'Two weeks ago,' Anne said, 'when my husband and I visited Comte de Serre in the Louvre, he told us that the countess died of a fall from her horse. He couldn't understand how it could have happened, for she was such an accomplished rider. Yet he also described her, with admiration, mind you, as daring, even reckless on a horse. Since then, I've wondered if she ever had any accidents before her fatal one.'

A strange, unguarded expression came over Cécile's face. For a significant moment she strained to gather her wits, her cheeks flushed from the effect of the wine. Finally, she said, 'Nothing serious, that I know of.' She raised the glass to her lips, as much to hide her embarrassment as to drink.

Anne pretended to have noticed nothing out of the ordinary. The conversation turned to other aspects of life at the château. But Anne promised herself to find out more about a possible, secret accident. Could it be the same matter that Pierre wanted to keep from the ears of the police?

After lunch Anne and Cécile drank tea fortified with punch in the countess's study, a richly paneled room, with fine furniture, Turkish rugs, and cases of leather-bound, gilt-edged books. Anne sensed nostalgia in Cécile, who must have been recalling with pleasure the best days in the years she lived in similar privileged surroundings.

Eventually, Anne brought the conversation around to Bouchard's recent murder.

'I know his wife,' Cécile remarked. 'She comes to me occasionally with gowns almost beyond repair. I feel sorry for her. Tight-lipped about her husband, to be sure, but everybody knows that he gambled away the family's money.'

'Who do you think killed him?' Anne asked.

'Gillet, the engraver, of course.'

'Really?' Anne wrinkled her brow.

'Yes. I heard from the watchman at the scene,' Cécile went on. 'Gillet killed Bouchard for the gambling money he was carrying.'

Cécile probably shared the view of most people in the neighborhood. Her attitude toward the incident seemed detached, uncomplicated, unlike the anxiety that Michou had observed in her at that mysterious encounter with Pierre in Saint-Roch. Suddenly, Anne received a shock of insight. Cécile was being followed for reasons unrelated to Bouchard's murder. Pierre and his master were hiding something else from the police. A serious matter, surely. A violent death? Anne shivered.

Lunch finished, Cécile returned to Rue Sainte-Anne, her gait somewhat unsteady. Anne followed in the hope of learning more about Pierre's hold on her. As Cécile approached her shop, the concierge studied her with a hostile eye. Anne chose a table in the café across the street and waited with a glass of wine. A half hour later, the concierge entered the room, glanced around with a familiar air, then walked over to Anne's table.

'Mind if I join you?' she asked with barely concealed impertinence. 'Men occupy all the other tables.'

'Please do,' Anne replied politely, though disconcerted that the woman appeared to know her. At first glance, the concierge seemed amiable enough—rosy cheeks, an easy smile, a stout body, and a hearty voice. But her eyes were keen, cold, shrewd.

The woman signaled the barman, then confronted Anne. 'I know you, madame. Saw you directing one of Quidor's agents this morning. You neatly took out the old flower woman who dogs Cécile. A few minutes later, you walked off with her. Clever trick!' The woman's eyes narrowed, her gaze hardened. 'For several days, you've been watching Cécile. Are you here on Quidor's business?'

'Yes,' Anne replied, a half truth at best. She had to be careful. This woman could alert Cécile to the investigation, frighten her off. 'The inspector doesn't suspect Cécile of any wrongdoing. But, up to a few months ago, she and Pierre Fauve worked for a countess who died under suspicious circumstances. We wonder why Pierre is now paying so much attention to Cécile. Could you help us?'

The concierge stared at Anne, hands clasped before her mouth, concealing the lower half of her face. Finally, she lowered her hands, gave Anne a crooked smile. 'Nothing happens in this neighborhood that escapes my eye. But I keep most of it to myself—I'm not a tattler. Still, from time to time, I've given the inspector's agents bits of useful information.' She paused, a cunning look in her eye. 'How much is a bit worth to you?'

At this point, the barman came with the woman's glass of wine. Anne paid him. 'That's for a start,' she said to the woman.

She took a deep drink, set the glass down firmly on the table, and spoke in a low voice. 'By now, you must know Pierre's business. He helps people, but he expects to be paid. If they can't give him money, they must offer service instead. Cécile owes him—I don't know why or how much. Maybe he found money for her to buy the shop. Each week, the old flower woman collects a sum for Pierre. If Cécile doesn't pay, Pierre *visits* her.'

'What do you mean?'

'I mean . . .' She bent forward, lowered her voice to a whisper. 'He goes up to her room and she pays him with her body. I've seen them at it. She doesn't look happy but she's willing enough. Pierre knows how to please a woman.' The concierge's face was pitiless. 'Don't be shocked. Madame Tremblay puts on airs, would have you believe she's a proper, respectable woman. More than once, she's brushed past me as if I were dirt under her feet. I'd have exposed her long ago, except I don't dare cross Pierre. He can be very nasty.'

Anne felt sorry for Cécile. Though laced with malice, the concierge's story had the ring of truth. Cécile's compliance with Pierre's demands, however, was probably not as crassly financial as the concierge inferred. If she were to refuse Pierre, he would harm not only her but also Laure and Vincenzo.

The concierge ordered another glass and Anne paid for it. There was no more to gain in conversation with the woman. Anne excused herself, promising the woman that Quidor would be grateful for her assistance. That seemed to please her.

Eighteen

A Gambler's Trail

September 11

Early Tuesday morning, a servant awakened Georges with a hastily written message.

> *Come to the Quai du Louvre. A suspicious death. Quidor.*

Georges hurried to the place and found the inspector bending over a sodden body that had been dragged from the river. Quidor's agents were pushing back a curious crowd. Georges waited with the others until the inspector straightened up, apparently finished with his macabre business.

He recognized Georges and beckoned. 'You know this one.' He pulled aside a cloth covering the body.

'The engraver Gillet,' Georges murmured. 'Foul play?'

'Accident or suicide, possibly. We won't know for sure until the autopsy.' Quidor wiped his wet hands with a grimace.

'But I can't find a blow to the head or any other sign of violence. A fisherman pulled him up an hour ago. He had hidden Bouchard's watch in his clothes.' Quidor handed the watch to Georges. The painter's initials were engraved on the back. The watch had stopped at a few minutes past two.

'You had him under observation at our request. What happened?'

'Last night, he slipped away from my agent, who then tried to find him at his usual gambling den on the Quai des Augustins. No luck.' The body was lifted on to a cart and carried away to the morgue at the Châtelet. 'Come with me, Georges, we'll search his room in the Louvre. If he killed himself, he may have left a note.'

On the way to the victim's room, Georges weighed the most dire alternative—Gillet might have been murdered because of his connection to the Bouchard case. Georges never seriously suspected that Gillet had killed Bouchard, merely that he had robbed the corpse. But he might have witnessed the killing. Or the killer might have thought he had—he was in the vicinity. In either case, the assassin would have made the death look like an accident or a suicide.

Quidor tried to open Gillet's door, but the key was too large. He handed it to Georges. 'I found it hidden in his clothes.'

Georges inspected it. 'Must be Bouchard's. It has a bow in the shape of the letter B on a fluted shank.' He showed the key to Quidor. 'So Gillet was the mysterious intruder who broke into Bouchard's apartment, probably to steal records of his debt to the painter.' He put the key into his pocket. 'Madame Cartier will recognize it and be relieved.'

Quidor tried another, smaller key in the lock. This one fit snugly. 'I found it in Gillet's pocket.'

Georges opened the door. The room was as Georges had last seen it. The bed had not been slept in. A careful search uncovered no note and no other indication of what Gillet had done after leaving the printing office early the previous evening.

At the Royal Printing Office, their next stop, the two policemen were also unsuccessful. Gillet hadn't told anyone what he had planned for the evening or where he might go.

108

On the other hand, he usually didn't confide such information to his colleagues. He hadn't looked or acted suicidal.

'Where did your agent last see him?' Georges and Quidor had stopped for a drink at the Café de Foy and sat at a garden table.

'Right here, Georges. The engraver had come from work, realized he was being followed, entered the café, and sneaked out a back door. A waiter saw him leave and told the agent, but Gillet was already out of sight.'

'Let's talk to the waiter. I have a suspicion.'

The waiter arrived shortly, an uncertain, wary expression on his face. Georges sympathized with him. Years ago, he had been one himself. The job could be dangerous. Policemen or their spies sometimes coerced waiters to give damaging information about a customer who would then retaliate against the waiter.

'My good man,' Georges began, a coin held discreetly in his hand, 'had Monsieur Gillet met someone here, before leaving through the back door?'

'No,' the waiter replied hesitantly. 'He had a drink at that table by himself.' He pointed with a jerk of his head. 'I served him.'

Georges produced another coin.

'But,' the waiter continued, 'another gentleman put a note for him on to my tray. I understood no one was to see it. A spy was sitting a few tables away. Shortly afterward, Monsieur Gillet got up and left.'

Georges drew a third coin from his pocket. 'Would you remember that gentleman who sent him the note?'

'He comes here frequently. Likes the ladies. They call him Pierre.'

Georges thanked the waiter, pressed the coins into his hand, and waved him off. Georges turned to Quidor. 'So Pierre must have warned Gillet about your spy and arranged a later meeting.'

'Pierre would deny everything, of course.'

'And so would his master, the count.'

'The Comte de Serre may or may not be involved. His valet,

I can tell you, Georges, works for himself as well as for his master.'

Early in the afternoon at his office desk, Saint-Martin glanced out the window and saw his adjutant crossing the courtyard, head bent forward in thought.

'What is it, Georges?' the colonel asked, as the older man took a seat facing him.

'Gillet is dead.' Georges went on to describe the scene by the river and his investigation with Quidor. 'He has gone to the morgue to hasten the autopsy, or at least get a preliminary report. Here's Bouchard's missing key and his watch. The inspector found them on the corpse.' Saint-Martin took them from Georges and put them into a drawer.

'I'll show them to Anne.' He reflected for a moment. 'Could Gillet have committed suicide?'

'He left no message, gave no indication he was thinking of killing himself. His escape from the police spy in the Palais-Royal suggests that he was planning something devious or illegal. Perhaps he was more involved with the King's enemies in the Duc d'Orléans's palace than we believed. Or maybe he wanted to get away for a wild night of drinking and gambling, in violation of the rules we imposed on him.'

'Assuming it's murder, who would want to kill him?'

'At this point, sir, we can only guess. He might have betrayed the duke's cause and was silenced before he could do any damage.'

'Slim conjecture, Georges.' The colonel leaned forward, arms resting on the desk. 'Gillet engraved scurrilous brochures for the duke's men, but according to Quidor, he didn't seem deeply involved in their cause.' He met Georges's eye. 'Gillet's death is more likely related to the painter Bouchard's. Suppose the engraver had witnessed more than he admitted to us. He might have been able to reveal the killer and had to be silenced.'

'I've considered that possibility, sir. But Bouchard's murder happened eleven days ago. Why would the killer have waited so long?'

Saint-Martin reflected for a moment before replying. 'Perhaps the engraver was personally involved in the killing.

The passage was dark. He pointed out the victim to his assailant. In return, he got the painter's money, watch, and key. Last night, Gillet wanted more money for his gambling addiction. He and the killer had a falling out and Gillet was the loser.'

A servant appeared at the door to announce that Inspecteur Quidor had arrived.

'By all means, show him in,' the colonel ordered.

Quidor entered and pulled up a chair. 'Gentlemen, we have a suspicious death on our hands. That's all the doctor can say at this point. We can't call it murder yet. Gillet's lungs were full of river water. No doubt, he drowned. There were no signs of violence on the body. Who knows, he could have been drunk and fallen in. That happens.'

'Or he was pushed,' Georges countered. 'That happens, too.'

Saint-Martin sighed. 'Now all we need to do, gentlemen, is find out where Gillet was last night and with whom.' The colonel rose from his desk and picked a file box from a shelf. 'He would have expected our spy to look for him at the gambling den on the Quai des Augustins, his favorite haunt.' He spread Gillet's papers on the table, studied them for a minute. 'Here's the only other place where he gambled, the Comte de Modène's establishment in the basement of the Luxembourg Palace off Rue de Vaugirard.'

Saint-Martin turned to his adjutant. 'You and I shall pay a visit to the palace now before the gaming tables become crowded. I hope to discover traces of the unfortunate Monsieur Gillet.'

Quidor stirred in his chair, slapped his thigh. 'I must return to my office. A report on Pierre Fauve should be there by now. By the way, Georges, I'm still waiting for permission to search for Hamel in the secret archive. But I've already spoken to the other inspectors. One of them recalled Hamel, gave me a knowing wink. I'll have to negotiate the information from him. That may cost me a favor or two.'

Saint-Martin and his adjutant donned civilian clothes and set out in a coach for the Palais-Luxembourg. The King's brother, the Comte de Provence, was the titular owner of the palace.

As royal property, it lay outside the jurisdiction of the Paris police, and was exempt from laws regulating games of chance. Hence, the count had rented the palace's basement rooms to an Italian prince, the Comte de Modène, who converted them into one of the city's largest gambling dens.

The entrance was a simple door at ground level. The count's footmen greeted them, showed them into a foyer, where a pair of muscular servants looked them over, then beckoned a manager, who, recognizing them as strangers, informed them of the games on offer.

'We are anxious to watch and perhaps play at the biribi table,' said Saint-Martin, recalling Gillet's preferred game. The manager escorted them through a series of simple, low vaulted rooms, furnished only with plain wooden chairs and green velvet-covered tables, in stark contrast to the sumptuous palace above. The contrast continued in the clientele. Every social class was represented, including many artisans and domestic servants.

'Our gamblers seem remarkably sober and well mannered, even though they are a mixed lot,' Saint-Martin remarked, casting a glance at several men dressed in beggars' rags.

'It's still early,' Georges replied. 'Wait until they've lost their shirts.'

The manager overheard this exchange. 'This is an orderly house. Women and children are not allowed. We admit only respectable men and tolerate neither drunkenness nor foul language.'

The official policy, thought Saint-Martin. The manager had already suspected that these two visitors were from the police.

As Saint-Martin and Georges arrived at the biribi table, two fashionably dressed young men were leaving crestfallen. The banker regarded the newcomers with hopeful, crafty eyes. No one else was in the room.

The colonel approached the banker with respect, as if asking for a favor. 'Before we place our bets, monsieur, can you recall a certain acquaintance of ours, the engraver Gillet, a slender fair-haired young man?'

For a few moments, brow creased with mental effort, the banker calculated the rising level of his risk. He recognized police even when disguised. 'No,' he said hesitantly, 'I can't recall him.'

'Try again,' Saint-Martin insisted. He was sure that the banker was lying. 'Gillet was here last night and wagered at this table. This morning he was found drowned in the river.'

The man started to shake his head. Before he could speak, the colonel remarked evenly, 'You work in a place exempt from the King's law, but you live in Paris. Shall I ask a police inspector to visit you at home?'

The banker's eyes wavered. His intransigence had become too risky. 'Now I remember him. Came to the table with about eighty louis d'or, probably borrowed. Bet it all, and won a huge sum, then bet again and lost most of it, then bet again and won. So it went through the evening. In the end, he lost it all, including fifty louis d'or advanced by the house. He looked wild-eyed and desperate. I felt sorry for him. Gave him a chit for a drink at the bar. He left. I didn't see him again.'

'Was anyone with him?'

'Other men watched him gamble, spoke a few words to him. But he seemed to be alone.'

'Among the onlookers, do you remember a handsome man with a pockmarked face?'

'Can't say. I keep my eyes on the money and the gambler.'

The two policemen left the table without placing any bets and made their way to a barroom.

As they entered, Georges turned to the colonel. 'Where did Gillet find eighty louis d'or? That's more than he earns in a year at the printing office and the Palais-Royal combined.'

'We can safely assume,' Saint-Martin replied, 'that a companion gave or lent it to him and was unhappy with how it was spent.'

They caught the barman's attention when he had a free minute. Had he served Gillet? Georges asked.

Yes, the engraver had been a pathetic figure. The barman took his chit, served him, and gave him an extra brandy for pity's sake. Yes, he left with a companion. No, the barman couldn't identify him. The room was crowded, the light poor. Saw him only from the rear.

113

'Well,' Georges remarked as they left the building, 'we've probably come to a dead end. Gillet and his companion could have gone to any one of a hundred taverns to continue drinking. Or the companion had hidden away a bottle or two, which they drank sitting on the riverbank opposite the Louvre. When Gillet passed out, the companion just shoved him into the water.'

'We'll withhold judgment, Georges, until we receive the official results of Gillet's autopsy. But I see signs that lead to Pierre Fauve. He's the only person I can think of who might lend eighty louis to Gillet—and not for pity's sake.'

Georges fell into a reflective mood. 'If I were Gillet, a penniless gambling addict rejected by my father, and I owed eighty louis to Pierre and fifty to the banker, I believe that I'd jump into the river. No one would have to push me.'

Nineteen

A Star-Crossed Love?

September 11

Meanwhile, Anne reached the Louvre a few minutes before Monsieur Hamel's customary dinner hour. Though she had come without an escort, the concierge at the ground-floor entrance merely glanced at her, smiled, didn't ask about her business. It sufficed, apparently, that Anne acted the part of a haughty noblewoman and wore Comtesse Marie's rose silk gown that Cécile had repaired. A maid had altered it slightly to fit Anne.

She waited outside the studio while students rushed past on their way to neighborhood taverns. Hamel noticed her and frowned. 'Madame Cartier, have you come to look at our work? I would like to assist you, but I have a dinner engagement.'

'I didn't intend to impose on you, sir. Monsieur Latour can show me the new work that might be of interest to my friend, the Comtesse Marie de Beaumont. She will come at a more opportune time.'

Hamel glanced at Anne's expensive gown, took note of her aristocratic manner, and considered the prospect of a commission. His irritation gave way to a forced smile. He assured her that his studio offered much that would please her, and he hoped to see her again when he had more time.

The studio was empty, except for Marc. Standing absorbed at an easel, he didn't notice her enter. She considered walking quietly up behind him to see what he was looking at. But she thought better of it and scratched on the open door.

Startled, he swung around, gaped at her. Then he politely bowed. 'What can I do for you, madame?' His expression was at first uncertain, then turned cool.

As she approached, he stood in front of the easel, blocking her view. Anne understood. He was embarrassed to reveal that he still cared for Michou. 'Monsieur Hamel said you could show me the new work being done in the studio, paintings that might be of interest to the Comtesse Marie de Beaumont.'

Marc appeared to relax a bit. 'I would be honored to assist you.' After reflecting for a moment, he guided her appropriately to Hamel's latest work, a half-finished portrait of a young woman. 'He had set this piece aside while he readied his works for the Salon. But over the past few days, he has resumed painting it.'

The portrait pleased Anne, and she said so. 'Has Hamel given up hope of repairing the Serre portrait?'

'He looks at it every day and shakes his head. Ever since Michou discovered the murder knife and cast suspicion on him, he has been angry at her. Says he won't work with her, even though the Comte de Serre urges him to. A troublemaker, he calls her. Told me to keep her out of the studio. I heard him say, "I'll see to it that she and Madame Bouchard soon leave the Louvre."'

'A mean-spirited man,' remarked Anne. 'But in the end, six thousand livres may change his attitude.' Still, Anne thought, this doesn't look promising. She inclined her head and asked gently, 'And how do *you* feel toward Michou?'

He didn't reply, just beckoned her back to his easel. As Anne had guessed, there was Michou, tenderly sketched, sadness in her eyes.

'It's been almost six days since I last saw her. I call her up in my imagination and express my feelings in the portrait. You've met my family so you know that our love is hopeless. It's best for her and for me that we don't see each other anymore.'

'Your situation is difficult, but I don't believe it's impossible. Would you consider working for someone other than Hamel?'

'Of course I would. That is, if another painter would accept me. I need a patron. I'm afraid to strike out on my own. Hamel refuses to give me a good reference, tells me to be satisfied with the job I have, warns that I lack what it takes to become a member of the Academy.'

'Hamel be damned!' Anne had to fight back her growing impatience. 'You are a talented painter and an excellent teacher. You could make a life and a career for yourself outside the Academy.'

He frowned with displeasure, not wishing to concede that his grand dream of becoming an academician was futile. But his eyes wavered. Anne was certain that she had sown a seed.

After a moment's hesitation, he lifted his head and spoke bravely. 'I'm not a coward, madame.' Then he added, 'I acknowledge now that Michou was right to take the knife to the police. I should not have objected. She must think badly of me. When she discovered the bloodstains, I thought first of the dreadful consequences—the studio in turmoil, accusations of murder leveled at prominent artists and patrons, and so forth. I should have shown better judgment. Tell her I'm sorry.'

'I shall tell her. I'm sure she would forgive you personally if you were to allow her.' Anne didn't wait for Marc's negative response but went on to ask, 'What happened to the knife?'

He hesitated a fraction before beginning in a low, halting voice. 'In the evening before Bouchard's murder, after the students had left the studio for supper, I routinely looked into the weapons cabinet, noticed the knife, and locked the door. Then Pierre, the Comte de Serre's valet, came to me. The count wanted to borrow a Corinthian helmet, he said. The request wasn't unusual. The count is an amateur artist and often borrows pieces from the cabinet. He just asks for the key and picks out what he wants. I lent Pierre my key. He came back with the helmet under his arm and returned the key. I didn't check the cabinet again.

'Shortly afterward, I closed the studio and retired to my room, unsuspecting. The next morning, as I was opening up the studio, he returned with the helmet, said he would put it back in its cabinet, asked for the key. I lent it to him as before. Later, I opened the cabinet and the knife was there.'

'When did you become concerned?'

'Perhaps that morning, when I first heard that a poniard had killed Bouchard. I gave a fleeting thought to our own knife. A suspicion must have grown. Then Michou questioned the knife portrayed in the Lucretia painting, inspired by the one in our collection. I realized it could be the murder weapon, though I was afraid to admit it at the time.'

'May I write down what you've just told me, and will you sign it?'

The request seemed at first to stun him, then he shook his head vigorously. 'I've said too much. I can't sign anything without Hamel's permission. You had better leave.' As he pointed to the door, his hand was trembling.

'You've given me something to think about, Marc. I'll leave you now.' She glanced at his sketch of Michou on the easel. 'I believe you two are meant for each other. There must be a way.'

As Anne walked home, she suddenly asked herself, why would the count have wanted to borrow that Corinthian helmet the evening prior to Bouchard's murder? After dinner with the Comte d'Angiviller, he returned late to his Louvre apartment and went to bed. He had no opportunity to sketch or to paint. So the helmet was merely a pretext to gain access to the weapons cabinet. And to the knife!

*　　*　　*

Anne returned from Hamel's studio to find Inspecteur Quidor on his way out the door of Paul's office, hat in hand.

'Madame Cartier, pleased to meet you. Sorry, I must leave.' He threw a glance at Georges and Paul, who had followed him. 'I'm expecting a report on Pierre Fauve.'

'Then, sir,' Anne said, 'you should wait a minute and hear what I've just learned from Marc Latour in Hamel's studio.'

The men returned to their seats. Anne pulled up a chair and joined them. 'The young man regrets having remained silent. Today he told me that the Bouchard murder weapon might have gone missing from the cabinet when Pierre Fauve borrowed a Greek helmet.' After describing the sequence of events, she concluded, 'Marc is witness to the fact that only Pierre and Hamel could have taken the knife that evening and returned it early the next morning.'

Quidor stroked his chin for a moment, then observed, 'Monsieur Latour didn't actually see the knife leave the cabinet. And he might take back what he told you, madame. After all, he didn't put it in writing and sign it. Nonetheless, supposing Fauve secretly took the knife, either he used it to kill Bouchard, or he stole it for his master, the Comte de Serre, who did the job himself, honor notwithstanding.'

Paul added, 'Or, by coincidence, Hamel took it. He had a key to the cabinet and a motive to kill the painter.'

'Why, then, did Pierre borrow the Corinthian helmet?' asked Anne.

'Perhaps for a reason entirely unrelated to Bouchard's death—for a *tableau vivant* in the brothel where he claims he spent the night,' replied Paul. He smiled cryptically. 'Pierre might have portrayed Achilles arming.'

'A lame idea,' Anne opined, recalling a recent visit to a prominent London artist's studio. She and Paul had admired a terracotta figure of the ancient Greek hero Achilles, striding forward, nude, placing the plumed helmet on his head. The sculpture's elegant body, noble posture, and sense of high purpose worked comically in Anne's imagination against her image of the sly, quasicriminal, pockmarked valet.

Paul agreed with a penitent smile.

'In any case,' Anne went on, 'Marc Latour's testimony appears to lessen suspicion of Monsieur Moretti. He didn't have access to the weapons cabinet that night.'

'Pierre *could* have given it to him, though more likely to the count,' observed Paul. 'We shall put Moretti to the side for a while, and explore the mystery of the engraver Gillet's death.' He nodded to his adjutant. 'Georges and I tracked Gillet to the gambling den at the Palais Luxembourg. He lost heavily and was last seen leaving early this morning with an unidentified companion.'

'Who could have been Pierre Fauve,' Georges added.

Paul turned to Quidor. 'Sir, while you investigate Fauve's background, you also need to know that he has shown a suspicious interest in Cécile, former personal maid to the late Comtesse de Serre.' Paul signaled Anne to speak.

'When I questioned Cécile last night,' she began, 'I learned that Pierre is attempting to keep her silent concerning an incident in the countess's history of reckless riding.' Anne went on to describe Pierre's sexual relationship with Cécile and their tense encounter in Saint-Roch. 'This has been going on for months before the Bouchard murder,' Anne noted.

Quidor nodded gravely, reached for his hat, rose to leave. 'The countess, the painter, the engraver—three separate violent deaths. They could have something in common.'

Saint-Martin rose, shook the inspector's hand. 'Probably something to do with Pierre Fauve.'

After Quidor left for his office and Paul settled back in his chair, Anne said, 'I've learned that Hamel intends to have Madame Bouchard evicted from her Louvre apartment and studio. Some of his hatred for her late husband has fallen on her. It's also a way to get back at Michou for discovering the murder weapon in his cabinet. He knows that Madame Bouchard is instructing her.'

Paul frowned. 'To evict Madame Bouchard, Hamel will need to persuade the Comte d'Angiviller. Previous directors have allowed the widows of deceased members of the Academy to retain at least their apartments if not their studios. The present director is eager to grant apartments to young, productive artists. I think the most we can expect is to gain time for Madame Bouchard to complete her husband's work. By all accounts, it is excellent. The director might be persuaded to buy it for the royal collection. In the meantime, how shall we persuade Monsieur Hamel to behave more reasonably toward Marc Latour, Michou, and Madame Bouchard?'

'Make use of his weaknesses,' Anne replied. 'He is vulnerable in two regards. The greedy part of him truly wants the six thousand livres that the Comte de Serre will pay for the finished portrait of his late wife. And his pride fears the ridicule he will experience from the exposure of his relationship with Jerôme Duby.'

Georges spoke up. 'I think ridicule is our strongest weapon, stronger than the six thousand livres. Hamel will do whatever we ask, rather than be arrested and exposed to public contempt. His friend, Jerôme, however, can't help us without incriminating himself. But there may be other more casual "friends". Quidor could seek evidence from a colleague, or in the secret archive, that Hamel is promiscuous. In addition, I suggest borrowing a spy from Quidor to lead Hamel into a compromising situation, as the police sometimes do. Then he will listen to reason.'

Anne threw a sharp, reproachful glance at Georges.

He smiled wryly. 'Unseemly, I admit, but is it wrong to nudge Hamel to do what is right? If he would rather be exposed, that's his choice.'

Anne could detect no pity in Georges's voice.

'There's great risk in your plan, Georges,' said the colonel, 'and I'm not sure that it would work.' He rose from his chair and began to pace the room. 'Hamel surely realizes that the Paris police routinely harass sodomites but usually those of the lower classes and men without connections. The police would be loath to expose Hamel, taint the reputation of the Academy, and threaten other well-placed, upper-class men like himself. For those reasons, I would also expect Baron Breteuil and Lieutenant-General DeCrosne to approve such a plan only as a last resort, if at all.'

'In that case, sir, I suggest that our spy merely discover

Hamel in an illicit encounter, rather than entrap him.'

Saint-Martin stopped pacing and stared at his adjutant for a moment, then nodded. 'Go ahead, Georges. Carefully.'

Shortly afterward, Anne entered the Louvre and climbed the stairs to the Bouchard apartment. A feeling of dread pressed upon her chest. Michou would want to know what she had learned from Marc in Hamel's studio, even though it would hurt.

Michou was alone in the kitchen, wearing a thin white dressing gown, staring into a cup of tea. Her hair hung loosely down her back. She must have come from the studio, having posed for the *Andromeda* painting. As Anne drew near, Michou looked up, mustered a sweet, tired smile, then frowned. She had read trouble on Anne's face.

'I've spoken to Marc,' Anne signed. 'He regrets having tried to keep the murder weapon from the police. You were right to insist. He's sorry if he offended you.'

Michou stared intently at Anne's signing. 'He is under great pressure. I forgive him.' She hesitated. 'But what did he say about us, me and him?'

Anne sighed inwardly, then went on to relate what Marc had told her. 'He loves you, Michou, but he feels trapped in a hopeless situation between his family and Hamel's studio. He doesn't see how your relationship can continue.'

'He doesn't want to see me anymore, right?' Michou's expression was stoic, dry-eyed. After a long silent moment, she rose stiffly from the table and went to the stove. 'Oh, I forgot to ask, would you like tea?'

Anne nodded, fighting back tears.

Twenty

Portrait of a Spy

September 12

'At every turn in our investigation we see Pierre Fauve lurking in the shadows,' remarked Saint-Martin. 'We need to know him better.' Georges nodded in agreement. They had just sat down in Quidor's office in the Hôtel de Police. The inspector had summoned them this morning for news about Fauve.

The inspector handed a file to Saint-Martin. 'Here's Pierre. Clever fellow. But you know that already. I'll give you the gist of the report now. Read the details at your leisure. When I find more, I'll send it to you.'

Saint-Martin opened the file, glanced at its contents, then put it into his portfolio. 'I noticed that the report begins with Fauve as a young man, when he joined the Comte de Serre's regiment.'

'Yes, my agent served with him in the army and is now looking into his family background. In any case, we know that he rose rapidly in the noncommissioned ranks, and for ten years was the count's eyes and ears among the rank and file.'

'When I was in the army,' Georges remarked, 'the count was notorious for his harsh discipline. Seemed to think that common soldiers were malevolent animals who had to be broken and then kept on a short leash.'

Quidor nodded. 'Consequently, when Fauve denounced a comrade, severe punishment followed. He also caused great harm to those who failed to show him respect.'

'It seems to me,' observed Saint-Martin, 'that his position was highly dangerous and he needed great skill to survive. If he were too zealous, he could provoke his comrades to shoot him in the back. If he were slack in this dirty work, the count would cast him off.'

'Right! Fauve is a peerless intriguer with a keen sense of the limits of his power and the challenges before him. He prefers to operate quietly out of sight. After leaving the army, the count took Fauve with him to the Louvre, called him a valet, but assigned him chiefly to spy among the domestic servants, prostitutes, and other common folk who were privy to the secrets of their wealthy masters.'

Saint-Martin met Quidor's eye. 'Inspector, you haven't yet mentioned any arrests. Are they in the written report? I sense in Fauve a deep contempt for the law.'

'At the Criminal Investigation Department we've questioned him on several occasions when we suspected him of beating persons, usually prostitutes, who had tried to trick him. But they wouldn't testify against him—too frightened. He's also suspected of extortion, but his victims refuse to cooperate with us. Strange as it may seem, he has never been convicted of a crime.'

'Strange, indeed,' Saint-Martin remarked. 'On the other hand, I'm not entirely surprised. Georges and I have seen him at work in the Palais-Royal and elsewhere.'

'There's more,' Quidor said smiling, 'something I'm sure you didn't know. Fauve is single, but he has a sister, Thérèse Fauve, who runs a brothel near the Louvre. She's as clever as her brother and unshakably loyal to him, supplies him with alibis, useful bits of information, and more.' Quidor gave a leering wink.

Saint-Martin grasped Quidor's meaning and wasn't surprised. Revelations of the Fauve family's knavery could no longer shock him. 'Fauve is formidable in his way, but we shall somehow get the truth out of him.'

'Good luck! He left Paris this morning. You'll find him at the Comte de Serre's château.'

Georges and Saint-Martin went immediately to the brothel, hidden in an old, tall, shabby building. 'We'll sniff in the dog's lair while he's away,' Georges had said. Quidor had directed them to an alley off Place du Palais-Royal, ideal for

123

Fauve's purposes. A few steps to the north were the busy shopping arcades and the garden of the Palais-Royal. A five-minute walk to the south was his room in Serre's Louvre apartment.

In the building's ground floor was a wine tavern, sparsely frequented late in the morning. As the colonel and his adjutant entered, a few bleary-eyed old men looked up, attracted by the uniforms. With a nod and a small coin to the barman, the visitors passed through the room, then climbed a steep narrow wooden stairway to the brothel on the first floor.

In a large plain room, a half-dozen women sat at tables, displaying themselves in gauzy dressing gowns to the clientele, a few artisans and domestic servants. Along the walls were bedded cubicles covered by drapes.

Saint-Martin noted that, unlike many prostitutes in the small, lower-class brothels, these women appeared healthy and robust. Probably peasants from near Paris. Some were comely and looked more intelligent than he had expected. All in all, the women's appearance attested to the brothel's good management. It could also mean that they worked in free time as spies for Pierre.

The mistress of the house sat at a table near the entrance. A commanding presence, Thérèse Fauve was a large-boned woman and rather tall, square-faced like her brother, with deep-set dark eyes, a high forehead, and a determined jaw. Her gown was of costly purple silk, low-cut, and flattering to her voluptuous figure.

On the table in front of her, neatly arranged, were a register, a cash box, a lamp and pen and ink. She abruptly shifted her gaze from the women of the house to the colonel and his adjutant. Her experienced, wary eyes scanned them from top to toe.

'To what do I owe the honor of this visit?' she asked the colonel, her contralto voice thick with ironic undertones.

'We'd like to know more about your brother's movements early yesterday morning when the engraver Gillet died in the river.' Before she could reply, the colonel added, 'We realize that Pierre has gone to the count's estate in the country.'

She was quiet for a moment, calculating her response.

Saint-Martin hoped that she and her brother might not have fully harmonized their stories before he left.

'He was here with me from midnight, when he left the Palais-Royal, until an hour past dawn.'

'Did anyone besides yourself observe him?'

A cloud of confusion momentarily darkened her brow. 'Probably not.'

'Wouldn't some of the women or visitors have seen him? Where did he stay?'

'There.' She waved in the direction of a door.

'Show us.'

She frowned, sighed deeply, but yielded to Saint-Martin's implacable expression. She slipped the register and the cash box into the table drawer, locked it, and led the two men into her apartment.

They passed through a small antechamber and into a parlor furnished with decent, comfortable tables and chairs. She lived well but not extravagantly, the colonel thought. Prints hung on the walls, but no books or musical instruments were in sight. 'When Pierre visits, he sleeps there.' She pointed to a covered alcove. 'He eats in the kitchen or dining room.' She waved toward another door.

'How does he come and go without anyone seeing him?'

She hesitated. Her reluctance was palpable. Finally, she realized that they would tear the rooms apart and discover her secret anyway. She opened a wall panel to a hidden stairway. 'The steps go down to a back door. It opens on to a passage to Place du Palais-Royal.'

Saint-Martin peeked into the dark, narrow, circular staircase and decided he didn't need to descend it. She was most likely telling the truth. Later, he and Georges would check the passage below.

After briefly studying the rest of the apartment and seeing nothing remarkable, Saint-Martin signaled Georges that it was time to leave.

Georges whispered in his ear, 'There's probably a small fortune of ill-gotten louis d'or hidden beneath the parlor floor.'

Saint-Martin nodded. 'But we'll leave it there for another day. We aren't charged with investigating Fauve's spy business.'

Madame Fauve led them back into the brothel. The young women were still idly chatting at the tables. Nothing had changed. Madame returned to her table, unlocked the drawer, and drew out the cash box and the register. Georges asked to see the register. She hesitated, grimaced but handed it to him. He scanned it for a few minutes, then turned toward the prostitutes. 'Which one of you is Louise?' A comely blonde young woman sat up, raised her hand.

Georges leaned toward the colonel and whispered, 'That's Moretti's woman. The register says she was away with him at the time Bouchard was killed. Confirms his alibi.'

'And that's what she would say if we questioned her. We won't waste our time.' Saint-Martin bowed and thanked Madame Fauve politely for her cooperation. Then, as he turned to leave, he asked, as if as an afterthought, 'Madame, would you remember if your brother came here with a fancy old plumed Greek helmet on the Friday evening before Bouchard was killed? Quite unusual, you could hardly forget it.'

She coolly met his eye and replied, 'No, monsieur, and I'm sure I would have remembered it.'

The colonel glanced at his adjutant, who had lagged behind. They showed themselves out of the brothel, passed through the tavern, and into the alley.

'Georges, tell me what you saw, as we were about to leave.'

The older man smiled slyly. 'When you mentioned the Greek helmet from Hamel's studio cabinet, I had my back to the young women, but I watched them in the mirror on the wall behind Madame Fauve. Their ears pricked up. Two of them glanced furtively toward her. She wasn't looking in their direction. They leaned toward each other, covering their faces. I'm sure they were giggling.'

'No doubt, Georges, he put on a show for them that night. Why would Thérèse choose to lie about it? Most likely, her brother had also dared to show the poniard. Later, he could have passed it on to Moretti just as well as to the count. Or he could have used it himself.'

When they reached Place du Palais-Royal, the colonel turned to his adjutant. 'Georges, what do you make of this Madame Fauve?'

'She's into more than prostitution, sir. At the very least, she's a partner in her brother's spy business. Big and strong, disguised as a man, she could have been the companion seen leaving the barroom with Gillet early yesterday morning.'

For a few minutes, they studied the buildings before them, trying to determine where the passage behind the brothel must be.

'There, sir.' Georges walked up to a locked door in a narrow recessed wall connecting two buildings. The lock was new, but easy to pick. The two men entered single file, stepping over decades of trash. The air was fetid. At the brothel's back door, Georges again picked the lock. Before them, barely visible in the darkness, were the first few steps of the circular stairway to Thérèse's apartment.

Georges took off his hat and wiped sweat from his bald pate. It was noon and the air was warm, though the sun's rays couldn't reach him. 'I wonder who else, besides her brother, uses this back entrance to her rooms.'

The colonel was silent for a long moment, staring into the open doorway. 'Georges, are you thinking perhaps of Monsieur Moretti? Considering his wealth and status, he wouldn't want to be seen walking in the front way. He probably has a key to the back entrance.'

'You'd think, sir, that if Moretti were bent merely on pleasure, he'd choose a luxurious brothel in the Palais-Royal. But he comes here instead. That's odd. He must have business to do with Pierre. And that's most likely neither honest nor legal.'

Twenty-One

Machiavelli's Daughter

September 12–14

In a shaded corner of her garden, Anne sat folding and unfolding her hands. She would have to sit on them, she felt so eager. An idea had taken shape in her mind that she wished to share with her husband. She hadn't seen him since breakfast. It was now late afternoon.

A servant appeared. 'Colonel Saint-Martin has arrived and is expecting you in his office.'

When she walked in, he was at his desk, assigning tasks to a clerk. Anne waited until he dismissed the man.

Before she could present her idea, Paul handed her a scrap of paper. 'Do you recognize this? It was waiting on my desk. A servant brought it from Comtesse Marie.'

Anne recognized it immediately. 'It's the mysterious Latin note that we found hidden in Bouchard's studio a week ago.'

'And here is the Comte de Savarin's analysis.' Paul gave her a folder.

She leaned forward and began to read. The message consisted of an address in the Beaujolais wing of the Palais-Royal and several names and recent dates. The only name that she recognized was Hamel's. She handed it back.

'The handwriting is Bouchard's,' Paul remarked. 'We can safely assume that he intended to use it somehow in his conflict with Hamel. I'll ask Georges to check the names and the address.' He put the folder and the note into a drawer.

Anne curbed her eagerness for a moment and asked her husband, 'What have you done today, Paul? Any progress in the investigation?'

'Georges and I spent the morning in a brothel,' he replied innocently.

Anne had grown accustomed to his teasing, so she dutifully frowned. 'For business or pleasure?'

'In fact, to learn more about Pierre Fauve's business. It's more extensive than we thought. He's a pimp as well as a spy, and most likely practices extortion as well. His sister Thérèse seems to be an equal partner in his enterprises.' He described Pierre's arrangements at the brothel. 'He and his confederates can come and go as they please without being observed.'

'After hours in such an environment, Paul, you need to relax in the beauty of our garden. I'll order cold drinks. Then I'll share with you an idea that I've had.'

They settled themselves at a shaded garden table, glasses of cider in hand, a basket of biscuits within reach. The sky was clear blue, the air warm. The raucous sounds of the city were distant and muted. A pair of hopeful sparrows hopped about near the table.

'What is on your mind, my dear?' He tossed crumbs to the birds.

'Marc Latour and his master, Monsieur Hamel. You need a written, signed copy of the statements Marc made to me yesterday, don't you?'

Paul nodded. 'Otherwise, he could change his mind under pressure from Hamel and claim you twisted his remarks. A magistrate hearing this case would want a signed statement.'

'And Marc won't sign while he is under Hamel's thumb. Correct?'

'True.' He gave her a quizzical glance. 'So what is your plan?'

'I've tried to bring together the ideas we discussed yesterday into the old strategy of a carrot and a stick. In fact, two carrots. The first is the six thousand livres Hamel would receive for completing the Serre portrait. Michou is willing to let him have her copy. Hamel is angry with her, but you could give it to him on her behalf. In return, he would pay her a few hundred.'

'He could probably digest that carrot. What's the other one?'

129

'Ease his mind of the fear that you might use his homosexuality against him.'

'I see, and the stick is that I might expose him or even arrest him, supposing that Georges and Quidor discover strong evidence.'

'In any case,' Anne went on, 'even if a trial were to end in acquittal, he would still be disgraced or, worse yet, ridiculed for being a hypocrite.'

Paul looked out over the garden thoughtfully. 'What exactly are we enticing or forcing him to do?'

'He must free Marc to give us a signed statement concerning the murder weapon.' Anne drank from her glass, brushed a crumb from her lap. 'Early this afternoon, I spoke with Adrienne Bouchard, who knows how the Academy functions. She suggests that Hamel, as a senior member, should give a glowing public testimonial of Marc Latour's character and his abilities as an artist, arrange for an exhibition of his work, and recommend him to become an associate of the Academy.'

'Hamel's stubborn and proud, Anne, as well as a suspect in Bouchard's murder. You are asking a great deal of him. Yet it's true, he's also greedy. By agreeing to your plan, he would gain thousands of livres, as well as preserve his reputation. That might work.' He paused for a moment, reflecting. 'And Marc should like an arrangement that frees him from Hamel's grip and allows him to give us helpful testimony. It also offers him the prospect of a career in art. But are his paintings up to the standard of the Academy? If not, Hamel's intervention would meet resistance and our plan would fail.'

She took a sip of the cider. 'I don't have a trained eye for painting, so I'm not fit to judge his works, even if I studied them. And I've only seen his portrait of Michou. It's lovely. But Adrienne Bouchard *is* qualified to judge. She thinks he has as much talent as her husband had. Marc's misfortune is to lack patronage. His family is poor and undistinguished.'

'Why has Hamel held him back?'

'Marc is an excellent teacher and manages the studio very well. That frees Hamel to do his own work. Marc would be difficult to replace, especially for the little that Hamel pays.'

'I believe, Anne, that the time has nearly come to approach

him, as soon as Quidor and Georges report back to me.'

'And let us hope, Paul, that several days of staring at his ruined Serre portrait will make him receptive to our solution.'

Connoisseurs des Estampes. Georges read the simple brass sign on the door of the apartment, one of many private clubs in the Palais-Royal. To judge from the sign, it was devoted to the collection and study of fine engravings. His ear to the door, Georges could hear very faint sounds and an occasional burst of laughter.

He had climbed to the second floor with Quidor's informant. The concierge could say only that the apartment consisted of several rooms. A certain marquis held the lease. Quidor's agent had followed Hamel to this door an hour ago, and twice in the past few days. He usually stayed for two or three hours, then left for the Louvre at midnight.

Earlier in the day, Quidor had gained access to the Lieutenant-General's secret police archives and shared his findings with Georges. The records mentioned Hamel and identified the other names on the Latin note, all of them well-connected wealthy or noble gentlemen, known to be libertines. Georges also learned that the club devoted itself to pornographic art. In view of its distinguished membership and since their activities were strictly private and didn't offend against public decency, the police tolerated the club. In any case, the Duc d'Orléans owned the apartment and its oversight.

After descending to the Beaujolais arcade, Georges conferred with the agent, who suggested following Hamel back to the Louvre. On previous occasions, he had stopped for an illicit encounter. Intrigued, Georges agreed. For a few moments, Colonel Saint-Martin's words of caution troubled him. But he reasoned that Hamel had to be unmasked. This was a good way—Georges wouldn't be setting a trap for Hamel, merely observing him. This night was as suitable as any.

After instructing the agent to alert him to Hamel's departure, Georges retreated to a nearby café's garden table. Promptly at midnight, the agent signaled. Georges hid his face behind a newspaper while Hamel walked by. They followed him to the duke's newly built circus, a large darkened structure for equestrian sports in the center of the garden.

'He's going in there,' the agent whispered, pointing to the scaffolding that still covered a section of the building's front wall. 'It's a sodomites' nest. They gather by the dozen. Hamel will pick up a companion, then go to the garden of the Tuileries, as they have several times before. I know their trysting place. Do you want to make an arrest? It would be easy.'

Quidor's agent had thus far proved to be competent and trustworthy. Georges thought for a moment, then said softly, 'Let's go.' He still wasn't quite sure the colonel would approve.

'We'll get there first.' The agent set off briskly, Georges following. In a remote corner of the garden, they hid in a hedge two paces from a wooden bench. The agent shuttered his lamp. A few minutes later, he touched Georges's arm and whispered, 'They're coming.'

Two shadowy figures approached the bench. Georges could barely make out their forms, but he soon recognized their movements and sounds.

'Now,' whispered the agent as he opened the shutters of his lamp.

The two delinquents were caught with their breeches down, Hamel on top of his companion. 'No!' he cried. 'Oh, God, no!'

Their hearing was held a day later. Colonel Saint-Martin peeked into his office. Hamel sat alone in front of the desk. The painter's companion, a domestic servant in the household of the painter Greuze, was in another room. Saint-Martin glanced at his watch. A quarter after nine. He had kept Hamel waiting, a traditional interrogator's device.

He turned to Georges standing behind him. 'You seem to have cowed Monsieur Hamel. I saw him arrive, neatly dressed and groomed, docile as a lamb. I had feared that he might come here in a rage, with the Comte d'Angiviller at his side. After a day to cool down and gather hope for leniency, he may be in a reasonable frame of mind.'

Georges's tone had been apologetic when he first informed

his superior of the arrests he had made. 'I didn't want to wake you so early in the morning, sir. There was no pressing reason for you to become immediately involved.'

'I'm grateful for your concern,' the colonel had replied in a slightly testy tone of voice. 'But, if there's a crisis, I don't want to be the last to hear of it.'

Saint-Martin gestured to the office door. 'Hamel has waited long enough. You go first, Georges.' The adjutant took a seat off to one side. The colonel sat at his desk. Both men were unsmiling.

The colonel began in a quiet, even voice. 'Monsieur Hamel, you and your companion were discovered yesterday in flagrante delicto, in the act of committing a capital crime. What do you have to say in your defense?'

'Colonel, I shall confess only to a crime that for decades the magistrates have not regarded as capital. You would not dare to burn a member of the Royal Academy of Painting and Sculpture at the stake on Place de Grève. The King, as well as enlightened opinion, would forbid you.'

'True, monsieur, your crime is commonly considered under the rubric of public indecency. And that is how I shall treat it. Nonetheless, a conviction even for this lesser offense could cause serious damage to a man of your professional stature. A month in prison. Banishment from Paris for two years. Shame and ridicule from your peers.' Saint-Martin paused to allow his words to sink in. 'And I may as well anticipate your likely complaint. You were not tricked or lured into the crime. The agents of the law simply observed you and your companion in a public, not a private place.'

For the most part, Hamel remained outwardly calm. But his eyes flickered with anxiety. 'Colonel,' he said tentatively, 'would you consider a way to spare me the punishment you have mentioned?'

Saint-Martin leaned forward, fixed Hamel with his gaze. 'Monsieur, I have, in fact, discussed that matter with Lieutenant-General DeCrosne. He agrees with my view that you must cooperate fully in the ongoing investigation of painter Bouchard's murder. Since you had a strong motive to kill him, you are one of the possible suspects. The alibi that Monsieur

133

Jerôme Duby has given you is doubtful. He initially stated he was alone that night. Furthermore, we believe you are intimidating your assistant, Marc Latour, into silence by threatening to use your influence in the Academy to stall his career. He may have knowledge that would be useful to us.'

Hamel opened his mouth to object. Saint-Martin's hand rose to stop him. 'Competent experts have assured me that his paintings are worthy of the Academy's notice. I conclude, therefore, that you must issue a written statement commending Monsieur Latour's art and his character. You must also allow him to exhibit his paintings in your studio and elsewhere and propose to the Academy that he be received as an associate. These measures will give him the independence to testify freely and truthfully. In brief, sir, if you wish to be treated humanely, you must act in the same spirit toward your assistant.'

The colonel left his desk, walked to the window, and gazed out over the courtyard. The scratching of Georges's pen stopped. The room fell unnaturally silent. Saint-Martin thought he could hear Hamel's labored breathing. Finally, he turned around and looked down at the man.

'Next, a word about Mademoiselle Micheline du Saint-Esprit, who discovered the murder weapon in your cabinet. In violation of my explicit warning against retaliation, you have denounced her in public as a troublemaker and prohibited her from entering your studio. Hence, you shall publicly apologize to her and open your studio to her on the same basis as to any other artist or patron. As a sign of her goodwill, she offers you her partial copy of the Serre portrait for a reasonable ten per cent of your commission from the count.'

Saint-Martin sat at his desk again. 'For the present, monsieur, I shall suspend judgment against you and your companion and store the records of this case in the police secret file. If you comply fully with my demands in a reasonable time, I will release both of you and destroy the records. If you refuse or attempt to evade, I shall charge you and him with public indecency.' He met Hamel's eye. 'You know the consequences.'

Throughout the colonel's remarks, Hamel hardly stirred. At the end, he remained silent for a long moment, then cleared his throat. 'I have little choice but to accept your conditions,

Colonel. For years I've dreaded the moment when I would be exposed. I've always imagined I would hang myself. Now I think differently.'

Twenty-Two

The Château

September 14

As the coach rolled south on the smooth stone highway toward the Serre estate, Anne felt apprehensive and touched the burnished box at her feet. It held her two pistols. Paul had told her to take them along. Even now he was glancing out the window, more sharp-eyed than usual. And she thought of Georges sitting outside, next to the coachman, armed with a musket.

The current unrest among peasants in the countryside occasionally exploded, striking travelers passing by. And bandits, said to roam in the forest near Fontainebleau, had become bolder. Paul's Highway Patrol was stretched thin, trying to keep the roads safe.

The dangers of traveling were real, she said to herself, but they didn't appear imminent on this sunny afternoon. So she turned to her husband sitting next to her. 'What happened to Hamel?' She had had to contain her curiosity. Paul had been occupied with the painter's case all morning. He hardly had a free minute until now.

'At a closed hearing in my office, he confessed to public indecency. I brought him and his companion to a magistrate who convicted them as charged. The companion, hardly more than a boy, was released with a warning. Since Hamel's offense was more reprehensible, given his maturity, his punishment was more severe.' Paul went into detail about the steps Hamel must take to free Marc and to atone for his injury to Michou's reputation.

Michou leaned forward, closely following Paul's account. Her eyes glistened while he described the new opportunities Marc would soon have to demonstrate the excellence of his painting and to advance his career. Then, a shadow of doubt crossed her face.

'Will Hamel really do as he was told?' she signed.

'He truly has no choice,' Paul replied. 'Exposure—and the ridicule that would surely follow—would ruin him. He must regularly report to Inspecteur Quidor, who is responsible for the Louvre district.'

'And when will he apologize for calling me a troublemaker?' Her eyes sparkled, her face folded into a broad grin.

'When we return from Serre's château, at the same time as you hand him your painting of the late Comtesse de Serre.'

Michou distractedly touched the portfolio where she had put the painting. Paul had returned it to her. The count had expressly asked to see it again. She leaned back, her eyes focused inwardly, an expression of great satisfaction on her face. After a few minutes, she cast an embarrassed glance at Anne, then at Paul.

'A penny for your thoughts, Michou.' Anne's signs were gentle, sympathetic.

'I was helping Marc select his paintings for an exhibition. His portrait of me, finished in oil, was among them.'

After a two-hour ride, the coach turned on to a country road at a simple sign announcing the Serre château. In the distance Anne observed low-lying hills covered with forest and meadows. On the flatland close to the road, peasants were hard at work in a vineyard, harvesting grapes.

The coach rolled through a black iron gate, past a porter's house into a paved courtyard, up to a large, rectangular three-storey stone château. Enclosing the courtyard to left and right were single-storey buildings housing the kitchen and a stable.

'What do you make of it, Paul?'

He surveyed the château with a critical eye. 'Built toward the end of the last century. Heavy, pompous, ill-proportioned. The owner had money but scant taste for fine architecture. Serre leased the estate ten years ago, when he left the army.

He spends no more than he must on repairs or improvements.' Paul pointed to unpainted window casements and missing tiles on the mansard roof.

As the coach came to a halt, an older man hurried out of the stables. 'That must be Vincenzo,' Anne remarked, drawing upon Cécile's description. He was short and thick-chested, his face creased and leathered by the sun. His gray hair was thick and tightly curled, his legs short and bowed. He hastened to the coach, lowered the steps, and helped the women descend.

A sturdy, sullen young stableboy approached, staring at the visitors, dragging his feet. Vincenzo glared at him. 'Benoît, see to the horses.'

Vincenzo turned to the visitors. 'Welcome to Château Serre.' He spoke with a distinct Italian accent. They followed him toward the château's main entrance. Before they reached the door, it was thrown open. Pierre Fauve stepped out, resplendent in the count's buff livery, embroidered with silver. His bearing had acquired a dignity that Anne hadn't noticed before.

He was followed by an older woman who had a housekeeper's ring of keys at her waist. She gazed at the visitors with an air of authority. Must be Laure, Anne concluded.

'The Comte de Serre will meet you in his study after you have settled in,' announced Pierre. 'Laure will show you to your rooms.'

Anne and Paul walked into a spacious, clean, and well-aired corner room on the second floor. Michou and Georges had adjacent rooms. Laure had placed a vase of cut flowers on a plain writing table. The rest of the furniture was also simple, mismatched, and worn. Anne looked out the window over a small formal garden. It appeared neglected, the boxwood hedges untrimmed.

'The count spends his money elsewhere,' said Anne, waving her hand over the room, then over the garden.

Paul joined her. 'In the past, he invested heavily in his art collection. I've learned that he may soon have to sell some pieces. He has sublet his lands to neighboring farmers, who manage them badly and yield him a low return. And this year's harvest was poor. His peasants, who are already unhappy, are likely to steal from his store of grain, poach in his woods, and cause other mischief.'

'Short of money? Selling his art? Is that why he invited Moretti?'

'Apparently. Moretti both buys and sells.' Paul leaned toward her conspiratorially. 'There may also be other reasons. The two men have had a curious relationship. They do not like each other. Yet they have been together more than their business affairs would seem to require.'

At that moment, a servant came to the door and led them downstairs to the count's study. Smiling politely, Serre came forward to greet them. After an exchange of courtesies, they sat at a tea table set for four.

The count answered their unspoken question. 'I'm expecting Monsieur Moretti in a few minutes.'

While they waited, and Paul chatted with the count, Anne glanced about the large L-shaped room. The study was located in its short arm. Shelves of leather-bound, gilt-edged books lined its walls. A writing table stood near a window. The long arm of the room served as a gallery. From her vantage point, Anne could see many paintings and sculptures.

The count noticed her interest. 'The best pieces have come to me through Monsieur Moretti. When we've finished tea, I'm sure he will be happy to show them to you.'

There were footsteps in the hall, then someone at the door. Moretti entered, bowing to everyone as he advanced to the table. He laid his cane on a chair near Anne. She wondered why he carried a cane. He appeared to be in excellent health and strong-limbed. His walk was graceful and easy, no sign of a limp.

She studied the cane as closely as she could without attracting attention to herself. The golden head appeared to have the features of a man. It could be Moretti himself, she imagined. A palm's width below the head was a thick gold ring, forming a grip for a sword or dagger. The cane might be a weapon. Her grandfather in Hampstead made similar canes, as well as pistols, in his shop. She had often admired their sinister beauty.

She sensed Moretti glancing at her and at the cane. Their

eyes met briefly, while they studied each other, then flicked back to the cane.

'An unusual head,' Anne remarked with appreciation of its workmanship. 'Your likeness?'

'Yes,' he replied as he handed the cane to her. 'A small masterpiece of the Florentine goldsmith's art.'

The head was incredibly accurate, even to details such as his hair. She ran her fingers lightly over its surface, furtively but in vain searching for a way to release the blade.

A smile of satisfaction came over his face. He leaned toward her and whispered, 'May I help you find it, madame?'

He lifted up the cane for all to see. Paul had begun to show keen interest. Holding the cane at the ring with one hand, Moretti turned the head clockwise with the other, and pulled. Out came . . . a small paring knife.

'One should always be prepared to peel an orange,' he said, directing a knowing smile toward Paul. 'Were you expecting a sword, Colonel? But you know that carrying concealed weapons is illegal in this country. In Italy, it's another matter.'

Anne understood that the sword blade for the cane was close at hand, probably hidden in Moretti's luggage.

When tea was finished, the count announced, 'Monsieur Moretti will guide us through my collection of ancient and Italian art.' As an afterthought, the count said to Anne, 'A servant will fetch your little friend, the painter, to join us with her copy of my wife's portrait.'

Michou arrived shortly and the tour began. The gallery was long and rather narrow, offering limited perspectives to viewers. Fortunately, the count had collected objects suitable to the space. Several months ago, Moretti had organized the collection, hung the paintings, and displayed the sculpture. Among the paintings Moretti chose to put on view were Venetian veduti by Canaletto and Guardi, Roman ruins by Piranesi, scenes of Rome by Belotto. The sculpture included a row of marble heads of Roman emperors, a reconstructed discus thrower, and a large ancient marble vase adorned with reliefs of Bacchanalian ritual processions.

Moretti spoke a mellifluous, slightly accented French, with an eloquence worthy of his subject. Anne translated for

Michou, though she seemed to understand Moretti well enough. Her eyes fixed on his lips and followed the elegant thrust of his cane toward the works of art that he was describing. Her face flushed from the exertion.

As they strolled in a leisurely fashion through the gallery, Anne fell in step with Paul. Together, they observed the Comte de Serre. Beneath the veneer of his mannered, jaded nonchalance, the count seemed almost as rapt as Michou.

'Art appears to make a remarkable impression on him, doesn't it,' Anne whispered to Paul, nodding toward the count. They had lagged a little behind the others.

'Yes, I'm surprised to see such feeling in a hardened military officer. The count's grand tour of Italy following his army career must have profoundly stirred his imagination. The sculpted and painted images of Rome's grandeur arouse in him a spirit akin to religious devotion. And he reads the ancient Roman authors Livy, Tacitus, and Plutarch with the fervor of a Christian convert reading the Bible.'

When they reached the end of the gallery, Anne noticed a conspicuously blank place on the narrow wall.

The count turned to the others and announced, 'There's where the portrait of my wife will hang, if Hamel ever completes it.'

Paul took a step forward. 'I can tell you now, with reasonable assurance, that he will set to work as soon as we return to Paris. Today, he has signed an agreement to pay six hundred livres to Michou for the use of her copy.'

Anne had anticipated Paul's announcement and had stepped back to better observe the others. The count seemed momentarily stunned. His head pitched forward, his mouth half open. He turned to the blank space, then swung around and sought out Michou. 'Bring your copy here!' he shouted, oblivious of her deafness.

She understood perfectly and hastened to the table where she had left her portfolio, then returned with the picture, and held it up to the wall. Serre gazed at it, tears came to his eyes. 'Impetuous, beautiful Virginie! She was the elixir of my life. Made me feel young again.'

Meanwhile, Anne also had a sharp eye on Moretti. What a

transformation! Gone for the moment was the guide's grace and eloquence. His back grew rigid, his neck stiffened. He glared at the count, gripping his cane with both hands, as if he would draw out the blade and commit mayhem. In the next instant, his body relaxed. With the cane tucked under his arm, he walked up to the portrait, examined it, then stepped back and inclined his head in an attitude of grave deliberation.

'That should do nicely,' he murmured.

'May I suggest a ride before dinner?' The count left the gallery with Anne and Paul. 'Monsieur Moretti will be working on a catalogue of items in my collection that I intend to sell.'

Anne and Paul exchanged glances, then spoke in unison. 'We would be delighted to ride with you.' Paul hesitated a moment, before asking, 'May Monsieur Charpentier, my adjutant, accompany us?'

'Of course,' the count replied.

An hour later, the riding party assembled at the countess's stable among farm buildings behind the château. For Anne, Vincenzo led out a sleek black hunter fitted with a sidesaddle. She stroked the animal, fed it a handful of oats, spoke soothingly. 'What's his name?' she asked.

'Midnight.' Vincenzo placed a stool for her and helped her into the saddle. The men mounted larger hunters. Vincenzo joined them. Anne and Paul rode around the paddock a few times to become familiar with their horses.

When they left the paddock, the count came between Anne and Paul. 'I suggest we follow the route taken by my wife that morning five months ago.' Without waiting for a response, he set out on a dirt road.

As they passed by barns and sheds, Anne noticed broken fences and other signs of neglect. They reached an open field from which grain had been harvested. Men and women in rags were gathering straw. Their wagons blocked the road. In a loud, harsh voice the count ordered them to push the wagons into the field.

Several peasants exchanged angry glances, then shrugged and threw down their tools. With much pulling and heaving, they moved the wagons off the hard packed surface of the road. The wheels sank into the soft earth of the field.

As Anne rode by, she studied their weathered, sullen faces. A feeling of impotent remorse welled up in her. She swung around to Paul. 'Couldn't we have left the road instead of forcing the wagons off?'

Paul's expression was grim. 'The count didn't wish to inconvenience himself. And there was a small risk that one of his horses might pull a tendon in the field's uneven footing. He truly despises the peasants, thinks of them as animals. This incident is typical of his attitude.'

The party rode on until they reached a stone wall separating the field from a forest beyond. A wooden gate was closed. It appeared to have been recently repaired.

The count beckoned Vincenzo forward. 'Tell my guests what happened here.'

The Italian dutifully rode up to the gate. 'The Comtesse de Serre reached this point and began to jump, but then a flock of grouse flew up in front of her. The horse stumbled, couldn't regain its footing, and crashed into the gate. She was thrown forward and hit that tree.' He waved in the direction of the forest, a grimace of pain on his face. 'Monsieur Moretti sent me back to the château for help while he tended to the countess. When I returned with the Comte de Serre, she was unconscious.'

The count motioned Vincenzo aside. 'That evening, she died without ever regaining consciousness. Later, when I had a quiet moment, I reflected on what had happened. I began to feel that this was a strange accident. Why should grouse be at the wall, and on the side of the gate she couldn't see, precisely at the moment she was about to jump? A remarkable, a lethal coincidence!

'The next day,' the count continued, 'I called troopers from the Royal Highway Patrol. They studied the site but couldn't find signs of evildoing.'

Saint-Martin had brought along the troopers' full report, which the count had not seen. It reported privately that they had found broken twigs and crushed leaves and plants in the forest near the wall. But in the twenty-four hours since the accident, the count and his valet had walked over the area. A poacher or a large animal might also have been there.

Paul beckoned Georges to join him. 'You have read our troopers' report of this incident. They could find nothing suspicious, only the unfortunate coincidence. Can you think of anything they overlooked?'

Georges dismounted, opened the gate, and began to inspect the wall. Like the gate, it was chest-high, built of large field-stones mortared together. The land behind it was cleared of underbrush to create a narrow footpath, preventing the forest from growing into the wall. Trees grew up to the edge of the path. It was shaded by thick branches hanging over the wall.

'Where does the path go?' asked Georges.

'To the mill and thence to the château,' replied the count.

Georges pushed aside the underbrush to peer into the forest. It was dense and dark. He returned to the gate, where the others had dismounted and gathered.

'The troopers investigated this site while it was still rather fresh. After five months, we're not going to find any traces of foul play that they missed. Still, at this point, I'll reserve judgment.'

Paul turned to the count. 'Have you any reason to believe that your wife's death was not an accident?'

'At the time, I accepted the troopers' verdict of a strange coincidence, but I wasn't fully satisfied. Then, three weeks ago, my wife's portrait was attacked. That forced me to wonder, was there a connection? She had no enemies, I have many— soldiers, poachers, and others whom I've had to punish over the years. Did one of them kill her to take revenge on me?'

'That seems unlikely,' Paul replied. 'An angry poacher or soldier might know the forest and how to capture birds and somehow plant them by the gate, but he would also have to know the countess's movements. And he'd be lost in the Louvre trying to find Hamel's studio and the countess's portrait. The two incidents seem unconnected.'

The count shook his head, then walked over to the spot where his wife had fallen and took off his hat. For a minute or so, arms crossed, he gazed at the leafy ground. The others remained silent. The song of distant birds echoed in the forest.

'We shall return now,' said the count in a low, strained

voice. 'Supper is at seven.' They mounted silently. Erect in the saddle, he led them back through the wheat fields to the château. Anne imagined this was how he had taken his unconscious wife home to die.

Twenty-Three

Scene of an Accident

September 14

'Paul, you and Georges go ahead. I'll join you upstairs in our room. I want to talk to Vincenzo alone.'

While riding on the dirt road to the gate and back, she had sensed Vincenzo's eyes on her. He had smiled pleasantly while helping her out of the saddle. 'You ride well, madame,' he had remarked, a shy smile in his eyes.

'Don't be too long, Anne,' said Paul. 'You should rest a little before supper.'

The riders had left their horses in the paddock. Anne leaned on a fence and watched while Vincenzo and his young assistant Benoît led them one by one into the stable. As she expected, the older man directed the boy to remove the saddles, feed and water the horses, and wipe them down.

When Vincenzo emerged from the stable door, she approached him. 'May I have a word with you, monsieur?' She spoke to him easily, for she felt a kinship with grooms, who spent a lifetime in the company of horses. Her grandfather's groom in Hampstead, an old cavalryman, was her friend, had taught her to ride, even to shoot her pistols at full tilt.

'Of course, madame.' There was a benevolent wariness in his eyes. He looked about for a suitable place.

'Perhaps you could show me the tackle room.' She wanted their conversation to attract as little attention as possible at the château. 'I understand this was the Comtesse de Serre's stable,' she remarked as they walked past a half-dozen horses feeding in their stalls. 'And these were hers as well?'

'Yes, we used to have many more.' He pointed to several empty stalls. 'After she died, the count sold her carriages and the carriage horses. He had enough of his own.'

The boy had lifted the saddles on to benches and was cleaning them.

'Just leave them here when you're done, Benoît. I'm going to show Madame Cartier the tackle room.'

Anne appreciated Vincenzo's discretion and his intelligence. A diamond in the rough. He seemed to know her. Had he heard already from Cécile about their conversation last Monday?

At the far end of the stable he opened a door to a large room that smelled of leather and oil. Along the walls were racks for whips, boots, harnesses, saddles, and other gear. In a corner at a window looking over the paddock were comfortable wooden chairs and a table and several cabinets. 'She loved to come here. That window was her favorite spot. She'd sit there with a thimble of brandy and watch her horses play.' He paused, then spoke less freely. 'The count told me to get rid of it all.' He waved his arm over the room. 'But I said, save it. One day, you might have guests who would like to ride or hunt. And he saved it. Surprised me.'

'You've kept her things in perfect condition. Were you fond of her?'

'She was good to me and Laure and Cécile. That's all I should say.'

'Then her death must have shocked you, especially since you nearly witnessed it.'

He nodded. 'It was almost like losing a daughter.'

'Was there anything that seemed strange to you that morning?'

'The birds . . . why would they be at the gate just when she was about to jump?'

'Yes, the odds of that happening are one in a million or more. Anything else?' She had watched him closely at the forest gate. A puzzled expression had come over his face. He had glanced several times toward a crevice in the wall a few paces immediately to the left of the gate. And he stared at a large tree behind the crevice. 'Did you notice perhaps something moving behind the wall?'

Alarm flashed across his face. She had hit a nerve.

'It was early in the morning,' he replied in a low voice. 'The sun was in the east behind the trees. At the wall it was very dark. I can't say for sure that I saw anything move.'

Anne realized she couldn't draw him out any further. And it was time to get ready for supper. 'Monsieur, I would like to ride tomorrow just after dawn, and use her saddle and boots and other gear. Would you ride with me? I'll ask Monsieur Charpentier to join us.' She met his eye. 'Do you understand, monsieur?'

'Yes, madame, I understand perfectly. I shall be ready.'

On the way up the stairs to her room, Anne heard steps above her and the rattle of keys. Laure was coming down. They met halfway and exchanged friendly greetings. Anne seized the opportunity to ask what the count would expect her to wear at supper.

'This won't be the King's table or the opera, madame.' With a broad movement of her hands, she drew the full skirts worn by ladies on formal occasions. 'The count's taste in fashion has always inclined to the simple. He's still a soldier at heart. Despises fops and courtiers.' She went on, 'He'd like a muslin gown, the kind favored by the Queen.' She studied Anne with the skilled eye of a woman who made her own clothes and had trained her daughter Cécile. 'You have a fine figure. Wear a white muslin gown. Add a few bright ribbons and you will surely please him.'

'You have set my mind at ease, madame.' Anne hesitated, then asked offhandedly, 'And how did the countess dress? I neglected to ask your daughter. I understand she was her personal maid.'

'Yes, Cécile wrote that you took her some work to do for the Comtesse de Beaumont.' The mother's expression became nostalgic. 'But, to answer your question, the countess was so beautiful that ornament was unnecessary. She shared the Queen's taste for light fabrics and simple gowns that allowed her freedom to move as she liked. Her hair was raven-black, her skin creamy white. Red was her favorite color. It was a delight to dress her.'

Anne thanked Laure and continued up the stairs. It wasn't a place suited for long conversation, even less for the question that Anne intended to ask Laure. What was the incident in the countess' life that had to be hidden?

Early in the evening, before the count and his guests dined upstairs, Georges and Michou joined the servants gathered for supper in a simple room off the kitchen. Pierre presided at one end of a long wooden table and the others clustered near him. Half the table was unoccupied, reflecting the reduction in staff during the past several months. Pierre nodded to a maid who ladled out bowls of soup. They helped themselves to bread and cheese and wine.

Conversation was sparse. Pierre seemed preoccupied, stared into his bowl. The presence of two strangers at the table, one of them deaf, the other a policeman, might have inhibited conversation. The servants seemed particularly uneasy with Michou's habit of staring while she tried to read their lips or to sketch them. More than once, Pierre glanced sharply at her, his eyes narrowed and unfriendly, as if he would do her harm. Georges grew concerned and promised himself to watch over her. Pierre must know that Michou had spied on him in the church of Saint-Roch.

For her part, Michou seemed unconcerned about Pierre's displeasure. She boldly sketched him in the book that she kept by her plate. Thereafter, she largely ignored him and focused her attention on Laure and Vincenzo. Finally, she turned to Benoît, the young stableboy sitting across the table from her. He became self-conscious, also anxious, as if she were stealing bits of his person. He glared at her to no avail, then turned to Pierre, who signaled Georges to stop her. He replied with a sympathetic but helpless shrug.

When the meal finished, Pierre and the young maids left to serve upstairs. Other servants went to their rooms. Vincenzo and Laure remained at the table.

The atmosphere immediately improved. Georges lifted his

glass, sniffed the wine, and toasted his companions. They smiled, at ease with him. But they glanced apprehensively at Michou, who was unlike any deaf person they knew.

'Michou's an artist,' said Georges, discerning their problem, 'especially good at portraits.' He caught Michou's eye and pointed to the sketchbook, then to Laure and Vincenzo.

She smiled, wrote a few words in the margin of a page, and handed the book to them.

'She's drawn our likeness,' remarked Laure, showing the page to her husband, 'and she writes that she'll finish the sketches and give them to us, with a copy for Cécile.' Laure rose from the table, embraced Michou, and returned the book. 'Your drawings are wonderful. Thank you.'

Michou bowed to them, tucked the book under her arm, and left for her room. As she passed Georges, she winked at him. He mouthed, 'Well done.'

A bell rang, and Anne and Paul set out for the count's dining room. At the foot of the stairs on the first floor they met Pierre Fauve in his buff and silver livery. He bowed politely. His hair was lightly powdered, gathered at the back of the neck, and tied with a black bow. His shoes were also black with silver buckles. No sign of the pimp and the master of spies, Anne noted. His sister at the brothel would be looking after those enterprises.

'You play many roles for the count,' Paul ventured to remark.

'Yes, Colonel, and I strive to play them well. Please follow me.'

A château as large as this one had more than one dining room, Anne surmised. Pierre led them through the formal one, a vast room with a high embossed ceiling. Judging from appearances, it was seldom used. White dust cloths covered its long mahogany table, its chairs and sideboards. The chandeliers and the wall sconces lacked candles. The dark paneled walls were decorated only with heavily varnished portraits of the count's male ancestors, a mixture of soldiers and magistrates. A stuffy-looking lot, Anne thought.

Their tour ended in an intimate dining room, furnished in

a restrained style of the previous reign—cream paneled walls and plaster ceiling, delicate gilt shell and floral decoration, moss-green drapes drawn over the windows, a dark-green marble fireplace. A pair of fanciful garden scenes graced one wall. A pair of still-life paintings hung above a sideboard. In the middle of the room stood a round table covered with a fine linen cloth. Sèvres porcelain and polished silverware had been set for four. Gilded wall sconces and a small crystal chandelier cast a lively golden light.

Anne wondered whose tastes were reflected here.

'The previous owner created this room,' said the count from behind her. He had just arrived with Monsieur Moretti. 'My wife liked it, so we kept it as it was.'

'It's charming,' Anne observed. The room subtly revealed yet another facet of the Comtesse de Serre's complicated personality, a taste for refined dining and conversation. She thrived here as well as in her tackle room.

'I often eat alone at this table,' he remarked with feeling, then quickly directed his guests to their places. Moretti seized the opportunity to seat Anne. As he bent low over her, she detected a scent like a delicate exotic perfume. A pleasing sensation, she confessed to herself.

The count announced that they would have a simple supper. The housekeeper, now serving as cook, had prepared a vegetable broth, a roast of lamb in a mild garlic sauce, green beans. The wine was a rich red Bordeaux from the Saint-Émilion region. The meal would conclude with a garden salad, then ripe grapes from the estate's vineyard and aged cheeses, followed by small custard tarts and a brandy.

In yet another role, Pierre Fauve served the soup. His movements were elegant, his manners impeccable. Amazing, Anne thought, for a former soldier. How easily he adapted to widely different circumstances that would confuse or intimidate ordinary men. Did the count appreciate him, pay him well? Her eyes shifted from Pierre to the count, who ignored him as well as the other servants, and probably paid him hardly what he was worth. She studied Pierre again, as he drew near, almost touched her, and poured her wine. Yes, she now felt certain that to take him for granted, to slight him, could be a costly mistake. Why did such a talented man remain in the count's service?

The count seemed so full of himself. Between the soup and the main course, he began to reminisce, though he was in the company of strangers. 'My wife used to give small parties and dinners for a dozen guests. For entertainment there was dancing, gambling, hunting, or horse racing. In fair summer weather, we had music or light comedy in the garden theater.'

Pierre came with the roast lamb. The count interrupted himself, glanced at the food, nodded his approval, and directed it toward his guests. Pierre began serving.

'Since my wife's death,' the count resumed, 'I find country life less pleasing, even distressing at times. I've dismissed many of the servants, closed most of the rooms of this house, and now live almost like a recluse. Riding and hunting are the only passions I indulge while I am here. For a spiritual respite I visit my gallery and contemplate views of beautiful Italy, or recreate in my imagination the magnificent world of ancient Rome.'

Pierre reached him with the lamb. He went on speaking while being served, ignoring the servant. 'I shall be happy when the vacation season ends in a month. I prefer the bustle of Paris. It draws my mind away from the sad memories of this place.' He sighed, shook his head, then began to taste the food before him.

Paul seized this opportunity to shift the topic of conversation. 'Lieutenant-General DeCrosne is concerned about the current unrest in the countryside.'

'What can be done to calm the peasants?' Anne directed her question to Paul.

'I frankly don't know the full extent of the problem,' he replied. 'It's more than conflict over rents and fees. Too many fields are small, scattered, and poorly cultivated. We need to learn from the English how to raise livestock and increase the land's fertility. Our nation's agriculture is as poorly organized as its public finances. This much is certain, the task of maintaining order is already more difficult than a few hundred troopers of the Royal Highway Patrol can master.'

'Something *must* be done,' Anne insisted. 'If next year's

harvest is as poor as this one, grain will become scarce and the price of bread will rise. People will starve.'

Moretti entered the discussion. 'I think, madame, that they are more likely to break into the granaries and bakeries and help themselves. Peasants bear their suffering less patiently today.' He turned to the count. 'Is that not true, sir?'

'Yes, indeed, they are a lazy, ungrateful lot.' The count glared at his guests as if they were ignorant recruits. 'The solution is simple. Call in the army. Peasants understand only the language of force. Round up the ringleaders and hang them in the village market. The rest will obey their masters like sheep.'

Anne felt herself cringing from the count's arrogant, brutal remarks. An urge to contradict him almost overwhelmed her. But she reminded herself that her task was to study the man. For that she needed to keep a cool, clear head.

The custard tarts arrived while the count was complaining about hordes of beggars infesting the area. Poachers also had grown bold, stealing game from the royal forest of Fontainebleau. 'It's hardly worth the King's trouble to hunt there anymore. But poachers know better than to invade my forest. I've ordered the guards to beat anyone they catch to within an inch of his life.'

Anne was again tempted to lash out at him. To divert her wrath, she set about comparing the count with Monsieur Moretti. Their relationship had often intrigued her. The former was a sixty-year-old man whose best days were behind him, whose resources were shrinking, his health fragile. Though still mentally alert, he seemed weary of life and jaded. He was still capable of passion but lacked a worthy outlet. Since retiring from the army, he had achieved little. His hopes for honor and recognition had withered away. The decade he lived with Virginie seemed to have given him happiness, but it was a lovely sunset rather than a challenging dawn.

In contrast, Moretti was forty years old—the age of the late countess—and at the peak of his powers. Like Serre, he had lost his wife, but he was still handsome and virile. He could surely find another woman to his taste. And he was rich. He could look forward to advancing in a society that increasingly valued wealth more than birth.

151

What drew them together? Anne wondered. A common interest in art, to be sure. But what else? She had wrestled before with that question. Now she sensed that these two men still somehow shared the Comtesse Virginie de Serre.

Twenty-Four

Death in a Distant Land

September 14

Peace and quiet had come to the servants' quarters on the ground floor. The meal upstairs had been served, the table cleared. In the kitchen, the dishes were washed and left to dry. Pierre and the young maids had gone. Before retiring for the night, Anne joined Georges for brandy together with Laure and Vincenzo in the room off the kitchen. Anne chose this moment to uncover the hidden incident in the countess's past.

Trusting in the goodwill of these servants, and hoping that the brandy would weaken their inhibitions, Anne probed ever so gently at first.

'In our investigation of the recent crimes at the Louvre, Pierre has come to our attention. We wonder why he keeps close watch on your daughter Cécile.' Anne paused, studied their faces, noticed some anxiety but no surprise, or shame for what Cécile had to do, nor any anger toward Pierre for exploiting her. They apparently didn't know that Cécile was indebted to him. 'Forgive me for asking, but could you tell us how Cécile and her husband paid for the shop on Rue Sainte-Anne? Could Pierre have lent a sum to them?'

Laure shook her head. 'Cécile told us that her husband had received the money from a cousin who died without an heir.'

Anne doubted the cousin's existence, but she pretended to be satisfied and went on to say, 'I've heard that Pierre threatens to punish Cécile and you if she ever speaks about a certain

152

mysterious incident in the Comtesse de Serre's past having to do with riding.' Anne paused, took a sip from her glass, stared first at Vincenzo, then at Laure. 'What can you tell me?'

Her question seemed, at first, to startle them, then fear flashed across their faces. They exchanged glances. Neither wished to speak.

Anne met Vincenzo's eye. 'My husband, Colonel Saint-Martin, is an honorable man. He will respect the countess's reputation. He will also ensure that no harm comes to you or to Cécile.'

'The countess made me promise never to tell,' he objected, 'not even the count, her husband.'

'Nothing you say can hurt her now,' Anne assured him. 'She wouldn't hold you to that promise. Neither Cécile nor Laure nor you should have to endure Pierre's tyranny.'

Georges leaned forward and added, 'You can be sure that Pierre intends to use the incident in question to his own advantage. We don't know how, but almost certainly at someone else's expense. Pierre is a professional extortioner.' Georges addressed Vincenzo. 'You know Pierre well. Can you believe that he is fond of the countess, and zealous for her reputation?'

'Pierre believes in no one but himself,' said Vincenzo with conviction. He looked at Anne. 'I have heard good reports about your colonel. He has worked hard with his troopers to keep peace in the countryside.'

'Then will you help us?' Anne asked.

There was a heavy silence. Finally, Vincenzo put down his glass, walked to the door and locked it, and returned to the table. He glanced at his wife. She nodded hesitantly, gathered courage and said, 'Go ahead, tell them.'

Vincenzo cleared his throat, apologized to Anne, and took a sip of his brandy. 'The incident happened in Italy a year and a half ago.' He paused for a moment, refreshing his memory. 'We were at the end of a two-year trip. Both the count and the countess were fond of the country and had made two shorter trips to the northern regions, the first to Piedmont and Lombardy, the second to Venice. He loved the art and antiquities, she preferred the picturesque beauty of the land.

153

'Pierre, Laure, Cécile, and I accompanied them. We sailed to the south and spent the winter in Sicily and Naples. Afterward, we lived in Rome for an entire year. And finally we visited Pisa, Sienna, and Florence.

'The incident took place during our next-to-last day in Florence, shortly before sailing from Livorno to Marseille. The count had rented a country house in Fiesole, a beautiful village on a hill above Florence. He spent the day in the city enjoying art at the Accademia and the monastery of San Marco. She entertained guests at a farewell dinner. After they left, she came to me. "Please saddle my horse. I must ride out into the country and revive my spirits." It was early in the evening and still light.

'Two hours later, she came back. Though it was now dark, I could tell that something was wrong. A ride usually refreshed her, banished all her cares, filled her face with happiness. This time, she seemed anxious and upset. While I helped her dismount, I asked, had the ride been pleasant? She nodded, then rushed away. I thought she was about to cry.' Vincenzo turned to Laure to continue.

'The countess went directly to her room. I alerted Cécile and we followed after her. She had shut her door. I knocked and asked through the door if we could help her change clothes, draw a bath, bring something to eat and drink. She replied that she had a headache but didn't want any help. She would be fine in the morning. So we left her.

'The next day, we began to pack for the trip to Livorno. The ship was in the harbor, waiting for us. The countess slept late. Cécile took her tea and biscuits, helped her dress. She seemed subdued but much better.'

Vincenzo took over the narrative again. 'Her horse had been rented. Before we departed, I had to return him to a stable in the city, a few miles downhill. About halfway, I noticed the horse had begun to limp. His left front leg was lame. I dismounted and examined it but could find no visible damage. He must have bruised a tendon. I led him the rest of the way to the stable, apologized to the stable owner, and paid him extra for the injury.

'Off and on for the rest of the day, I thought about that

injured leg. How could the horse have hurt it? Perhaps he stepped into a hole in the road and twisted his leg trying to keep his balance. Late in the afternoon, as was my custom, I walked into the village to a trattoria for coffee and gossip. The men were discussing a terrible accident. A young boy, the only son of a widow, had been found dead alongside a country road. He had been run over by a horse the night before and had lain unnoticed for hours in a ditch. The rider was unknown. No one had yet admitted responsibility.

'Right away, I thought of the horse's lame leg. But I held my tongue. As soon as I could, I hurried to the house and discussed the incident with Laure and Cécile. Perhaps the countess had had nothing to do with the boy's death. Other riders had also used the road. But if she killed him by accident, his mother had a right to at least a sign of regret, maybe even compensation. And, if the countess had been reckless, then the police should be notified. They might hold her indefinitely, the ship would have to sail without her. There might be a trial, conviction, prison in a foreign country.'

'Did you confront the countess?' asked Anne, gazing first at Vincenzo, then at Laure.

She shook her head. 'How would the countess—and especially the count—react if three servants were to accuse her of killing the boy and expose her to possible scandal or prosecution?' She lowered her voice. 'The count is *not* a kind man.'

'We decided,' resumed Vincenzo, 'that I shouldn't accuse the countess when I spoke to her, but simply mention the horse's lame leg and ask her how it happened. If the occasion arose, I might also mention the news about the young boy's death.

'That evening, in a small paddock behind the house, I was feeding the carriage horses we had rented for the trip to Livorno. Two porters were out front with Pierre loading our trunks on to the carriage. The countess came up to me, petted the horses, helped me feed them. She liked to do that, but I could tell she had something on her mind. Finally, she asked, "When you returned my horse, was the stable owner satisfied?"

'"No, Comtesse," I replied simply. "The horse's left front leg was lame. I had to pay compensation."

155

'She became very still, then spoke in a casual voice. "A few minutes ago, I overheard the porters talking. Someone killed a young boy on a country road yesterday. Have you heard any more news?"

'I'm sure my face gave me away. She drew very close, looked me in the eye. "Tell me what you know."

'So I did, as gently as I could.

'"Then you must think that I killed the boy and left him dying in the ditch," she said.

'"I don't know the circumstances, Comtesse. I've not jumped to that conclusion."

'She was silent again. When she finally spoke, her voice was low and tense. "I was riding at a gallop on a narrow straight stretch of the road. Suddenly, the boy stepped out in front of me. I hadn't seen him. The horse hit him and stumbled, then struggled for balance. I managed to keep him from falling. I dismounted, found the boy lying on the road, and felt for a pulse. He was dead. I was shocked, could hardly think. I looked around, nobody saw me. I could do nothing for the boy. If I reported his death, I would be held by the police while they investigated. I would miss the boat at Livorno. The count would be angry with me. People would accuse me of reckless riding." She hesitated a moment, her voice so taut that she couldn't speak. She drew a deep breath. "I'm ashamed to tell you this, Vincenzo, I pulled the body off the road and covered it with leaves and twigs and rode away." She paused again, her eyes moist and pleading. "Do you believe me?"

'"Yes," I assured her. "I understand how people might react in a sudden crisis. I must tell your story to Laure and Cécile. They know much of it already, but their view needs to be corrected. I see no reason to speak to anyone else."'

Anne leaned back in her chair and gazed at Vincenzo. 'You are courageous and very wise.'

Georges sighed. 'I've been a soldier or policeman most of my life. I should be as hard as nails. But when I hear your story, Vincenzo, I feel pain.' He touched his heart. 'How sad!'

The room was quiet for a moment until Anne spoke again. 'Did you learn any more about the widow and the boy?'

'A little. Their names. Maria and Benedetto Falzone. He

156

was about ten, sickly. They came from the city to escape the summer's heat and filth. Rented a cottage near the road.'

The mood in the room was somber and pensive. A wall clock ticked away the minutes. Anne and Georges finished their drinks and started to rise from the table. Vincenzo waved them down. 'There's one more unfortunate detail I must share with you.' His face became grim. Laure shifted uncomfortably in her chair. 'When the countess left me alone with the horses, I heard a rustling sound. I immediately raised my lantern and peered over a nearby hedge. Pierre was sneaking away. He must have heard everything the countess and I had said.'

'*Merde!*' said Georges, as he clapped his hands to his head. He glanced at Vincenzo, then at Laure. 'When did he begin to warn you to remain silent and threaten you?'

Laure spoke up this time. 'When the countess died. Pierre said the count wanted to protect his wife's reputation. He must have supposed that we now felt freed from Vincenzo's promise to the countess.'

Anne asked, 'Do you know for a fact that the count had found out about his wife's incident?'

'No, we don't,' replied Laure. 'The count has never spoken about it. He usually deals with us through Pierre. But isn't it likely that the count would know? Behind the stiff, aristocratic facade, there's a sly, crafty man.'

'Yes, of course,' Anne agreed. 'And I'll never underestimate him.'

Twenty-Five

Suspects

September 15

Anne was up at dawn and woke Paul. He rose eagerly. Before going to bed, she had shared Vincenzo's story with him. 'At

157

the moment,' he had said, 'I can't see how that incident in Fiesole could be connected to the vandalizing of her portrait or to Bouchard's murder. But any event in her life as serious as a homicide is potentially relevant.'

They dressed for riding, she in buff breeches and white shirt like the countess, then made their way in the early light to the stable. The air was cool and fresh, the sky was clear. Georges and Vincenzo were already saddling the horses. In the tackle room Anne put on the countess's boots, black riding coat, and black jockey cap. From there she went to the paddock, where she found Paul and Georges already mounted.

Vincenzo approached her, leading the black hunter. When the groom got close, he blinked. 'I'd have sworn you were the countess come alive.' He handed her the reins. 'I've brought you Midnight again. He was one of the countess's favorite jumpers and a brother of Blackie, the horse she rode on the morning she died. Broke its front legs against the gate. We had to put him down.'

Midnight whinnied in anticipation of a good run. Anne stroked his refined head, then stepped back and admired the rest of him. Powerful hindquarters and slender legs. A pure color, no mixing of hair, but a small white marking on his left front foot. That means good luck, she recalled. What a pair they must have been, he and his black brother. Vincenzo stood by while Anne swung into the saddle and sat astride. With a little calf pressure, she urged the horse out into the paddock. They trotted amiably around a few times. 'I think we're friends, Midnight.' She leaned forward and stroked him. He shook his head, hot-blooded, eager to go.

Georges rode up to her. 'Vincenzo tells me that the light and the weather will be like it was at the time of the accident.'

Anne corrected him. 'But then, in early April, the trees were beginning to leaf. Today, they are still in full leaf.'

'Yes,' he admitted, 'we must allow for the difference.'

They rode out of the paddock, past barns and a small shed and on to the dirt road to the forest. At the gate, they stopped in a circle. Georges laid out his plan. 'We'll reenact the countess's fatal accident. I'll hide behind the wall. When I give the signal, Madame Cartier will ride up the road at a full gallop and jump the gate. That's how the countess used to ride. Colonel Saint-Martin will follow her, pretending to be Monsieur Moretti. At the gate, sir, you will dismount, and cross the wall to assist her. Vincenzo, you do exactly what you did that morning.'

Georges tethered his horse out of the way, climbed to the far side of the wall, and ducked out of sight.

Anne rode back toward the château a short distance and waited facing the wall.

Georges waved his arm.

Anne spurred her hunter to a gallop. The wind whistled in her ears. A worry crept into her mind. Midnight was a new, mostly untested acquaintance. He might have doubts about her, then suddenly balk at the gate, and send her flying. But he's also an experienced, sensible jumper, she told herself. He knows this gate and has jumped it many times before. Just be calm. Maintain constant, insistent calf pressure.

She felt Midnight pull on the reins. So he's eager. This should be fun. She settled herself in the saddle, balanced for the jump. And just in time. Midnight took off in a powerful leap, soared over the gate, flew through the air. What a thrill! They landed smoothly on the other side, galloped on a few lengths, turned around and trotted back. Anne gratefully stroked him, then tethered him to a sapling by the road.

Anne was still enjoying the exhilaration of the jump when she recalled Georges's instructions. Her mood altered immediately. She hurried to the tree where the countess had fallen and reclined against it. A profound distress gripped her. The unfortunate woman might have experienced pain, even though the accident occurred suddenly. Anne now lived the horror at a slower pace in her imagination. This wasn't sport but the replay of a brutal death. Her body suddenly began shaking.

Paul came to her side. 'Are you all right, Anne?' he asked, putting his arms around her. He had given the reins of his horse to Vincenzo and climbed over the wall. Then, like Moretti, he had called out to the groom to seek help at the château.

'How dreadful, Paul. Her life snuffed out in an instant. Right here.' She touched the spot. 'I must mark it.'

'Do mark the spot,' Paul said gently. 'But, in fact, she died later in the château.' He looked up. 'Let's watch Vincenzo.'

The Italian had started down the road to the château.

'That's enough!' Georges shouted. 'Vincenzo, come back. Tell us what you saw.'

They all gathered at the gate.

'Nothing unusual,' the groom replied. 'If anything had moved, I might have noticed it. But maybe not. The forest is dark and casts shadows over the wall. I also kept my eye chiefly on Madame Cartier, then on Colonel Saint-Martin, and gave the wall only a brief, sweeping glance.'

'Colonel, what did you see?'

'Even though I focused on my wife, I caught a glimpse of you sneaking into the forest.'

'Good, that's what I expected.' Georges crouched behind the wall a few paces to the right of the gate and in front of a large tree. 'From here, I watched you all approach. You couldn't see my head because of the shadows and because the top of the wall is uneven and partially covered with debris from the forest. In front of me is a broken leafy branch that I can see through but still conceals me.

'When Madame Cartier's horse began to jump, I ducked down and pulled on an imaginary cord, releasing a flock of imaginary grouse from a trap at the gate. Had they been real, they would have flown up into the air, fluttering their wings and frightening her horse. It would have crashed into the gate. She would have gone flying headfirst into the forest.'

Anne felt faint and leaned against Paul. They hadn't had breakfast before setting out. He held her again. 'This will soon be over,' he said softly.

Georges went on with his story. 'I grabbed the imaginary trap and slipped into the forest. But not quickly enough.' He pointed to Paul. 'You, Monsieur Moretti, saw me. That might be significant.' He paused, reflecting. 'Or it might not. Our imaginary killer could have moved faster than I did. Then Moretti wouldn't have seen him.'

'Who is our killer?' asked Anne, pointing the question to her companions.

'A poacher,' suggested Vincenzo. 'A poacher would have such a trap.'

'And the Comte de Serre might have given him a motive to use it,' Anne remarked. 'I'm thinking of his harsh measures toward poachers.'

Paul turned to Vincenzo. 'Can you recall anyone caught poaching birds and severely punished?'

'Yes, two years ago, there was one, but he later died from the beating he received. Still, he probably had friends or relatives who might want to avenge him.' He paused, stared at the spot where the birds had once been. 'The dead poacher's trap!' He struck his forehead a glancing blow. 'Why hadn't I thought of it before? Follow me.'

Vincenzo led them into the small shed that they had passed on their way to the gate. 'It should be here,' he said, lifting an old canvas, then reaching into a low pile of broken tools and pieces of wood. 'It's gone!' he exclaimed. 'That's strange. I used it perhaps a month before the countess's death. It was in working order. The count demanded a pair of roasted birds for his dinner. I went to the forest with the trap and caught them. Where could it be?'

Georges removed his hat and palmed his bald head. 'If the killer used it, he might have hidden it in the forest, not too far from the gate. He wouldn't have walked out with it in the daylight, wouldn't care to be noticed.'

Paul turned to Vincenzo. 'I'd like you to spend a few hours looking for it.' Then he met Georges's eye. 'Get a couple of troopers from the nearest post and question the servants, past and present, who might have connections to poachers. Talk to people in the nearby village. We must narrow down a list of suspects.'

As they left the shed, Anne said to Paul, 'We may not find the trap, but we can be almost certain that someone deliberately put the grouse in front of the gate. If so, the Comtesse de Serre was murdered.'

Colonel Saint-Martin found the count in a dressing gown at breakfast in his study. It was about nine o'clock. He had groomed for the day's routine, a fresh wig on his head. A discreet touch of rouge brightened his pallid cheeks. Moretti was with him, dressed in a black silk suit with delicate floral silver embroidery, a perfect image of good taste. His gold-headed cane leaned against his chair. Several paintings rested on easels near the library table where the two men sat, a tray of coffee and half-eaten bread between them. To judge from the expression on the count's face, he disliked having to choose any of his treasures to sell.

Among the possible explanations for the countess's death competing in his mind, Saint-Martin selected for this occasion the one that would appeal to the count, not the one that he himself thought most likely. He needed to hold the count in a complacent mood until more evidence was gathered. Otherwise, if provoked, the count might take countermeasures that would impede the investigation, such as expelling his visitors from the château and persecuting Vincenzo and Laure.

As the colonel approached, the two men looked up. Serre appeared relieved by the distraction. Moretti seemed annoyed. The colonel excused himself for interrupting their business, then addressed the count. 'Sir, I must tell you that I am reopening the Highway Patrol's investigation into the death of your wife, the countess. It's a hard decision, since our resources are already stretched thin. I'm also reluctant to spoil the pleasure of your vacation. But I have no choice.'

'A sudden decision, Colonel?' The count raised an eyebrow, pointed Saint-Martin to a seat.

'No,' he replied, 'a gradual one. On several occasions during the summer, especially since arriving here, I've observed unrest among your peasants. They've already moved to acts of violence toward your property. I thought it possible that they might try to injure your person or someone dear to you.

'The poaching on your estate and your strong measures to curb it set me to thinking about the circumstances of your wife's death. Early this morning at the forest gate, my adjutant organized a reenactment. We reached a more plausible explanation than the coincidence of a few grouse at the gate, rising with a great flutter at the moment the countess began her jump.

'I believe she was killed by a person with a well-thought-out plan and a poacher's skills. His weapon was a trap full of birds. He had learned somehow from inside the château the countess's movements. Otherwise, he couldn't have known when to lay the trap.'

The count nodded. 'That is true, Colonel. When she was residing at the château, the countess rode out into the country and jumped the gate frequently, but not every morning nor at the same hour.'

Saint-Martin paused as if to take note of the count's observation, then added, 'The killer may have been an aggrieved poacher who was avenging the death or beating of a relative or friend. He had help from one or more of the servants in the château.'

The count sat through this narrative, tight-lipped, his head tilted to one side, arms crossed on his chest. When the colonel finished, the count waited for a few moments, then spoke in a low, taut voice. 'Over the past month, and especially since her portrait was defaced, I've come to nearly the same conclusion. A poacher murdered her to punish me. One of the several servants whom I have dismissed could have helped him.'

Meanwhile, Moretti's brow furrowed with doubt. He took up his cane and laid it across his lap. 'Your conjecture is clever, Colonel, but lacks evidence. The putative killer left no trace of himself. Neither Vincenzo nor I saw him.'

'That's true,' Saint-Martin granted. 'But the probability of my theory is strong enough to call for an investigation and point it in a certain direction.'

Saint-Martin turned to the count. 'Sir, to help my adjutant search for suspects, I have brought in a few troopers. They are questioning the servants you dismissed and those you still employ, as well as certain men in the neighborhood suspected or convicted of poaching. I've sent Vincenzo to the forest to look for the missing trap.'

The count reared back in his chair. 'Rather high-handed, don't you think, Colonel, for a guest to order the host's servants about?'

'I grant that guests should know the limits of hospitality. But this guest happens to be in charge of a murder investigation.'

With a curt gesture, the count indicated that he had heard enough. 'Will there be anything else, Colonel?'

'Yes,' replied Saint-Martin, 'I have more questions for you and Monsieur Moretti separately. Would this room after dinner be convenient?'

The count frowned, sighed. 'If you insist, though I've told you all I know.'

Moretti affected a mixture of nonchalance and irritation. 'The count shall be first. I'll follow him.' But his fingers tapped the head of his cane nervously.

Serre glanced at the pictures around him, then at Moretti. 'We shall discuss the sales again tomorrow. This business of my wife's murder has distracted my mind.'

Saint-Martin thought he detected a new, harsher tone in the count's voice. Woe to the poacher caught in his forest.

Anne and Paul walked out into the garden where they couldn't be heard. Paul recounted to her what he had told the count and Moretti. 'They have several hours to figure out why I want to question them. Both are hiding something from us.'

The sun was bright and warm. They made their way into the shade of a decrepit pergola. Anne grimaced with disgust. The floor was littered with dead blossoms, leaves, and other debris from the untended vines overhead. Bird droppings soiled the benches attached to the sides of the structure.

Her husband gazed with a critical eye at the flower beds, overgrown with weeds. His eyes shifted to the dense *Clematis vitalba* vines covering the pergola. 'What a pity!' he exclaimed. 'This place will soon become a jungle. No one is picking off the dead blossoms. The count must have dismissed the gardener when his wife died.'

Anne understood that it hurt him to see such neglect. He approached gardening sometimes as if it were an act of worship, working together with the hand of God in nature.

She cleared her throat to gain his attention. 'What can I do, Paul, to help the investigation?'

He faced her and smiled. 'Speak to Laure again. Find out, if you can, whether the countess and Moretti had an intimate relationship. If so, did the count know about it? When we

164

raised this issue with him earlier, he brushed it aside. The countess liked to play games with men, he said, and Moretti was happy to oblige. I believe the count told us less than the truth.'

'I'll look for an opportunity this afternoon.' She hoped Laure didn't feel that she had already revealed more than was prudent for a servant. Vincenzo seemed more caught up in solving the mystery of the countess's death than his wife. She might also fear for her daughter's well-being.

'Meanwhile,' Paul continued, 'I will, first, probe the count's feelings toward his wife and, then, Monsieur Moretti's background.'

'Yes,' she added, 'it's surprising how little we know about Moretti, considering that he keeps himself in the public eye.'

Paul paused for a moment. A cluster of lovely white clematis amid a wall of withered blossoms had caught his eye. Lines of concern cleared from his broad forehead. 'If we look carefully, we can find beauty in unexpected places.' As he spoke, his eyes shifted to Anne. He took her hands in his and said softly, 'I love you.'

She felt a rush of tenderness and stepped forward to kiss him. They embraced for a long moment until a distant shout from the courtyard distracted them. Someone had arrived at the château.

'Until later,' Paul said. They left the garden hand in hand.

Anne was approaching the servants' room off the kitchen when she heard Cécile's familiar voice. Why had she come? Was something wrong?

She was sitting at the table drinking tea. Her mother was by the stove, stirring the fragrant contents of a pot. A young maid was cutting and cleaning greens for a salad.

Anne greeted Cécile in a normal voice, quieting her concern. She replied with a tentative, almost forced smile. She had arrived unexpectedly. Questions were hanging in the air. But they would have to wait. Preparations for dinner came first.

Cécile finished her tea and joined her mother at the stove. Anne helped with the greens. Hours passed before she found an opportunity to speak with Cécile and Laure alone.

'We need to talk,' she whispered to them, when the dinner was ready. Pierre and a maid would serve it. He was still running in and out of the kitchen.

'Come to our room, but don't let Pierre see you,' was Laure's reply, as she and her daughter left.

Anne waited a few minutes until Pierre could no longer be heard. She hastened down a hallway to the far end of the building, and knocked softly. A voice called her into a simple room with two sleeping alcoves in opposite walls. A large armoire stood against another wall. A writing table and several wooden chairs occupied the middle. Several windows facing south admitted abundant light.

The women sat by the hearth, conversing softly. Between them was a basket of clothes to mend. A low fire helped dispel the chill in the air.

Anne pulled up a chair and went directly to the point. 'This is a surprise visit, is it not?'

Cécile nodded, her eyes tinged with reproach. 'Since Monday, when we met, I've grown anxious for Laure and Vincenzo. Something bad might happen to them because I started you thinking about the accident in Fiesole. Pierre's spies continue to watch me. After four days of worrying, I couldn't bear the suspense, so I took this morning's coach for Fontainebleau. A kind peasant brought me from the highway to the château.'

'There's no cause for worry here. That unfortunate incident hasn't been discussed beyond our circle.' Not yet, Anne thought. 'We've been mostly concerned about the circumstances of her death.'

Laure looked up, met her daughter's eye. 'Vincenzo has told me how she died. It wasn't an accident. He claims he's always wondered about it. Now he's convinced someone set loose those birds that startled her horse.'

'Someone in this house?'

'Most likely. No one else could know that she would ride in the morning at that time.'

Cécile stared at her mother, a tremor in her voice. 'Aren't you frightened? A killer might be hiding here.'

'Quite possibly,' Anne interjected. 'And we won't be safe

until we find out who he is.' She paused, then abruptly asked, 'What can you tell me about Pierre Fauve's relationship with the countess?'

Both Cécile and Laure looked at Anne, wide-eyed. 'Are you implying that he's the one?'

'He's only a suspect at this point. I can't tell you why he would kill her. But he knew her movements.'

'This much I can say,' Laure remarked, 'his behavior toward her was always correct. He must have realized that was what the count expected of him. Still, he never smiled when her name was mentioned. That's not enough to brand him a murderer. He wasn't the only one who didn't like her.'

'Many peasants hated her,' Cécile added. 'She'd lead the hunt through their grain fields in pursuit of a deer, regardless of the damage to the crops. It was her right, she'd say.'

'As her personal maid,' Anne observed, 'you must have known Monsieur Moretti quite well.' She paused, then asked carefully, 'Was he ever intimate with the countess?'

'Not to my knowledge.' Cécile grimaced with displeasure. 'I really shouldn't speak about such a private matter. They might have looked like they were in love. They were occasionally alone together. But I think they were only playing games; at least she was.'

Anne sensed that Cécile was still withholding something. 'Did Moretti ever question you about the countess?'

Cécile's reluctance grew stronger. She looked for support from her mother. Laure nodded. Cécile sighed. 'Once, he asked me about our visit to Fiesole. Had we seen this or that? Did we enjoy the view over Florence? Was the house to our liking? And so on. Finally, he asked, had the countess ridden on a certain road out of Fiesole for a view of the picturesque countryside? I told him I didn't know.' She met Anne's eye. 'That road was where her accident took place.'

Why should that accident particularly concern Moretti? Anne wondered. 'He probably had asked the countess the same line of questions and had received a less than satisfactory answer. So he hoped to learn more from you.'

'Pierre must have told him the story,' Cécile contended.

167

'No one else knew about it. But would Pierre disobey the count who insists on protecting his wife's reputation?'

'I frankly don't know, yet,' Anne replied, filing the question with others that needed more thought. She shifted to another topic. 'How did the count and countess behave toward each other? With love and respect?'

'As far as I could see, she behaved correctly, never spoke ill of him, complied with his wishes. But she never referred to him with affection. I think she feared his wrath. When he exploded at the peasants for whatever reason, she would tremble. He gave her everything she wanted—horses, carriages, a stable, her own groom. But he showed more affection toward his horses.'

'Would you agree that the count could become jealous of another man's attention to her? If so, how would the count react to his wife's infidelity?'

'Violently,' Laure broke in forcefully. 'He pretends to be zealous and forthright in defense of his honor. But his nature is devious and crafty—and brutal. He had a peasant killed who poached grouse in his forest. You can hardly imagine what he would do to a man who seduced his wife.'

Anne nodded. 'Still, he might bide his time and cover his tracks.'

Twenty-Six

Pointed Questions

September 15

As the dinner hour drew near, Saint-Martin went to his room and put on his coat of light green silk with silver embroidery. It was rather more elegant than he cared to wear on a country visit. But he would be dining with two of the count's neighbors, a marquis and a banker. Their conversation might touch on problems of the countryside. He could learn something useful for the Highway Patrol at such a meal.

His mind shifted to Anne downstairs among the servants. She and he often moved on different social levels. But their friendship and love brought them together where social barriers vanished. They were harmonious, well-matched partners. Whatever society might think, he considered himself fortunate. In the year or more that they had worked together, she had become a skillful investigator, a valuable aid to Georges, especially among women and children in the lower classes.

A servant came to the door. 'There's a messenger in the front parlor to see you, Colonel. Just arrived from the city.'

Saint-Martin followed the servant to the waiting visitor, one of Quidor's agents.

'The inspector thought you would want this information immediately. I'll be outside in case you wish to send a return message.'

'Please wait.' When the agent had left the room, Saint-Martin broke the seal and began to read.

Colonel, during almost two weeks of digging, I have uncovered secret information you should know. First, I have on good authority that Pierre Fauve is the bastard son of the Comte de Serre. Like Thérèse his sister, Pierre was born of the count's youthful affair with a camp follower of his regiment. Though the count has never acknowledged paternity, he has always treated Pierre with special regard: supporting him through childhood, promoting him in the army, engaging him as a valet, and so forth. And there's more. After the count's first wife died, Pierre became his principal heir. When the count married Virginie, she replaced Pierre. Following her death in April, the count made Pierre again his heir. Were the count to die today, Pierre would become a wealthy man. Though at present the count is short of ready money, he inherited from his wife

169

a large fortune in government bonds and other investments.

Quidor

Saint-Martin found paper, pen, and ink and immediately wrote to assure Quidor that the information would prove useful. He gave it to the agent and sent him off.

As he stood at the window, watching the agent ride out of the courtyard on his way back to Paris, the colonel wondered how this new information applied to the death of the countess. *Cui bonum?* he asked himself. Who benefited from her death? A poacher lurking behind the forest wall? Her death would satisfy his need for revenge.

Or was it someone within the household who believed that she stood in his way? The count was elderly, his health doubtful. With the death of the countess, Pierre could have expected to receive a large fortune in the not too distant future. That fortune could even have tempted the count.

The dinner lasted for only an hour. The count wasn't inclined to linger at the table. His guests, the marquis and the banker, had arrived early for drinks. Whatever serious matter these men had to talk about was dispatched then, perhaps a scheme unsuitable for the ears of a police officer. By the time they came to the dinner table and joined Moretti and Saint-Martin, they were ready for fine wine, good food, and light conversation.

When they realized that Saint-Martin had recently been on a mission to England, they busied him with questions about fashion, gambling, horses, cuisine, and the like. 'Tell us about the strange English sport of boxing,' said the marquis, who sniffed at the current French bent for things English.

Saint-Martin described the match he witnessed between a black slave and an English champion, both men stripped to the waist. For an hour they battered each other before a large excited crowd amid the ruins of an ancient monastery in the rural west of England. Thousands of pounds in wagers changed hands that day. For good measure, Saint-Martin added, 'The Prince of Wales is the sport's principal patron.'

'The English call that a sport? How bizarre!' The marquis shook his head vigorously. 'That's one English custom the French will never accept.'

'Is our hunting any less strange?' asked Saint-Martin. 'The odds are far more unfair to the animal or bird. At least in boxing both contestants usually survive.'

The dinner ended peacefully enough. Saint-Martin left the table feeling he hadn't learned much of use for his troopers, but he had enjoyed a delicious meal. He was on his way from the dining room to the count's study when he heard his name whispered. Anne beckoned him into a parlor.

'Paul, before you speak to the count and to Moretti, you need to know that Pierre has told Moretti about the countess's accident near Fiesole. Moretti might doubt the accuracy of Pierre's report, and has asked Cécile for confirmation.'

'And what did Cécile tell him?'

'That she didn't know about any such accident.'

Paul reflected for a moment, disturbed by his wife's report. 'When Pierre revealed the secret to Moretti, he probably told him that she had deliberately killed the boy or left him dying. That might seem doubtful to Moretti. Cécile should have given him a true account of the accident. By refusing to do so, she probably confirmed in his mind Pierre's version that the countess had done something unspeakably evil.'

Anne grimaced. 'Why is Moretti so interested in the accident and why has Pierre disobeyed his master's command to refrain from speaking about it? Pierre and Moretti appear to be working together more than anyone would have suspected.'

'I have recent news from Quidor that may partly answer your question. He has discovered that Pierre is the count's bastard son and heir.'

'Now I see,' Anne said. 'It was in Pierre's interest that the countess be removed from his path to wealth. Still, why should he try to persuade Moretti of her guilt? To involve him in a plot to kill her?' She paused for a moment with a puzzled expression. 'I can see Moretti despising the countess, but not killing her. She hadn't harmed him personally.'

'We agree entirely.' He patted her hand. 'I must go now,

171

my dear.' He got up and walked to the door. 'I'll take these concerns with me.'

The Comte de Serre was seated at the writing table in his study. Michou's painting of his wife stood on an easel to one side. He gazed at it with attention so intense that Saint-Martin hesitated to interrupt him. It was impossible to tell what he was thinking.

Finally, he became aware of the colonel's presence and stood up. 'Yes, Colonel, what do you want to know?'

They sat down facing each other across the table.

'If my theory is correct,' Saint-Martin began, 'that a vengeful poacher would need information from within the château, then I must wonder who among your servants is the most likely suspect. Several of them would have known her plans for the following morning. In our investigation, my adjutant, Georges Charpentier, and my wife and I could find no apparent reason for any of your servants to betray the countess to a poacher, except Pierre . . .'

The count frowned, his eyes widened with alarm.

'Except Pierre, whom we have yet to examine. Because of his importance in the household, I thought I should turn to you for an understanding of the man. You would know him better than anyone.'

'Yes, of course. Go ahead.'

'I believe he has been close to you virtually since birth.'

'His mother, Victoire, was the widow of one of my men, an intelligent, spirited woman, left with two small children but with no resources. I took pity, found work for her among the regimental suttlers, gave her small amounts of money. Her boy, Pierre, was a precocious little fellow. I saw to his education. When he was old enough, I enrolled him in the regiment. He proved to be loyal and helpful, advanced rapidly in the ranks, left the service with me, and became my valet. I have learned to trust him implicitly.'

'His mother's husband had died a few years before Pierre was born. Would you know who was his father?'

'Of course not. His mother never identified him.'

And you rewarded her silence, thought Saint-Martin. He

could see no point in pursuing any further the issue of paternity, so he shifted his tack. 'This question may appear to intrude into your private affairs, but it's necessary. Who is your heir?'

'Pierre,' he replied evenly. 'I have no family. The Serre line will end with me.' The count glared at the colonel. 'You'd better not draw any hasty conclusions from what I've told you.'

'It's too early for conclusions, sir.' Saint-Martin nonetheless couldn't help wondering how long Pierre would be willing to wait for his inheritance.

Before Monsieur Moretti arrived, Colonel Saint-Martin had a moment of leisure. He walked to the window and looked out over Serre's estate stretching north to the horizon. The neglected flower garden was to his left, a better-tended kitchen garden to his right, and a grassy terrace in between. Beyond were farm buildings, in the distance the fields and forest. The sun sank low in the west, casting long shadows.

The count merely leased this property and wouldn't be leaving it to Pierre. Nor would he want it, in any case, an unprofitable enterprise and expensive to maintain. As for the prestige of a château, Saint-Martin couldn't imagine the pimp, the master of spies, enjoying the role of seigneur on a country estate.

Footsteps echoed in the hall. By the time Saint-Martin turned around, Monsieur Moretti stood framed in the open doorway. He had changed into a moss-green patterned silk suit and carried his emblematic cane.

'May I come in?' he asked, flashing an ironic smile.

'Please do,' replied the colonel evenly, as he motioned to a chair facing him at the writing table. 'Brandy?' He glanced toward a decanter and a tray of glasses.

Moretti stood his cane against the chair and nodded. Saint-Martin poured. The two men raised their glasses, then sipped.

There were more footsteps in the hall. This time, Anne appeared at the door. Moretti glanced at her with surprise, then at the colonel.

'I've asked Madame Cartier to join us. She's familiar with many of the circumstances of the countess's life and death and will also take notes.'

173

Moretti gave a little shrug to the colonel and a slight bow to his wife.

Anne sat at the end of the table by a set of writing utensils and sheets of paper. She declined an offer of brandy.

Saint-Martin relaxed in his chair, head tilted slightly to one side. 'Tell me about yourself, Monsieur Moretti, your home and family, your career. Though you are prominent in the city's artistic circles, I don't know you well. That's not surprising, since previously you've not come to the attention of the police. But you *were* close to the late Comtesse de Serre, whose death I'm investigating.'

Moretti took another sip from his glass, shifted in his seat. 'I was born into a wealthy Florentine merchant's family forty years ago.' He went on to describe his deceased parents and his older brother, who inherited the father's business, sold it and moved to Milan. 'I have a widowed sister who still lives in Florence. I was also married for several years, but my wife died in childbirth and I have not married again. Buying and selling art is my life.'

Saint-Martin asked, 'Is my impression correct that you are at odds with your brother?'

'By law and my father's will, he was entitled to the inheritance. I thought he could have given something to me; but he took it all and left me penniless. I haven't seen him in years.'

'How did you amass your present fortune?'

'I married a wealthy woman, who helped me start a business. It has since thrived. At her death, I inherited her fortune.'

'You mentioned a widowed sister. Are you close to her?'

'Yes, a capable woman. She manages my business in Florence when I am away.'

'What is her name?'

'Maria.'

'Maria who?'

'Falzone.'

A bell rang in Saint-Martin's head. He threw a quick sidelong glance at Anne. Her pen paused for a second in midair, then carefully wrote a line.

Moretti noticed their reaction and heaved a sigh. 'Yes,

Colonel, you have recognized my sister's married name. Her husband, Antonio Falzone, died several years ago.'

'Leaving her with a son . . .'

'Benedetto. My dear nephew and godson, who died along-side a road near Fiesole over a year ago.'

Saint-Martin remained silent for a moment as the significance of this revelation sank into his mind. He leaned forward and measured his words. 'Now, sir, tell me what you think happened on that road.'

Moretti's lips quavered. He laid the cane on his lap and gripped it with both hands, as if trying to rein in his feelings. 'I was away from the city on business at the time. At first report, I thought the boy's death was a simple, most unfortunate accident. I hastened to Fiesole to comfort my sister and arrange for the burial.

'After learning the details and examining the site of his death, I began to wonder. The body appeared to have been moved from the road into a ditch, then covered with leaves and twigs. For several hours, it lay there scarcely visible. Many persons passed by, some on foot, before the body was noticed. I reasoned that the killer had arranged the body to delay its discovery until he could make his escape undetected.

'As I pondered the matter, a horrid image forced its way into my mind. Little Benedetto, gravely injured and unconscious, lay in the road. The rider, looking furtively left and right and seeing no one, pulled the boy into the ditch, covered him and fled. The boy's life slowly ebbed away while other unsuspecting riders passed him by.

'At that moment, I swore by all that was holy to discover the truth and to make sure justice was done. I turned to the police. For a week they focused their investigation on Fiesole, since the road was used only by local people. They questioned everyone who might have information, checked all the horses for unaccounted injuries. Finally, a stable owner in Florence learned of the case and came forward. On the day of the boy's death, a groom in the service of a wealthy, aristocratic French family had returned a rented horse with a lame left leg.

'The police then identified the family with the Comte and Comtesse de Serre, who had lived in the village for several weeks. They left for France the day after the boy's death, though not in haste. Their departure had been arranged long before. Now, however, the public's imagination became excited. Villagers reported that the countess rode her horse astride like a bold, reckless young man. Some claimed that rich foreigners had little regard for the safety of others on the road. And so forth.

'Through the Grand Duke Leopold's representative in Paris, the police inquired after the French family. The Comte de Serre denied any knowledge of the matter and maintained that he, his wife, and his servants had behaved responsibly at all times. None of them had hit the child, nor would any of them have abandoned an injured one.

'The Tuscan police could do no more. But I would not let the matter rest. I had many contacts in Paris. I decided to open a business there and pursue an investigation on my own. I introduced myself to the count, secured art for him at bargain prices, and became acquainted with his wife.'

'And with his servants,' added Saint-Martin. 'From Pierre you learned that the countess had ridden over the boy. But you still weren't sure of the gravity of her offense. Had Pierre suggested that she left the boy to die in the ditch?'

'Yes, he had. But I found it hard to believe she would do something so monstrous.'

'So you determined to know her better.'

'Yes, I did.' Moretti smiled slightly. His gaze appeared to turn inward to certain pleasures of that experience. 'For three months, I courted her at the château and at the Louvre apartment. The count didn't seem to mind. I suppose he thought we were just playing games. The countess probably was.

'From the beginning I appreciated her beauty. I eventually also discovered that she was an intelligent, spoiled child-woman, certainly not cruel or heartless, but impulsive, self-indulgent, and sometimes reckless. Still I wasn't sure that she had allowed my nephew to die. She avoided any discussion of an accident in Fiesole, so I asked Cécile, her personal maid. She neither confirmed nor denied my suspicions but seemed to be hiding a dreadful secret. Near the end, the countess tired of our relationship. I decided to confront her during our ride

176

in the forest and accuse her of the death of Benedetto. But she died before I had the opportunity.'

'Did playing games with the countess,' Paul asked in a matter-of-fact tone, 'ever include signs of personal affection or sexual intimacy?'

Moretti reacted as if slapped in the face. His eyes narrowed, his jaw stiffened. He raised his cane with both hands to ward off the blow. 'What can you mean, Colonel? Are you a gentleman?'

Saint-Martin remained unruffled. 'Your relationship with the countess may be crucial to solving the mystery of her death. Did you and she give the Comte de Serre any reason to believe he was being cuckolded? However gullible he might have appeared, he could well have wondered what you and his wife were up to. If he were then to have discovered evidence of infidelity, he might have taken revenge on her at the forest gate. And, finally, sir, he may surprise you. Take care.'

'Well, whatever the count may have thought, his wife and I were never intimate. She didn't want sex, seemed afraid of it. And I didn't want it either, but for different reasons. I saw in her the killer of my dear nephew. Sometimes when we were close, her face changed into a . . .' He was speaking quickly, stumbling over the words. He paused, took a deep breath, and said simply, 'She looked ugly.'

Saint-Martin smiled inwardly. Moretti had had the presence of mind to stop short of saying that the woman's beautiful face had become a hideous skull.

Moretti went on without embarrassment. 'The count's attitude was curious. He would leave us alone together, as if encouraging us to dally. On at least one occasion, he spied on us, not like a jealous husband but for pleasure, like a voyeur.'

'Can you explain why he would do that?'

'I've overheard servants talking. They say he's been impotent since before marrying the countess. Finds his pleasure watching others.'

The colonel remained silent for a few moments, taking in what Moretti had told him. The count now appeared in a new, garish light, testing his wife's fidelity, perversely enjoying her illicit pleasures.

Saint-Martin looked at his watch. 'It's time to bring this conversation to a close. You are most likely wrong to believe that she murdered your nephew.' He paused again. 'I can tell you this much, she admitted to having hit the boy but claimed she had left him only after seeing that he was dead. She couldn't explain why she moved his body into the ditch and covered it. I believe that may be as much as we shall ever know.'

'As you have suspected, Colonel, I did have a strong motive for killing her. But I didn't do it. I was riding with her at the time of her fatal jump. Vincenzo is my witness.'

'I never thought *you* killed her, sir.' The colonel left a question in the air: had Moretti paid someone?

'Are we finished, Colonel?' He loosened his grip on the cane.

'Yes, you are free to go.' The colonel raised a warning hand. 'The countess's death is but one of three that I am investigating. The motive that led you to pursue the countess did not vanish with her death. Several months later, it could have led you to take revenge on her portrait and murder the painter Bouchard in a cover-up. You are a suspect and may not leave the Paris region without my permission.'

Anne glanced at the notes she had taken. 'He told his story well,' she said to Paul, as he returned to his seat. He had seen Moretti to the door. 'And I suppose most of it is true.'

Paul sat down next to her and glanced at her notes. 'A letter to Florence could check the parts about his family, so I doubt that he would try to deceive us. His account of courting the countess is consistent with what Cécile and others have described. The question of intimacy remains unanswered. His version is plausible but not fully convincing. He also left open the possibility that he might have hired someone else to kill the countess.'

Anne took a minute to add to her notes. 'And I'm troubled by what he told us about the count. He could be both an impotent voyeur and a jealous husband.'

Twenty-Seven

A Villain Unmasked

September 15–16

Late in the evening after a tiring day, Anne stood for a moment in the doorway to the servants' room off the kitchen. Supper was at the long table—pea soup, bread and cheese, grapes. Conversation was sporadic, subdued. Anne sat down across from Michou and signed a greeting. She smiled back distractedly and went on eating her soup.

Anne filled her own bowl. Pierre gave her a quick sharp glance, then turned his attention to one of the young maids at his side. Farther down the table, other servants ate silently, while Cécile, Laure, and Vincenzo carried on a quiet chat. Anne tried to listen in. Her ears pricked up when she heard Vincenzo say a little louder than usual, 'I found the bird trap in the forest just before dusk.'

Too late, Laure tried to shush him. Pierre's face had frozen suddenly into an expression of alarm. He swung to the young maid on his left and glared at her. She stared rigidly into her soup bowl. Then he became aware that Anne was looking at him. He shrugged and said to Vincenzo, 'Someone was careless. Put it back in the toolshed.' He returned to eating as if nothing had happened.

This incident puzzled Anne. Why had Vincenzo's announcement startled Pierre? And what did the bird trap have to do with the young maid?

From across the table Michou signed to Anne. 'I can explain. Don't look now. That young maid is pregnant.' She pointed with her eyes. 'I'll tell you more about her later.' Michou's face was tense. She was on to something. Anne encouraged her to continue.

179

During the day, Michou explained, she had been busy helping Laure in the kitchen, sewing with Cécile, working in the kitchen garden alongside the pregnant maid. And in free moments, she had sketched almost everyone and everything in sight.

After the meal, Anne and Michou stepped outside into the cool evening air and breathed deeply, then walked along the back of the château past the dark, closed windows of empty ground-floor rooms. As they came to a lighted one, Anne noticed it was open, then heard the sound of voices, one of them familiar. With a touch she alerted Michou. They crept up to the window and looked into the tiny room.

Pierre was pacing the floor, speaking to the young kitchen maid sitting on the bed. Clad only in a flimsy nightdress, she seemed frightened and was crying. Anne tried to piece together the words and phrases she could hear. Pierre appeared to blame the girl for the trap's being found. He suddenly seized her by the shoulder, shook her, and told her to stop crying. Then he said something about her father. Finally, he left the room, obviously angry. For a few minutes, the girl continued to sit there dejectedly, heaving great sobs. She doused the candle and disappeared in the darkness, still whimpering.

'What was that all about?' Anne signed to Michou. They had retreated to the privacy of Michou's room upstairs to exchange impressions of the day's visit.

'I'll tell you what I've learned,' Michou signed. The maid, about eighteen years old, came from the neighboring village and had worked at Château Serre for almost two years. She couldn't read or write, though she seemed intelligent enough. Michou communicated with her only by signs and gestures.

Early on, Pierre had taken an interest in her, an unhealthy one, Anne was sure. For a poor country girl, the maid was unusually attractive, with a perfect set of teeth, clear complexion, bright brown eyes, thick brown hair, and a shapely body.

'I don't know the details,' Michou signed, 'but Pierre treats her as his mistress—as you could see through the window. He felt free to be alone with her in her room and make her cry.'

180

'And that's probably his baby she's carrying,' Anne remarked.

Michou nodded. 'Laure could probably tell you more about her, but she's afraid of Pierre and won't do anything that might provoke him.'

'What's the maid's name?'

'Paulette Rivard.'

'With Georges's help we shall watch her closely tomorrow and perhaps find out what she and her father have to do with that newly found bird trap.'

The next morning, Anne took a breakfast tray upstairs to her room. Georges and Paul had already discussed the Fiesole incident and Moretti's strong motive for revenge against the countess. After coffee was poured, Paul asked Georges for a report on his search for clues in the Serre estate's village and outlying hamlets.

'The troopers and I have questioned the most likely suspects. You won't be surprised to hear that no one would admit to poaching in the count's forest, or to knowing anyone who did.'

Anne glanced at him over the rim of her cup. 'Have you spoken to a Monsieur Rivard, whose daughter Paulette works at the château?'

'Yes,' Georges replied. 'He's the villager living closest to the forest gate. The bird trap was hidden within sight of his cottage, baited and set to catch grouse. He's a day laborer, thin as a rail, about forty, looks sixty. Since this year's harvest is poor, he has earned very little money. He and his wife appear to be desperate—can't pay the rent and fear the count will soon evict them with no place to go.'

'Did he show any hatred toward the countess?'

'No, he didn't. He spoke of her with respect. She had given clothes and food for his daughter to take home. His wife had little to say. Never smiled. They both looked sour, when I mentioned the count. Had reason to, I suppose. He's the landlord.'

'How shall we deal with the Rivards?' Paul asked, spreading butter on a piece of bread. He glanced at Anne.

181

She finished her coffee before replying. 'Michou and I shall keep our eyes on Paulette this morning. If she goes to her father, I'll follow her. She might carry a message from Pierre.'

'And I'll keep track of Pierre,' said Georges. 'He'll probably wait for Paulette to return. Then he might leave the château and meet Monsieur Rivard somewhere, perhaps in the forest away from prying ears. Vincenzo might know a likely spot where we could eavesdrop.'

Anne added, 'Paulette's pregnancy seems to have become an issue. I imagine that Pierre now wants to get rid of her and needs to talk to her father. He also must make sure that the Rivards will keep their mouths shut. They might incriminate him in the countess's death.'

'The Rivards are vulnerable,' Paul agreed. 'We may have to take them into protective custody. They won't speak frankly to us unless they feel safe.'

About midmorning, Anne heard someone at her door. It was Michou with news from the kitchen. Paulette was about to leave. At a lull in the work, she had excused herself in order to pay a brief visit to her parents. Laure frowned but agreed and reminded the girl to be back in time for the dinner's preparations. The count would again have guests.

Anne donned a servant's dress and hurried downstairs, just in time to see the girl walking away on a dirt road to the village. Other travelers were also using the road, so Anne didn't attract attention. Paulette turned off at a short lane to the Rivard cottage. A hedge along the lane allowed Anne to sneak up to the rear of the building. Shielded from the view of passersby, she peeked into an open unglazed window.

The family had huddled at a table in the middle of the room.

The father, a small, wiry, unshaven man, held a note in his hands. 'Pierre wants to talk to me. "Come to the woodcutter's hut in the forest," he says. The village and the château aren't safe. Crawling with police. They've found the bird trap and think they know how it was used.' He glared at his daughter. 'Says he also wants to talk about you. Why?'

She looked down at the table and spoke too softly for Anne to hear.

'Pregnant, you say, girl! I suppose Pierre wants to get rid of you. As if the harvest weren't bad enough, now this.' His thin face flushed, his eyes blazed with anger. 'You dumb cow, I've a mind to beat sense into your head.' He raised an arm to strike her, but his wife leaped up and seized him.

'If you must beat someone, try Pierre. He's the cause of our misery.' She left her husband and comforted her daughter. 'Paulette's done the best she could. That devil's taken advantage of her.'

Rivard got up and began pacing the floor, muttering to himself. When he had apparently made up his mind, he took a long sheathed knife hanging on the wall, fastened it to his belt, and put on a ragged brown smock that concealed the weapon.

He turned to his daughter. 'You go back and tell him I'll meet him at the woodcutter's hut in an hour.'

Anne quietly slipped away from the window, retreated along the hedge, and hurried on the dirt road to the château.

She found Georges alone in his room and reported what she had learned at the cottage.

He listened intently, then leaped to his feet. 'If I leave immediately, I'll reach the hut before Rivard and Fauve. Vincenzo will guide me. If we are lucky, we can hide close enough to hear what they say.' He strapped on his pistols and rushed out of the room.

Anne pondered what to do next. Her husband was at dinner with the count. Perhaps Paulette Rivard needed a sympathetic shoulder to cry on. The girl had returned to the kitchen to find a long list of chores to do. Anne approached her gently. 'I see you could use some help. I've nothing to do for an hour. Find me an apron and some soap and water and I'll wash.' She waved a hand over stacks of dirty dishes and pots and pans. 'You clean up the kitchen. When these things have drained, you can put them back where they belong.'

The girl stared at Anne with large bewildered eyes. 'You're a lady, you can't do that.'

'You've seen me eating at the servants' table. Why can't I

183

wash my own dishes and those of my friend Michou, and the others?'

'You're the wife of a colonel, an aristocrat. Does he allow this? Laure will scold me if she sees you doing my chores.'

Anne began to wonder if being helpful in this way was going to increase rather than disarm the maid's apprehension. She looked her in the eye, put a hand on her shoulder. 'My husband approves of what I'm doing. And, if necessary, I'll explain it to Laure. I'm convinced, Paulette, that a true lady, like a true gentleman, helps other people in need. That's what I'm doing here. Your pregnancy has made you tired and sick. And because you took time to visit your family, you are behind in your work. So let's do this together and get to know each other better.'

That line of reasoning seemed to satisfy the girl. She ventured a smile and began to show Anne the routine. In an hour, when Laure arrived, the kitchen was clean and in good order. She surveyed her domain, nodded her approval. Then, seeing Anne remove her apron, she let out a soft gasp. 'Madame Cartier! What are you doing?' She turned on the maid. 'Paulette!'

Anne came to the maid's rescue. 'I wanted to become better acquainted with this young woman. I'm sure you will allow me.' Anne reinforced her message with a telling look in her eye.

Laure, a perceptive woman, caught Anne's meaning. 'Yes, of course, I understand.'

'Could Paulette have a little free time? I'd like to visit further with her.'

'I believe I can manage without her. The other maid will soon be here to help me with the dinner upstairs.'

This exchange between the ladies seemed to confuse Paulette. Anne took her under the arm and walked her out of the kitchen. 'Let's go to my room, where we won't be disturbed. We'll have a talk.' Pierre was most likely on his way to the forest, but Anne didn't want to risk his showing up un-expectedly. The girl offered no resistance, so off they went.

In the upstairs room, Paulette's apprehension changed to amazement. Anne showed her the rose silk dress, embroidered in silver, that Cécile had altered. After first glancing at Anne, who nodded, the girl fingered the fabric as if it were priceless. 'Madame the housekeeper has me sew sometimes. I'd like to learn how to make a dress like this.'

Anne asked herself if Cécile could use a willing, inexpensive apprentice in her shop on Rue Sainte-Anne, especially if Paul's aunt would direct more customers there and make arrangements to care for the baby. Then Paulette could escape from Pierre's clutches.

After a few sips of brandy and a couple of orange sweetmeats, Anne judged the time right for more serious issues.

'I would like your help, Paulette, to find out who killed the Comtesse de Serre last spring. You know, don't you, that her death was no accident? That's why the police are here.'

Fear had begun to creep into the maid's eyes, but she nodded. 'I've heard the housekeeper and the groom talking about it.'

'Then you also know that Pierre Fauve is the chief suspect. Correct?'

'They think so, but no one dares to say it. Pierre is so clever and has the count's trust.'

'The police think your father supplied the birds—the trap was found near your cottage. But he didn't know what Pierre would do with them. Correct again?' Anne gave Rivard the benefit of the doubt.

The maid hesitated, tried to avoid Anne's gaze. 'I mustn't say anything to hurt my father.'

'He's innocent of the countess's death, isn't he?'

'Yes, he thought Pierre meant to sell the birds in Paris. He and Pierre had done that before.'

Anne wasn't surprised. She suspected that he had organized an earlier attempt on the countess's life, foiled by changes in her plans. Paulette was now giving information more freely. Anne offered another sweetmeat and took one herself.

'Where were you the night before the countess died?'

'With Monsieur Fauve in his room. Late at night, he sent me to my father with a message. I couldn't read it, but I was curious, so I showed it first to my mother. She said that Father was supposed to do something with the birds he had recently caught. "Cursed birds," my mother said. "Nothing but

185

trouble." I was never to speak about them to anybody.

'It was nearly midnight when I returned to the château. Monsieur Fauve was waiting for me, very nervous. I handed him a note from my father. Pierre seemed pleased. He told me we would celebrate his good fortune. We drank wine and went to bed. He was restless, tossed and turned, snored. I couldn't sleep, but I pretended. He rose before dawn, didn't try to wake me. I still pretended, didn't want to get up so early. He came back about seven o'clock. Sneaked in the door very quietly, saw that I was awake. He grabbed me by the shoulders and stared me in the face. "If anyone ever asks you where I was, you say I was with you all night. Understand? I want you to promise. If anything bad happens to me, your father and mother will suffer." So I crossed my heart and promised him.'

Her lips began to quiver, her eyes moistened. 'I shouldn't have talked to you. Now Pierre will beat me and ruin my parents. They'll lose the cottage and starve.'

'That wasn't a promise, Paulette, he forced you to make it. Don't worry, he will no longer hurt anyone. When he's convicted of the countess's murder, he will be locked up and the count will disown him. My husband the colonel will find ways to help your parents. You will all be better off when you are free from Pierre's grip.'

These words seemed to calm the maid, if not entirely convince her. Anne gave her a kerchief and she dabbed at her eyes. Anne accompanied her back to the kitchen. Laure met them with a harried expression. Anne warded off any complaint by quickly saying, 'Paulette has been very helpful. We should all be grateful to her.'

Laure understood what Anne meant. Her face brightened. She took Paulette's hand, patted it, and told her to prepare some greens for dinner.

Anne hurried to her room and jotted down the gist of Paulette's testimony. Then she made a full and fair copy. The maid would put her mark to it, Laure as witness. Pierre might have met his match.

Twenty-Eight

The Woodcutter's Hut

September 16

Dark clouds heavy with rain scudded in from the west, dimming the early-afternoon sun. Georges, Vincenzo, and a trooper galloped into the forest by a back way to avoid being seen by either Rivard or Fauve. In the stable Vincenzo had told Benoît a misleading tale about riding to a distant hamlet. The boy was too much in Pierre's confidence to be trusted with the truth.

At a safe distance from the woodcutter's hut, they tethered the horses in the trooper's care. Vincenzo led Georges to the hut. No one there yet. Built to give shelter during the winter, when most cutting took place, it was larger and more substantial than Georges had expected. The windows were unglazed but shuttered, the door latched but unlocked. It was occasionally used during the summer. Brush had been cleared away from the front and a path beaten to the door. A low stack of cut wood stood alongside the building. Taking care not to leave evidence of their presence, the two men entered the hut.

'I was here a month ago after a storm,' said Vincenzo, 'and repaired damage to the roof, cleaned the chimney, and chased out a family of rats.' In the light from the open door, he pointed to a ladder leading to an open loft. 'A man could hide there and overhear everything said inside and see through cracks between the boards.'

Georges had to squint to study the loft, almost hidden in darkness. 'I'll go up there. You hide in the brush nearby. If Pierre opens the shutters, you may also be able to hear what's said inside. If something happens that I can't handle, I'll shout.

187

You call the trooper.' Georges patted his pistols. Vincenzo and the trooper were also armed.

Georges climbed up the ladder into the loft. Only at its peak could he stand. The air was musty, the floor gritty under his feet. 'Rat droppings,' he muttered. He brushed off a floorboard, laid down, and peered through a large knothole. The room lay open beneath him.

He had hardly made himself comfortable when he heard noises outside. The latch was lifted and Rivard walked in. He opened the shutters and looked out, then stepped back and glanced about the room. For a moment, he stood still, head bent in thought. Finally, he drew a deep breath and walked out the open door.

For a few minutes Georges heard nothing but the rustle of leaves in the forest. The light from the windows grew dim as clouds began to block the sun. Even in the loft he caught the scent of oncoming rain. Then he heard voices, at first indistinct.

'Let's go inside. It looks like the rain will be heavy.' That sounded like Pierre, thought Georges.

The two men sat at a table, facing each other. Pierre leaned back, nonchalant, relaxed. Rivard bent forward, shoulders hunched, neck taut. He spoke first, 'What did you want to see me about?'

'Your daughter. She has to leave the château. We can't use her anymore. She's sick half the time, and in a few months she'll be nursing a baby. We need to hire a new maid.'

'It's *your* baby, damn it to hell. You can't just throw the girl out. How will she live? My wife and I can't take her in. We can hardly feed ourselves.'

'Who knows whose baby it is? She's a lusty bitch. I'm not the only man in this area who has had her. She's your problem now, baby and all. You can take her home this evening.' With a thin, ironic smile on his face, Pierre dug a coin from his pocket and tossed it on to the table. 'A louis d'or for your trouble, Rivard. That's all you'll get from me.'

'That's less than a month's wages in a good year. This was a bad one. I'll have two more mouths to feed. The count says he's going to raise the rent. I won't be able to make it through the winter.' Rivard was standing now and shouting. 'You give me ten louis or else.' Vincenzo could hear him easily. Maybe even the trooper.

'Or else what?' Pierre's voice was calm, his words carefully measured.

'Or else I'll tell the troopers who killed the countess at the forest gate.' He paused, his eyes narrowed, his lips curled into an ugly grin. 'And I'll tell them exactly how you did it.'

Georges felt his heart begin to beat as though it would break his ribs.

'Please tell me. I'm anxious to know.'

'Smooth bastard! I left the bird cage behind the big oak tree early that morning, like we agreed. But I didn't go home. I was curious what kind of game you were playing. Nothing honest, I was sure. So I hid and watched while you put the birds behind the gate. After a while I heard horses coming and saw you duck behind the stone wall. When the countess was about to jump, you pulled on a cord that opened the trap door. The birds flew up, her horse stumbled, and she flew over the gate. You pulled the trap into the brush and stole away. Then you hid the trap near my cottage where you usually kept it.'

'I underestimated you, Rivard. I never imagined that you would figure out my plan.' He shifted in his seat, rubbed his jaw. 'Let's discuss again what you would need in order to support your daughter. Shall we say five louis d'or?' He paused, gazed at Rivard's hard face. 'No? How about ten?'

Rivard guffawed, waved off the offer with contempt. 'Ten was a minute ago. I've changed my mind. The servants say you became the count's heir, when the countess passed on. Well, the count's old. You'll soon come into a fortune.' He paused, pretending to reflect. 'Since you've raised the question, I'd say I need a hundred now. When the count's gone and you're rich, we'll see how much more I'll need.'

Pierre shook his head. 'You drive a hard bargain, Rivard. But I have no choice. I came prepared to give you ten. I'll need some time to raise the rest.' He stood up, reached into his pocket. 'Here it is.' He pulled out a small pistol and aimed

189

it at Rivard's head. 'Don't reach for your knife or I'll shoot. We must take a walk in the woods. No one will ever find your body.'

'Drop that pistol!' Georges's voice boomed down from the loft. Pierre glanced up into the barrels of two large military pistols. An instant later Vincenzo appeared at an open window with two more pistols and called out to the trooper.

Within a minute, both Pierre and Rivard were disarmed and bound. Georges and the trooper guarded the prisoners inside the hut while Vincenzo rode to the château for a cart. The rain began to fall.

At the château, it had rained off and on. Seated by an open window, Saint-Martin breathed in the scented air from the wet fields outside. Dinner was drawing to a close with a dessert, *tarte aux fruits*. The count's guests, local landowners, had expressed their fears and concerns to Saint-Martin. As the officer in charge of public order for the region around Paris, he should clear the area of marauding bands of beggars, and should curb the growing insolence of the local peasantry. The ministers at the palace in Versailles turned a deaf ear to these complaints.

Saint-Martin had listened patiently, then pointed out what seemed obvious to him, if not to the men around him. The rural poor lived on the edge of starvation. A poor harvest had made them desperate. This was a bad time for landowners to raise rents and fees, even though their own income had declined. In any case, the colonel insisted, his men had to devote themselves mainly to chasing bold armed bandits from the royal highways. They had little time or energy for anything else.

The colonel's place at the table had a view overlooking the grassy terrace at the rear of the château. During a lull in the conversation, he gazed out the window. Then he stared. A strange procession of horsemen and a cart came from the forest through the open fields. They mounted the gravel walkway through the terrace and stopped at the rear entrance to the château. Georges and Vincenzo were in front. Behind them, a servant drove a cart with Rivard and Fauve bound by ropes. In the rear was a trooper.

Others had noticed Saint-Martin's reaction and followed the direction of his eyes. The Comte de Serre frowned at the colonel.

A guest suddenly exclaimed, 'Good God! What's going on?'

The count strode to the window and looked out. All color left his face. His knees began to buckle. He collapsed in the guest's arms.

'Anne, you say Pierre confessed? Amazing.' Saint-Martin sat with Anne and Georges at the writing table in the count's study. Serre had been put to bed in a state of nervous exhaustion. His guests had gone home to their châteaux more anxious about their security than when they had arrived. The Comtesse de Serre had not died accidentally. Evil men from the lower classes had murdered her.

'Tell me more, Anne.'

'Gladly.' Her eyes shone with excitement. 'I followed Paulette to her parents' cottage, spied on the family, and learned that Rivard would secretly meet Fauve at the woodcutter's hut in the forest. I alerted Georges.' She nodded at him to continue.

He shifted his weight, tugged at his lapels. 'At the hut Vincenzo and I overheard Rivard declare that he had seen Fauve murder the countess. Fauve admitted the truth of the accusation. Rivard threatened to expose him unless he paid a large sum in gold. When they appeared about to kill each other, I arrested them. End of story.'

'Well done!' exclaimed the colonel. 'I'll confine the two suspects separately in strong rooms in the château's basement. Two troopers shall stand guard there.'

Anne handed him a sheet of paper. 'Here's Paulette's statement concerning Fauve's movements the night before he killed the countess.'

Saint-Martin scanned the paper, noted the girl's mark, witnessed by Laure and Cécile. 'This establishes his opportunity for the crime. Anne, would you try to get a similar statement from Madame Rivard?'

She agreed with a nod and left the room.

'Now, Georges, I shall interrogate Fauve and Rivard.'

A trooper led Pierre into the study, hands manacled, and sat him down in front of the colonel, then backed away to the wall. Georges sat at the end of the table to take notes.

Pierre put a brave face on his situation. When asked what he had to say in his defense, he replied, 'Rivard killed the countess out of hatred for the count, who was about to raise the rent on the cottage.'

'However, in the woodcutter's hut, Monsieur Fauve, you accepted Rivard's account of the murder and agreed to pay him.'

'I only appeared to confess to the crime, Colonel, because I didn't want to argue with him. He was carrying a knife, and angry about my relationship with his daughter. If I had known that the police were eavesdropping, I would have taken the risk and declared my innocence.'

The colonel gave Fauve credit for mental agility. 'Where were you at the time of the countess's death?'

'In bed with Paulette Rivard.'

'Oh?' Saint-Martin paused, lifted up a document. 'In a sworn statement, she says you left the room before dawn and didn't return until seven.'

'She lies because I told her that our relationship is over.'

'A final question. When did you learn that the countess would ride to the forest that morning?'

'Like other servants, I heard Vincenzo mention it the night before at supper in the servants' room.'

So far the interrogation had unfolded as Saint-Martin expected. Fauve's defense was facile but unconvincing. A court would surely convict him. It would be more difficult to determine whether Fauve had a silent partner and whether the two of them were involved in the deaths of Bouchard and Gillet.

Saint-Martin signaled to the trooper, who took Fauve away, unabashed, unrepentant. In a few minutes the trooper returned with Rivard. A pitiable sight, the image of despair, a man for whom everything appeared to have gone wrong in his life.

'Monsieur Rivard,' the colonel began, 'what do you have to say for yourself?'

'Because I earned a few small coins selling birds, I'm now suspected of murder. It isn't fair.'

'The law might show you consideration if you prove to be a credible witness in the case before us.' Saint-Martin's task was to determine the degree of Rivard's complicity. Perhaps Rivard believed he was cooperating with Fauve only in a poaching scheme. Unfortunately for Rivard, a court might be swayed by the rise of unrest in the countryside and choose to make a severe judicial example of him. At the least, DeCrosne would say, hold Rivard in custody until the final disposition of the case.

Rivard nodded but without a glimmer of hope in his eyes. 'Fauve asked me to catch a few birds for him, gave me the trap, said the guards would look the other way. Paid me. Told me to leave them hidden by the forest gate and he'd pick them up. He'd usually tell me the night before he wanted them. So I kept a few on hand behind my cottage. Twice, I sold birds to him. No problem. I thought he might be selling them in Paris for a little extra money. But I grew curious. The third time that he ordered birds, I spied on him, saw him kill the countess.'

'Why didn't you report him?'

'I'd be accused of being his accomplice, or of killing the countess myself. There's bad blood between the château and the village over rent for the cottages and fees for use of the mill.'

'Then why did you confront him in the woodcutter's hut?'

'He arranged the meeting. Wanted to cast off my daughter like trash under his feet. I can't afford to support her and her baby.'

'You carried a hidden knife to the meeting.'

'I knew he would be armed. If your men had given me another minute, I'd have knocked the pistol out of his hand and killed him in self-defense, with the police watching.'

The colonel gazed at Rivard's brown, stubbled face. Poverty had brutalized him. Still, he was entitled to a fair hearing. His story was credible. Saint-Martin would discuss his fate with

Georges and Anne. At the moment, he was leaning toward clemency. 'You may go now, Rivard.' Saint-Martin nodded to the trooper, who led the man away.

After supper, Anne joined Paul and Georges in the study. She had just come from visiting the count.

'How is he?' asked Paul.

Anne replied, 'He's pale and appeared weak, but as harsh and opinionated as ever. I asked how he felt about Pierre. He said it was too soon to condemn him. Rivard might have killed the countess and cleverly passed the blame on to Pierre.'

'And Rivard's family?'

'The count has discharged Paulette Rivard and given orders to evict the family from their cottage. Behind in the rent, he claimed. I talked to the village priest. He will find temporary shelter for mother and daughter. Madame Rivard gave me a signed statement of her husband's dealings with Pierre.'

Georges spoke up. 'In your report to Lieutenant-General DeCrosne, you should recommend leniency for Rivard. I'm persuaded that he was Fauve's unwitting accomplice in the murder. Rivard was also innocent of poaching, since Fauve in effect gave him permission to do it.'

'I shall focus on Fauve. He killed the countess, and he is the key to solving the remaining mysteries,' said Paul.

Georges added, 'We could try to bargain with him. Offer a lighter sentence if he would tell us who killed Bouchard and Gillet.'

Paul shook his head. 'Fauve has a keen mind and might doubt that we could deliver on that offer.' He paused. 'Check on him before you go to bed.'

Twenty-Nine

Escape in the Night

September 17

At dawn Anne was awakened by loud banging on the door. She pummeled her husband, who could sleep through cannon fire. He stumbled to the door in his nightshirt. One of the troopers stood there shaking with anger.

'Fauve has escaped. My comrade is unconscious. Poisoned, I think.'

'Wake up Charpentier and Vincenzo. We must organize a pursuit.'

In ten minutes, Anne and Paul were dressed and on their way downstairs. Vincenzo and Georges met them at the entrance to the basement. 'My wife will come in a few minutes,' said Vincenzo as he led the way down a circular flight of stone steps.

At the end of a hallway, a trooper lay on the floor, his comrade bending over him. 'I found him sitting slumped against the wall. I laid him down. This was next to him.' He pointed to a tea tray. A cup was half empty.

Georges knelt down and examined the victim. 'Shallow breathing. He has vomited. Might be a dose of arsenic.' Georges looked up at the comrade. 'How was he poisoned?'

'The cook made tea for us and left it on the stove. Before going on duty in the evening, I drank a cup. Felt fine. A little after midnight, my comrade and I were checking the prisoners in the basement. A boy came down with a tray— a small pot of tea, sugar, cream, a sweetmeat—then left. My comrade put the tray aside. We finished with the prisoners and I went upstairs. As I left, he was pouring a cup for himself.'

Georges stood up, palmed his head. 'Whoever poisoned the tea hid until the guard drank it and passed out, then took his keys, and freed Pierre. Maybe three or four hours ago.' Georges glanced at the victim's holster and his scabbard. 'His pistol and his sword are gone. Pierre is armed.'

Saint-Martin turned to Vincenzo. 'Check the stable. He probably stole a horse and is miles from here by now. But arm yourself, just in case.'

'What can we do for this poor fellow?' Anne pointed to the sick trooper on the floor.

'I may be able to help.' Laure had arrived. 'Through trial and error, I've had to learn the physician's art.' She bent over the victim and examined him. 'There's rat poison in the kitchen. Someone must have put it in the tea.' She motioned to the men. 'Take him upstairs to Vincenzo's bed. I'll go to the kitchen and prepare a potion. I need to empty his stomach. That he's still alive means that he's strong and didn't drink much. He may recover.'

Anne asked Paul, 'Might the poisoner have deliberately prepared a weak mixture of tea and arsenic, so that it would incapacitate the guard but not kill him?'

'Possibly,' he replied. 'That could be a clue to his identity.' A worried look came over his face. 'Anne, go up to our room and get your pistols and mine. We must search the house and the farm buildings. Pierre's accomplice may still be here.'

Paul, Georges, and the trooper began to carry the victim down the hall. Anne felt a sudden rush of anxiety. 'Has anyone checked on Rivard?' The men immediately lowered their burden. 'I've looked into his room,' said the trooper. 'He was asleep.'

'Better look again,' said Paul.

The trooper unlocked the door, stepped into the room, and shouted, 'He's still asleep . . . No! My God! His throat's been cut. From ear to ear.'

Anne poured hot coffee for her husband. The day had turned cool and rainy. They sat at the table near the glowing fireplace in their room, drying their damp clothes. She and Paul were resting for a few minutes after searching the château and the farm buildings.

Benoît the stableboy was missing, most likely Pierre's accomplice. They had each taken a horse and might be traveling together or separately. Italy was a probable destination, since Pierre was familiar with the country and spoke the language. But they might also ride to Paris, whose nooks and crannies Pierre knew so well. He could hide there indefinitely.

Georges had set off for the Highway Patrol's post at Villejuif. From there, an alert would go out to all the posts between Paris and the Italian border. He would continue on to Paris, engage the police in the search, and put a watch on Thérèse Fauve's brothel.

Meanwhile, Vincenzo had moved Rivard's body from the château's basement to a vault under the parish church. It would be buried the next day in the adjacent graveyard. Cécile had visited his widow and daughter.

Paul gazed at Anne with a pained expression. 'This hurts. Everything's gone wrong. Our principal witness is dead, our chief suspect has escaped.'

'True, but you have Rivard's sworn testimony, and you may yet capture Pierre.' Anne broke off a piece of bread and buttered it. 'Didn't Vincenzo ever suspect that the stableboy couldn't be trusted?'

'No. He was hired a month ago, kept to himself, did his work well. Vincenzo recalls often seeing him in conversation with Pierre, but that didn't seem remarkable at the time. Pierre had recommended him for the job. He ate at the servants' table, was also familiar with the kitchen, and had borrowed the rat poison to use in the stable.'

'I truly doubt,' said Anne, 'that the boy could organize Pierre's escape on his own initiative. A more mature mind must have directed him.'

'I agree.' He drained his cup and set it down. He gazed at Anne with a teasing smile. 'Madame, whom shall we visit first, Monsieur Moretti or the Comte de Serre?'

'I say we should begin with our disagreeable count and save the charming, handsome Moretti to the last.'

*   *   *

It was nearly noon when a servant came to their door and announced that the Comte de Serre was ready to meet them. He had felt ill and had not ventured downstairs to see for himself what had happened. Vincenzo and Laure were temporarily in charge of the household. Seated in a comfortable upholstered chair, at his side the remnants of a breakfast tray, he received his visitors coldly, didn't invite them to sit. Paul pulled up a chair for Anne and one for himself.

The count frowned. 'During the past hour, I have been negotiating with Monsieur Moretti the final arrangements for the sale of pieces of my art collection. Distressing business. Now perhaps you will explain in detail what has happened downstairs. I have learned the gist of it.'

'I shall give you a full account, sir.' Paul then offered a carefully worded version of events, leaving out speculation concerning where the culprits might flee.

'Colonel, I'm not sorry about Rivard. I hold him and his birds responsible for my wife's death. Your wrongheaded investigation led to the arrest of Pierre, an innocent man. I can understand that he might flee rather than trust his life to magistrates who would judge him on the evidence you would present. If Pierre killed the villain Rivard, I applaud him. He has saved the country the costs of an execution and taught my enemies in the village a lesson.'

What a perverse line of reasoning! Anne thought. How can the count believe in Pierre's innocence? He must realize that he has put himself under suspicion of having aided and abetted Pierre's escape? He appeared not to care.

Paul went on in a matter-of-fact tone, ignoring the count's provocation. 'The evidence we've gathered points to Pierre. Lieutenant-General DeCrosne will decide what action to take in this case.' Paul paused for a moment to shift to another topic. 'Tell me, sir, what were you doing between midnight and dawn?'

The count grimaced with irritation. 'What can you possibly mean, Colonel? Do you imply that I might have been in the kitchen, preparing a concoction of rat poison for your trooper? To answer your question, I was asleep in bed.'

'Do you know the stableboy, sir?'

198

'Of course, he has often saddled my horse.'

'He has aided Pierre's escape and has fled with him.'

'I'm not surprised, Colonel. Didn't you know that the boy is Pierre's son?'

How should Paul know? muttered Anne to herself. It was a secret kept even from Vincenzo.

If the count's mocking tone and taunting defence of Pierre irritated Paul, he hadn't shown it. He had plodded ahead, searching for what might lie behind the count's arrogant posturing, a motive still hidden.

On the way to visit Moretti, Paul and Anne chanced to meet Michou, quite agitated. She beckoned them into her room. 'What happened in the basement?' she asked. 'The servants are talking about Monsieur Rivard's murder.'

Anne gave her a quick explanation.

Michou's lips parted, her green eyes widened in amazement. 'I'm sorry for his wife and daughter. Will the trooper recover?'

'Most likely,' Anne replied.

Michou lapsed into thought for a few moments, then signed, 'I remember the stableboy very well, never trusted him. He was more clever than he let on. Same shifty eyes as Pierre, spied for him downstairs. I sketched both of them.'

Interest sparked in Paul's eyes. 'May I see your sketches?'

Michou flipped through the loose leaves in her portfolio and pulled out two of them. 'These are the best.'

Paul held them up to the light from a window. 'They are excellent likenesses. May I have them, Michou? I want to make prints to circulate among the police of Paris and the Highway Patrol.'

'Of course you may. I'm pleased when I can be helpful.' She paused with an afterthought. 'Once when the stableboy was excited and thought no one could hear him, he addressed Pierre as *Père*. Even though the words are similar, I'm sure I read his lips correctly. Pierre scolded him.'

'Pierre, the boy's father,' Anne remarked to Paul. 'A revealing slip of the tongue, don't you agree?'

'Yes, indeed!' he replied. 'It confirms what the count said.

I wonder who could be the boy's mother? Pierre might seek refuge with her.'

They found Moretti in his room, looking out the window at the rain. He was dressed in a plain, well-tailored brown silk suit, ready to travel. They stood aside at the door while two servants hauled a trunk past them. Moretti turned to greet his visitors with his usual courtesy and sat with them by the fireplace.

'I have finished my work with the count this morning, and will leave for Paris in an hour with a dozen of his paintings, engravings, and precious objects to sell.'

Anne reckoned that the art dealer had made good use of his time at the château. In four days, he had selected each piece, studied its provenance, and written a draft of a sales catalogue.

At first glance, he appeared relaxed, obviously relieved to depart from the château. 'If you need me, Colonel, come to my gallery on Place Dauphine.' He explained that the count, an irascible and demanding client, wanted at least 50,000 livres net from the sale. Anne guessed that if all went as planned, Moretti's commission would be 5,000, enough to make this long weekend at the château worthwhile.

Paul congratulated Moretti on his apparent success, then remarked, 'You are aware, I'm sure, of Rivard's murder and of Pierre's arrest and escape.'

'The servants who packed my trunk have told me.' Moretti's voice changed abruptly, became a bit shrill. 'I am trying to understand why Pierre would kill Virginie. True, he has no conscience, but he's also shrewd, judges everything in the light of his own self-interest. So what would he gain by killing her? Nothing that I can see. He had no grudge against her and treated her with respect. She feared him and took pains to avoid displeasing him. If he had nothing to gain, why take the risk?'

Paul stared at Moretti, then asked, 'Didn't you know that Pierre Fauve is the natural son of the Comte de Serre?'

An expression of disbelief swept over Moretti's face. 'Like everyone close to the count, I recognized his remarkable trust in Fauve, but he never acknowledged paternity.'

'What's even more interesting,' Paul continued, 'according to a will drawn up after the countess's death, Fauve became heir to the count's fortune.'

'What?' exclaimed Moretti in a tone of displeased surprise. 'Fauve led me to believe that, for lack of an heir, the count would leave his possessions to the Crown or to a philanthropic institution. The count's will is none of my business, but it obviously gives Pierre a strong reason to remove Virginie from his path.'

During this discussion, Anne observed Moretti closely. He struggled to maintain a mask of cool self-control. Tension worked the corners of his mouth. He clutched his cane until his knuckles turned white.

When Moretti left the room, Anne asked Paul, 'Why should Moretti care so much if Pierre were arrested for the murder of the countess?'

Paul thought for a minute. 'That depends. If Moretti had learned to love the countess, as he has led us to believe, then he would hate Pierre and perhaps become angry enough to avenge her death. On the other hand, Moretti might have deceived us and only pretended to love her. He might even have conspired with Pierre to kill her. With Pierre's arrest, Moretti might fear being exposed.'

The rain continued into the afternoon. From a parlor window, Anne and Paul watched Moretti's coach being loaded with his trunk and several sturdy boxes of the count's art. A cape over his shoulders and the gold-headed cane under his arm, Moretti stepped quickly into the coach and it set off for Paris.

Anne and Paul left the parlor and climbed the stairs to their room. Paul began putting papers into his portfolio.

'We must also return to Paris, Anne. That's where we shall find Pierre and Benoît. They may stay there in hiding or, more likely, gather resources to flee the country and live comfortably abroad. The troopers shall remain here until the sick one can be moved. The healthy one will offer a measure of protection to Vincenzo, Laure, Cécile, and the other servants.'

201

'If we leave in an hour, Paul, we'll be home before dark.' She started for the door. 'I'll tell Michou and begin packing.'

Paul closed his portfolio. 'I expect the count will soon follow us. He and Moretti are closely connected to Pierre Fauve, the key to solving the murders of Bouchard and Gillet.'

Anne stopped in the doorway, gazed at her husband. 'Yes, they were all caught, one way or another, in Pierre's web of intrigue. He's a master spider, and dangerous as well.'

Thirty

Pursuit

September 18

'How *shall* we find Pierre?' Anne asked, an impatient edge on her voice. 'Paris is the haystack, and he's the needle.' She and Georges had joined Paul for breakfast at the conference table in his office.

'The police have made a huge effort,' Georges sighed. 'They've put a price on his head and searched his usual haunts, including his sister's brothel and the count's apartment. All the likely places of refuge are under surveillance.'

Paul replied with a calming gesture, 'Let's put ourselves in his situation and imagine what he would do. Think of an unlikely solution. Remember he has few options and he's desperate.'

'He may turn to Monsieur Moretti,' Georges suggested. 'Suppose that he had paid Pierre to kill the countess and promised him shelter or retirement in Italy. Fauve might ask him to honor that promise.'

'But,' countered Anne, 'suppose instead that Moretti had no part in her death. Wouldn't he hate Fauve for killing the countess?'

'I agree,' Georges replied. 'But even then, he might force

202

Moretti's hand. Fauve could perhaps prove that Moretti defaced the Serre portrait—or did something equally scandalous. As a master extortioner, he probably has found dirt in Moretti's past. Fauve could threaten to expose him, unless he helped him escape to Italy.'

'True,' observed Saint-Martin, 'Fauve may have no better option. He doesn't have connections to any country other than Italy and would not want to hide in Paris indefinitely and risk being caught and convicted. But he can't go directly to Moretti, whose house is under surveillance.'

Georges stirred in his chair, preparing to leave. 'We need help from the public. I'll take Michou's sketches of Pierre and the boy Benoît to the Royal Printing Office. Within a few days, the likenesses of these fugitives will spread across the country.'

'Good plan,' the colonel agreed. He rose from the table. 'I'm confident we'll soon have Pierre in custody with enough evidence to convict him.'

Anne gave him a reassuring smile, but she had an uncomfortable feeling that they had overlooked something.

Pierre was not her only concern. At midmorning, she, Paul, and Michou found Hamel at the writing table in his office. He greeted them politely but with an unsmiling, resigned expression. Paul had earlier informed the painter of the visit: he would check Hamel's compliance with his orders concerning Michou. In her portfolio she carried her copy of the Serre portrait. As they took seats facing Hamel, Anne noticed that the countess's damaged portrait had been placed on an easel.

Paul pointed to Michou's portfolio, then at the painting on the easel. 'Michou has come prepared to give you her painting of the Comtesse de Serre's portrait. But first, here is a contract.' He handed two copies over to Hamel, who scanned them.

Anne translated for Michou. 'She is asking ten per cent of the sum that you will receive for the finished portrait.'

Hamel glumly nodded, signed the two copies, and handed them to Michou. She signed them and handed one back to Hamel together with her painting.

He held the portrait in his hands, fixed his eyes on it. The room grew still. Then he smiled for the first time. 'This image brings the countess back to my mind. It's as if she were sitting before me. I hope to exhibit the finished portrait before the Salon closes.' He hesitated for a moment, a cryptic expression on his face. 'Now is as good a time as any,' he said, then handed a sealed envelope over to Michou. 'My letter of apology to you, mademoiselle.'

Anne didn't have to translate. Michou received the envelope with a steady hand and gave him in return a polite smile and a bow of her head. After breaking the seal and opening the envelope, she stared for a moment at the message. Then she handed it to Anne. 'Please read it aloud,' she signed.

It was brief and straightforward.

> *I herewith apologize to you, Mademoiselle Micheline du Saint-Esprit, for having called you a trouble-maker. In fact, you were only doing your duty to assist the police investigation of a serious crime. To make amends, I allow you to visit my studio at the appropriate hours.*

'Are you satisfied, Michou?' Paul asked.

'Yes,' she signed, and held her chin a little higher.

'Then we shall leave you now, monsieur,' Paul said to Hamel, 'and visit with Monsieur Latour. We need to discuss the progress of his career.'

Hamel looked annoyed. It was, after all, only four days since he had been ordered to treat his assistant fairly. The blow to his pride still hurt. 'I believe you will find him satisfied.'

'I hope so,' Paul replied. There was no smile in his voice.

The visitors stood just inside the studio and watched Marc instructing a student. They were both smiling. After a few minutes, Marc's gaze met theirs. He finished with the student and joined his visitors, giving Michou a sidelong glance.

'You are busy,' Paul began. 'We shall take only a minute of your time. How does Hamel treat you?'

'Yesterday, he increased my wages to what others in my

position earn. He also told me to think ahead to an exhibition in the next few months. If all goes well, he would recommend me to the Academy for the status of an associate. Your words to him have had an effect.'

'Are you willing now to confirm in writing what you told my wife several days ago concerning the knife that killed Bouchard?'

'Yes, I should have been more courageous at the time. Both Hamel and Pierre Fauve had access to the knife on the eve of the murder.'

'Madame Cartier has written out your statement.'

Anne handed it to him. He read it and signed.

All this took place while Michou stood off to one side, reading lips as best she could. Marc cast quick glances in her direction. Anne signed the gist of what was said. Then she took Michou under the arm and presented her to Marc. 'I think you two should be friends again.'

Marc flushed and hesitantly reached out his hands.

Michou held them in hers, then kissed him on both cheeks.

'Will you come during Hamel's dinner hour?' he signed to her.

'Yes,' she replied. 'You could show me the pictures you'd like to exhibit.' She stepped back.

Anne uttered a silent prayer of thanks. 'We had better allow Marc to return to his students.' She moved toward the door.

Paul joined her. 'I must speak with Lieutenant-General DeCrosne about the investigation.'

Michou followed them out of the studio. 'And I'll visit Madame Bouchard.' She gave Anne a heartwarming glance.

On the way home, Anne came to Saint-Roch, her husband's parish church, where she and he had repeated their marriage vows in the spring. This was, therefore, a special place for her, and she often spent a minute inside or at least offered a thankful prayer as she walked by.

On weekdays, the broad steps leading to the front entrance resembled a small neighborhood market, where one could buy roasted chestnuts, fruits and vegetables, flowers, bits of clothing, and the like. Men and women gathered to exchange gossip. Beggars and thieves plied their trade. Over time, Anne had become intrigued by the old flower woman who usually perched on these steps, one of Pierre Fauve's spies, the one who had followed Cécile.

Now, Anne searched in vain for the woman. With Michou's sketch of Pierre fresh in mind, Anne suddenly recollected a family resemblance—a similar square face, crafty blue eyes, and wiry body. She must be his mother, the camp follower Victoire, whom Serre mentioned three days ago. The age was right. About sixty.

She could simply have left the place in order to relieve herself, but Anne was curious. 'Where's Victoire?' she asked an alert old woman who sold sweetmeats, but chiefly served as a conduit of gossip. 'She left just a few minutes ago to run an errand. One of the beggars overheard her mention Place Dauphine. She was there once this morning.'

Anne immediately recalled that Moretti lived there. The flower woman could be carrying Fauve's messages. Instead of walking on to her home, Anne turned around. The old woman would have to cross the Pont Neuf. If Anne hurried, she could reach the bridge first.

Several minutes later, Anne arrived nearly breathless at the statue of Henri IV in the middle of the bridge. There she could observe traffic in both directions. In a few minutes, the woman appeared, carrying a basket of dried flowers. Anne pretended to examine a peddler's oranges until the woman turned left off the bridge and entered Place Dauphine.

Anne followed her at a safe distance. She put her basket on a bench in front of Moretti's house. A hedge concealed Anne from his view, should he be watching from a window. With the small spyglass she carried in her bag, she watched the woman offer her flowers for sale. In a short while, a servant came from the building and drew close to the woman. While pretending to admire the flowers, he slipped a small package into her basket. Then he stepped back and handed the woman a coin. She reached into her basket, pulled out a dried flower, wrapped its stem with a piece of paper—a message, Anne assumed—and handed it to him.

There had already been one exchange, earlier in the day.

There could be more. The flower woman's significance grew in Anne's eyes.

She picked up her basket and left the place with Anne following her. Instead of returning to Saint-Roch, the woman stopped at a wine tavern just off Place du Palais-Royal near the Louvre. Anne didn't dare enter. A well-dressed woman sitting alone would attract far too much attention. But it must be in the same building as Thérèse Fauve's brothel. So, Anne surmised, this was where the flower woman picked up and dropped off Pierre's messages. He must be hiding in the neighborhood.

Anne took her new insights to Inspecteur Quidor's office near Place Vendôme. In the anteroom, a clerk received her and offered her a chair. 'I'll ask if the inspector will see you.' Quidor was a busy man; Anne expected to wait. But in a minute the clerk was back and showed her in.

'What can I do for you, Madame Cartier?' The inspector was a gruff man, but he treated Anne with the respect due to the colonel's wife. They had also worked together on an earlier investigation. He listened with keen interest to her brief account of the events at Serre's château and her spying on the flower lady that morning.

'What can you tell me about Victoire?' asked Anne.

'I'll send for her file.' He gave a note to his clerk. 'We should have something. I questioned her last night, searched her room in a garret above Thérèse's brothel. Like the others, she claims she hasn't seen or heard from Pierre.' In a few minutes, the clerk arrived with a file. Quidor took out a sheet, scanned it, then looked up. 'As you know, madame, she's one of Pierre Fauve's spies, called Victoire. Uses various family names, including Fauve. Most likely a relative.'

'The Comte de Serre told me, sir, that she's Pierre's mother.'

'The Fauve family begins to resemble a viper's brood. I thank you, madame. That information shall go into her file.' Quidor continued, 'Madame Victoire has a record of minor offenses, such as pandering. Hm, I see here that she's known to carry a knife. A few years ago, she stabbed a man to death who attempted to assault her. Never charged. She probably has a powerful patron. Witnesses testified it was self-defense.'

'My respect for Victoire has grown,' Anne admitted. 'I wonder if the Comte de Serre might be that patron. She's not a person to trifle with. Pierre might use her again as his messenger to Moretti. I realize your agents have Moretti's house under surveillance. Perhaps they should pay more attention to Madame Victoire.'

'In view of what you have just reported, madame, I shall alert them.'

At midafternoon, Anne left the Hôtel de Police and returned home. Georges was in his office, at work at his desk. He stood up to greet her and ordered tea. The Royal Printing Office, he reported, would have Michou's sketches ready for distribution by tomorrow morning. She told him about the flower woman's visit to Place Dauphine.

'The odds are slim, but this woman might inadvertently lead you to Pierre and the boy,' said Georges.

'I'll change into a servant's clothes and follow her.'

The tea arrived and was poured. Georges drank from his cup, then lowered it thoughtfully. 'Pierre knows that Quidor's agents here in Paris and the Royal Highway Patrol throughout the country can maintain the present level of intense surveillance for a week at most. They will soon be overwhelmed by pressure to solve other crimes. Pierre's making preparations but won't leave until then.'

'What practical steps can we take?'

'While you investigate the flower woman, I'll study Paris underground. At least for a short while, Pierre could be hiding in a deeply buried chamber and move about through the sewers.'

'How dreadful!' Anne could almost smell the stench. 'He would have to be desperate.'

Georges lifted his cup and stared into it. 'I'm sure he is. And I doubt that he knows the underground. It's a dark, stinking jungle. He would need help.' Georges scratched his head. 'Who could he turn to?'

'A man who has worked in the sewers,' Anne replied,

'another relative, perhaps an uncle, someone Pierre knows and trusts. He may have gone directly to that man, rather than to his sister. It's a remarkable family!'

Georges's investigation started with Quidor, who thought the idea worth pursuing and sent him on to the office of the lieutenant-general, whose jurisdiction included sewers as well as streets, lights, fire protection, and other urban services. By late afternoon, Georges was sitting at a small table and a clerk was laying a thick register of documents before him.

'I would need years to go through this,' Georges complained. 'Do you know someone who is expert on the subject? I'd like to talk to him.' Georges jingled the coins in his pocket.

'Let me think.' The clerk screwed up his face with the effort. 'Yes, he retired recently after thirty years with us, knows the system better than anyone.'

'His name?'

'Jean Fauve.'

'We may be on to something,' said the colonel, sitting behind his desk. Georges had just described his discovery. Jean Fauve had retired to a room in the parish of Saint-Roch, on the street of the same name. 'The members of this family live within a five-minute walk from one another.'

'Since Jean Fauve is likely to be sympathetic to Pierre, I also found another expert on the sewers, Bernard Noel, the man who took Jean's place. The clerk thought there was bad blood between the two men.'

'We shall ask Quidor to assign one of his spies to follow Jean Fauve. Meanwhile, pay a visit to Monsieur Noel.'

Hours later, Georges found him in a wine tavern in the central markets near the merchants' church of Saint-Eustache. To avoid drawing attention to himself, Georges had donned commoner's clothing. Still, as a stranger to the place, he attracted a few wary glances. He sat by himself, ordered bread and wine, and guardedly studied Noel.

He was a thick-bodied man, with rheumy eyes, mottled complexion, and a hacking cough. Before him stood a pitcher of wine, on his plate a half-eaten loaf of bread. He was with

209

a comrade, to judge from the easy familiarity of their conversation and the bits that Georges could overhear.

In a short while, the other patrons were ignoring Georges. So when Noel's comrade left, Georges approached his table. 'May I have a word with you, monsieur?' Georges began in his most persuasive manner. 'You'll find it to your advantage.'

Noel had changed from his working clothes, but the pungent odor of the sewers wafted from his skin and his hair. He nodded to the empty chair facing him, studying Georges through narrowed eyes. 'I'm listening.' He broke off bread from his loaf, soaked it in his wine, and popped it into his mouth. He had no teeth.

'Could a man live in the sewers, or at least hide there for a week?'

'Why would you want to know?' He sucked on his empty gums.

'Let's say I'm curious.' Georges shoved a coin across the table. Noel threw a glance at it, put it into his pocket.

'I've spent most of my life in the sewers. Can't say rightly that I've lived there. Never stayed overnight. Could be done. Your man wouldn't get much sleep fighting off the rats.'

'Where would be the best place to hide?' Georges reached into his pocket for another coin.

'I'm working in an old tunnel under Rue Montmartre, not far from here. I wouldn't recommend it. Rats as big as hunting dogs—and as fierce.' He paused, thought for a moment. 'Then again, your man would be safe from the police. They wouldn't care to search for him there.'

'You know Jean Fauve, I believe.'

'Bastard that he is. For years, he made me do the hard work he got paid for.'

'His nephew is on the run, charged with murder. I think Jean may be hiding him.'

Noel's face brightened, his toothless mouth broke into a wide, malign grin. 'Would you like some help finding him?'

Georges nodded.

'Jean Fauve had us working on the Great Sewer just before

he retired. It runs from the Montmartre tunnel westward under Rue de Provence and the Champs-Elysées and exits into the river west of the city center. As good an escape route as his nephew could hope for. We'll set a trap at the exit, then go down into the sewer and flush him out.'

'First thing tomorrow,' Georges declared with a grimace, the scent of the sewer already assaulting his nose. 'The colonel will owe me a favor for this.'

Thirty-One

Into the Depths

September 19

Shortly after dawn, Anne set out for Saint-Roch, disguised in a domestic servant's plain brown woolen dress and armed with a small hidden loaded pistol. Paul had given her a note with his seal, authorizing her to carry the weapon and to request aid from the police. She told herself that these precautions were unnecessary. Nonetheless, she felt exhilarated, as if setting out on a dangerous adventure.

Victoire, the flower woman, and her companions were already on the church steps, locked together in a heated discussion. When Anne heard 'Police . . . Pierre Fauve,' she drew close and listened. For a moment, she wondered, had they caught him? Victoire looked anxious.

'No, he's still in hiding,' a fruit seller announced. 'Clever rascal.'

'The police will never find him,' said a beggar. 'Like Cartouche, he's gone underground.' He pointed toward a drain in the street that emptied into a sewer. 'The police are afraid to go in there, get lost, die of the pest and be eaten by monstrous rats.'

Anne had heard of Cartouche, the legendary bandit, whose

211

exploits decades ago lived on in the people's imagination. She continued through the crowd and entered the church. Priests were saying Mass at the side altars. The murmured sounds of worship and the smell of burning candles seemed to gently stir the air. Rays of thin early-morning light sifted through the windows on to paintings and sculptures, bringing them to life. She stood still for a minute, allowing the mood of the church to beguile her senses and lift her spirit.

With a parting prayer, she returned to the steps outside. She had brought with her a few ribbons to sell, a simple way to mask her identity as a spy and to fit in. No one else sold ribbons. And she took a spot that no one else had claimed. For a minute or two, the women nearest her looked askance, as they would at any newcomer. But since she offered them no competition, they eventually ignored her.

An hour passed. Then a young woman ran up to Victoire and whispered in her ear. In an instant, her neck grew taut, her back stiffened. She sent the messenger off with a jerk of her head, then rushed from the steps in the direction of the Palais-Royal.

Anne sensed immediately that this was no ordinary errand. A crisis had occurred. Standing on the edge of the crowd, she could slip away without being noticed. For a moment, the flower woman disappeared from view in the crowded street, but Anne caught up with her at the entrance to the Montpensier Arcade.

Victoire stopped at the door to a shop, hesitated, then entered. Anne hastened to the shop, peered through a window. Victoire was speaking earnestly to a shop girl, who glanced anxiously at the older woman in charge. The shop girl shook her head and the flower woman left. In the same arcade, she approached another girl in a pastry shop and a third selling sweetmeats, all with the same result.

Victoire left the arcade, muttering to herself and clenching her fists. Finally, she approached a young woman seated in the garden. By her bold manner and heavily painted appearance, Anne judged her to be a prostitute enjoying a few moments of leisure. In contrast to the embarrassed, even fearful reaction of the three other young girls, this woman smiled easily at the flower woman, invited her to take a nearby chair. They talked for a minute, Victoire growing increasingly agitated.

Sheltered by a hedge, Anne drew out her spyglass and attempted to read their lips. Too far away, she missed most of their conversation, but she deciphered the words they stressed and repeated, 'Boy . . . disappeared . . . this morning.' Pierre's boy, probably. The prostitute reflected for a moment. Her face brightened. She said something, pointed eastward, nodded.

For Anne, this was fast becoming more than she could hope to deal with. The old woman was usually armed with a knife and had already demonstrated that she was willing and able to use it. The boy was almost a full-grown man, broad-shouldered, tall and strong beyond his fourteen years, and also might be armed and dangerous. It seemed foolish to confront these two alone. Anne looked about for help.

Meanwhile, Victoire thanked the young woman and set off across the garden of the Palais-Royal in the direction of the central markets, Anne nervously following. A few minutes later, the old woman entered Rue du Pélican, a short, narrow street, whose shabby buildings appeared to be devoted to the oldest profession. Many of the women were leaning out the windows, advertising themselves. Midway down the street Victoire stopped at the sign of a wine tavern, peered in, then entered.

Anne began to feel panic, wondering what to do. She was still standing undecided at the head of the street when three guardsmen from the city police strode rapidly toward her.

'Mademoiselle!' called out the oldest of them, a burly sergeant. His voice was stern, inquisitorial. 'What are you up to?'

Anne found herself momentarily at a loss for words, alone without a shopping basket in this notorious part of the city.

'Why were you following that old woman?' asked the sergeant. The men had surrounded her. Were they going to search her?

As calmly as she could, she explained, 'The flower woman is armed and looking for the young fugitive Benoît Fauve.

213

She may have found him as we speak.' Anne showed the guards Michou's sketch of the boy. The printing office had sent Paul several copies that morning, and he had given one to Anne. She also gave them Paul's note authorizing her to be armed and to request police assistance.

The sergeant studied the note, examined Paul's seal, showed the sketch to his comrades. Their attitude suddenly became deferential, even a little embarrassed. The sergeant bowed. 'I know your husband, madame. Your papers are in order. We must act quickly. Follow the old woman into the tavern. If she's there with the boy, give us a signal. We'll come immediately. We can't go with you now, or we'll rouse the entire neighborhood. They'll pitch garbage at us from the windows. The boy might escape.'

Relieved, Anne squared her shoulders and walked down the street, stopped at the tavern, and looked into a long, dark, crowded room. On the left was the bar. Patrons lined up with jugs to be filled. On the right were several battered tables and chairs. Even at midmorning, prostitutes occupied most of them, waiting for customers. Men from the central markets to the east walked in, looked over the women, picked out one, or left perhaps to try next door. In the back of the shop, a flight of stairs led to the upper floors.

With all the coming and going, the place lacked the feeling of a tight community. Anne sensed she could blend in. She bought a glass of wine and sat down at a table next to an older, fine-boned prostitute, whose beauty had long since faded and now was any man's last choice in this room. 'What are you doing here?' asked the older woman. 'This isn't your line of work, is it?' She waved a hand contemptuously over her comrades.

'No, it isn't. I'm in domestic service.' Anne paused, attempting to gauge the woman's intelligence and powers of observation. In a moment, she was satisfied. 'I'm looking for my younger brother, a wayward lad. Our parents are worried about him.' Anne showed the woman the printed sketch of Benoît Fauve. 'I was told he used to come here, so I thought I'd see for myself.'

The woman gazed at the print, her face wrinkled into an ironic smile. 'That's him, hardly fourteen years old, but as lusty as a wild boar. He and one of the younger girls get on well together.' She met Anne's eye. 'You're in luck. He's upstairs now. She's gone to the market. A lady calling herself his grandmother just went up to him.'

The woman's expression hardened. 'Tell me, darling, what's going on? Are you from the police?' Her fingers curled around a sharp bread knife.

'Madame, I see you're a clever woman.' Anne spoke softly, carefully measuring her words. 'The boy may have killed a man. There's a reward for his capture. Interested?'

'What do I have to do?' Her tone was doubtful, but her fingers relaxed a bit. 'How much will I get?'

'Thirty louis d'or, what you'd earn in a year if you were lucky.' Anne tried to sound convincing. It was a likely sum, though she couldn't know for sure how much the reward would be. 'Where's the boy and his grandmother?'

'Fourth floor. Up those stairs. I could show you the room.'

'Is there a back way?'

'There's a rope out the window to a ladder below into an alley.'

'I'll be back in a minute.' Anne left the shop, signaled the police at the end of the street. They came on the trot. She quickly instructed them. The younger ones went around the building into the alley, the sergeant followed Anne into the shop. A sudden hush came over the place. The barman stared, eyes wide, mouth open but speechless. The old prostitute was already at the foot of the stairs. Anne and the officer walked quickly through the crowd and climbed after her. He drew his pistol, touched the saber at his side.

On the fourth floor, the woman stopped at a door. 'This is it.'

Anne heard sounds within. Two voices rose in anger.

'Ungrateful wretch!' cried a shrill female voice.

'Old bitch! Get out!' shouted a male voice in turn.

Then came a piercing scream, followed by a loud crash. The sergeant tried the door. Locked. He pounded on it. No response. He threw himself against it and burst it open.

The boy lay on his back, bleeding profusely from a wound to his chest. The window was open and the rope thrown out.

215

The sergeant rushed to the window and called to his comrades below. 'She's climbing down. Catch her!'

Anne knelt over the boy. He was still alive. His half-opened eyes fixed on her, seemed to recognize her. 'He's in the sewer,' he whispered.

'Where?'

'Louvre.' The eyes closed.

The old prostitute bent over the boy, stanched his wound with a towel, covered him with blankets to ward off shock. Anxious to earn that reward, Anne thought, then corrected herself. The woman appeared to be genuinely concerned for the boy.

The sergeant studied him, glanced at Michou's sketch. 'He's the one. I'll summon help.'

Anne reported what the boy had told her. 'I must go now and tell my husband and his adjutant. They will search the Louvre sewer.'

Downstairs, the barroom had emptied. The flower woman sat bound, subdued after a brief battle with the two younger guardsmen. She appeared unrepentant, and would not tell where Pierre was hiding.

'The boy has told us,' Anne said coldly.

'Treacherous scum!'

'The boy Benoît is in police custody, seriously wounded,' Anne told Georges. They were together with Bernard Noel in Georges' office. Both men appeared dejected.

'Good! I hope he lives.' Georges leaned forward, immediately attentive, his spirit improving. 'What did he say?'

'Pierre's in the Louvre sewer.'

Georges and his companion Noel had spent the morning in the Great Sewer. Though they had changed clothes, the stench had lodged in their hair and skin and hung in the air. The runoff from heavy rain during the past few days had left the tunnel littered with stinking debris. Their search had proved fruitless.

At the word 'Louvre', Bernard stirred in his chair. 'There's a tunnel *near* the Louvre, built a hundred years ago. Several drains and sewers empty into it. The flow goes down to the river. Haven't been there in a while. Don't know its condition. Should be tolerable.' He paused, rubbed his chin. 'Come to think of it, that tunnel has a couple of chambers for storing tiles, tools, and the like. Yes, a man could hide out there. I suppose it's been done before.'

Georges reached for his hat. 'Let's go.'

By midafternoon, the two men had figured out that a connecting tunnel might run from the basement of the brothel to the main Louvre tunnel. They entered the ground-floor tavern and ordered the barman to show them to the basement. With a reluctant expression on his face, he led them to the rear of the room, then down a circular stone stairway into a musty, windowless, vaulted stone wine cellar. Racks of bottles covered the walls. Georges held up the lantern while Bernard studied the room. The floor sloped to a small drain in the middle.

'This drain flows to a larger one nearby,' Bernard observed, then turned to the barman. 'Is there another basement room?'

He shifted his weight from one leg to the other. 'This is the only one I know of. I must go back upstairs and tend to my customers.'

'No, you stay with us.' Georges paced the room, measuring its dimensions, comparing them to those of the room upstairs. 'I'd guess there's another room on the other side of this wall.' It took him a half hour, but he eventually found a hidden latch in a section of wooden shelves. When he pulled, the entire section rolled out, leaving an opening for a man to squeeze through.

The room was empty and also windowless. The scent of the sewer was powerful. There was a round opening in the middle of the floor. He held the lantern over it. Iron rungs led down into a black abyss.

'I want you to go down there first.' Georges held a pistol to the barman's head. 'You know what we're looking for. And you know the way—I smelled it on you. If you cooperate, you will receive a reward. If you don't, well, you will go into that hole anyway—as a dead man. "Shot attempting to escape," the report will say. You have five seconds to make up your mind.'

The man was trembling so hard that his teeth chattered. Finally, he nodded and started down the rungs, Georges and Bernard following. The tunnel's stone vault was high enough for a man to stand. Thick, stinking mud nearly filled the channel where a trickle of water flowed. The narrow walkway along one side was littered with slippery, foul-smelling debris. Prodded by Georges's pistol, the barman led the way through the connector tunnel into the main tunnel. Cautiously, they worked their way downstream toward the river.

In the distance, Georges began to see a glimmer of light. 'That's the first storage chamber,' Bernard whispered in his ear. 'The light's coming from a vent in the ceiling.'

The barman stiffened, slowed down to a crawl. Georges whispered to him, 'If Pierre calls out, tell him you have a message.' The three men continued toward the light. Georges shuttered his lantern, handed it to Bernard.

They almost reached the opening, when a voice called out, 'Antoine, is that you?'

'Yes,' croaked the barman. 'I'm bringing a message.'

In the next instant, a dark figure appeared in the opening, a pistol in each hand. The barman dropped to the walkway. Georges and Bernard pressed against the wall. A flame burst from one of Pierre's guns. An ear-shattering explosion shook the tunnel. The ball struck the vault above Georges's head, sending down a shower of stone fragments. Before Pierre could raise the second pistol, Georges fired. Another huge explosion. Pierre spun around, dropping his pistol, then sank to one knee.

Georges rushed forward and seized the man by the collar. 'I arrest you, Pierre Fauve, for the murder of Monsieur Rivard and the Comtesse de Serre.'

Something stirred behind him.

'Look, Georges, what I've found.' Bernard had gone around a pile of stones and, with his pistol and a broad crooked smile, flushed out Jean Fauve, his retired master.

'What, may I ask, are you doing here?' Georges glared at the culprit.

Crestfallen, trembling, the retired sewer expert struggled for words.

Bernard searched the man's sack and pulled out a large tool.

'Pincers. He intended to cut the lock on the grate at the end of this tunnel.'

In another sack, Bernard found a pouch full of louis d'or, and a sealed envelope. In yet another sack, he found a change of clothes and a wig.

'Well, Monsieur Noel,' Georges addressed his companion with a chuckle, 'it appears that Pierre and Jean were about to leave. I suppose we'll find a boat waiting on the river. We came just in time.'

Thirty-Two

Revelations

September 19–20

Anne stepped into Paul's darkened office, raised her lantern, and looked around. His desk was clear of clutter—no tilting piles of loose paper as in Georges's office. Thick file boxes stood in serried ranks on the shelves. Anne smiled. Her husband's mind, like his office, was rational, ordered. Fortunately, his heart was warm, his love passionate. She gazed at Michou's portrait of her, centered on the wall where one might expect to see the King or Queen.

Paul wouldn't be home until nightfall. He had planned to spend the day in Versailles with DeCrosne and Breteuil, discussing the progress of the investigation, especially as it concerned Hamel, Moretti, and Serre. To place men of such prominence under suspicion of murder called for caution at the highest levels of authority.

She had begun to worry, when Georges and then Paul arrived, tired but well. They all gathered at the conference table in Paul's office for a light supper and began to share news of the day. The servants brought in bread and soup, fruit and cheese, and wine, then withdrew.

219

'Anne, tell us about the wounded boy Benoît.' Paul's fore-head creased with concern. 'We need him as a witness.'

'In the early afternoon, I went to the Hôtel-Dieu, the hospital on the island near Notre-Dame. The guardsmen had given custody of the boy to one of Quidor's agents. I waited three hours, hoping that the boy might regain consciousness. At times, he became delirious and called out to his girlfriend. I couldn't question him, but I got a medical report. Victoire's blade missed his heart by an inch. He's hovering between life and death. Fortunately, he's strong.'

Paul turned to Georges. 'What did you learn from Victoire?'

'She's one tough old lady. When Pierre discovered that Benoît had fled from the tunnel, he sent Victoire to bring him back. The boy knew too much and would talk, if captured. When she caught up with him on Rue du Pélican, he refused to return. Infatuated with the girl, he was angry at his father for taking him away from her. He and Victoire argued. He insulted her. She lost her temper and stabbed him.'

'Did she throw any light on Pierre's activities?'

'No. I asked. She refused.'

Georges went on to describe his investigation of the sewer tunnel, ending with the capture of Pierre and his uncle Jean. 'I notified Quidor, who transported Pierre to the Hôtel-Dieu and put him under guard. The shot had smashed his right shoulder. He was in great pain, needed an operation to remove the ball, so he was in no condition to be interrogated.'

'And Jean Fauve? What's happened to him?'

'I turned him over to Quidor, who imprisoned him at the Châtelet, along with Victoire and the boatmen hired to trans-port Pierre to the coast.' Georges paused, drank deep of his wine. 'This was their scheme: Pierre and the boy fled from the Serre château to Uncle Jean, who hid them in the Louvre tunnel. Victoire got a sealed envelope with travel documents, a testimonial letter, and a large letter of credit from Moretti. Jean gathered three hundred louis d'or from a hiding place in the brothel and hired a boat to take Pierre and the boy to the Channel. They were to cross over to England, board a ship bound for Livorno, and settle down in Florence.'

At the mention of Moretti, Anne gasped. 'Why would

Moretti take such a risk, so compromise himself, unless he's deeply involved in Pierre's crimes?'

'Good point, Anne,' Paul replied. 'He has much to explain. We'll question him tomorrow.'

Thursday morning was cool and cloudy. Low clouds scudded over Paris, loosing bursts of rain on the flowers outside. At breakfast in the garden room, Anne didn't complain. It had been a dry summer, and the garden needed moisture. The peasants in the countryside must feel as she did.

A servant handed her a message. Paul was in the midst of buttering a roll. 'It's from Michou,' she told him. 'The Comte de Serre unexpectedly returned to his Louvre apartment late last night. She and Adrienne are keeping an eye on him. Michou thought the colonel would want to know.'

'Indeed!' Paul put down the roll and took the message from Anne. After reading it, he leaned back in his chair and stared out over the garden for a few moments. 'Why would he cut short his vacation by several weeks?' Paul fell into an uneasy silence.

'We shall certainly hear from him,' Anne replied. 'He is bent on mischief.'

'I was expecting you,' Moretti said, as a servant showed Anne and Paul into the first-floor drawing room that overlooked Place Dauphine. Anne had brought pen and ink and paper to take notes. Moretti glanced nervously at her. At midmorning, he was well groomed as usual, but his red-rimmed eyes witnessed to a sleepless night. He led them to chairs by the glowing fire. 'This will draw the dampness from your clothes.'

Paul raised an eyebrow in surprise. 'Why should you expect us? I haven't said we were coming.'

Moretti's voice grew tentative. 'I've heard that Pierre's been arrested while attempting to escape.'

'That's correct. And, as you have surmised, we discovered a sealed envelope containing travel papers, a letter of credit, and a letter of recommendation. These documents must have taken weeks to prepare. Tell me why you gave them to Pierre.'

'I won't insult your intelligence, Colonel. The contents of

221

that envelope were in response to extortion. No surprise there. That was Pierre's chief profession, and he was very good at it.' Moretti paused, looked plaintively at Paul, then at Anne, as if embarrassed to proceed.

'Continue, monsieur.'

'A noble woman's honor is at stake, Colonel. I promised to protect her name.'

'Would you rather that we ask Pierre? He has no reason to preserve the secret now. Inspecteur Quidor, you can be sure, will persuade him to reveal all.'

Moretti capitulated. 'I'd rather that you hear it from me. Pierre will present a distorted version.' He stopped to take a deep breath. 'Despite what had happened to my nephew, Virginie and I did fall in love and were intimate. I had come to realize that she could not have left him dying. For all her faults, she was really a decent person. A few days before her death, we had decided to separate. She could not marry me, she also feared the count. He could be heartless and brutal.'

'Did Pierre find out?' asked Paul.

'Yes. He spied on us. Discovered our secret. But he needed solid evidence. The morning Virginie died, he searched through her papers, found letters she had written but never sent to me, and a diary.'

How could Pierre find intimate papers so easily? Anne wondered. The countess must have hidden them. Anne raised her hand. 'May I ask, did someone help Pierre spy on you and find the papers?'

Moretti replied with a bitter smile. 'Your suspicion is correct, madame. A servant helped him.'

'Cécile?'

'Yes. She and her husband saved nothing. The count paid them poorly. Yet, after the countess's death, they left Château Serre and immediately opened a shop on Rue Sainte-Anne.'

Anne wondered, what kind of transaction had Cécile secretly entered into with Pierre. Had he paid for the papers? That didn't seem likely. Contrary to what Cécile told her parents, the money for the shop must have come from an illegal source. Pierre discovered it and forced Cécile's hand. Anne's curiosity was further aroused, but she signaled Paul to continue.

He asked Moretti, 'Has Pierre given the intimate papers to you in return for the envelope?'

'No, his sister has them and was supposed to send them to me when he arrived safely in Italy. That dubious arrangement rested upon a thief's honor, I realize, but I had no choice. Apart from the indecency of exposing our relationship to the public's prurient eyes, I also was reluctant to anger the count. Our business association was useful. And, more important, it was unwise to shame him, to expose him as a cuckolded husband. He could become violent and try to harm me or challenge me to a duel.'

'How would you describe your relationship to the Fauve family?'

'Prior to Pierre's theft of Virginie's papers, there wasn't any relationship. After the extortion began, he tried to keep me in sight, arranged meetings, sometimes at his sister's brothel. And the old lady, Victoire, spied on me. I wanted to hold his goodwill, so I complied with his demands for money, the travel papers, and the like. In return, he supplied Louise to me on several occasions.' Moretti's brown eyes had grown dark with anger and shame. 'In hindsight,' he said in a low voice, more to himself than to Anne and Paul, 'Fauve made a fool of me. I should have killed him.'

Anne felt uncomfortable witnessing Moretti's abject confession. This rich, cultivated, proud gentleman was forced to dance to the tunes of the count's bastard son, a pimp, a spy, a criminal hiding in the sewers of Paris.

Paul let several seconds pass in heavy silence, then said quietly, 'That will be all for now, monsieur. You have aided a fugitive in his attempt to escape from the King's justice. And you are still a suspect in Bouchard's murder. For the time being, you are confined to Paris and its environs.'

On the way home, Anne stopped at the Louvre to visit Michou and Adrienne Bouchard. Paul continued on to Thérèse Fauve's brothel. He would try to secure the countess's diary and other stolen papers. Anne hadn't seen Michou since yesterday in Hamel's studio. She hadn't seen Adrienne since almost two weeks ago, and wondered how far her work on the *Andromeda* had progressed.

Anne found the two women busy in the studio. Michou was posing nude, tied to a makeshift cliff. Adrienne beckoned Anne to the easel. The painting seemed completed. The figure of Andromeda was now quite plainly Michou, her body stretched to escape from the menacing sea monster. Her large green eyes looked hopefully at handsome young Perseus coming to save her.

At a break in the work, Michou wrapped herself in a robe and reported that she and Adrienne had organized a watch on the count's apartment, to see who came and went. Michou had hardly finished signing, when one of Adrienne's acquaintances among Serre's servants entered the studio and said that Serre was dressing to go out in his finest silk suit, a sword at his side—and a package of rat poison in his pocket. The acquaintance was sure of the last item. The count took it from the kitchen when he thought no one was watching.

Anne decided to follow him in disguise. She pinned up her hair, darkened her face with powder, then rushed to the dead Bouchard's wardrobe and put on one of his suits and a hat. Passing a mirror, she cast a glance. The fit was loose in the shoulders but good enough.

She left just in time. Serre was crossing the Cour Carrée toward the east portal. She hurried after him, but when she reached the portal, he had disappeared in the crowd. Where would he go with a package of rat poison? She could think of only one place, the Hôtel-Dieu, where he might try to silence the wounded Pierre. She had noticed that the count moved slowly. If she hastened, she could reach the hospital before he did.

At the hospital, Georges and the guard were talking outside the room where Pierre lay. They didn't recognize Anne at first. 'What brings you here?' Georges exclaimed.

'The Comte de Serre is coming with a package of rat poison.'

'What?' Georges gaped.

Anne quickly described Serre's unexpected arrival in Paris and his strange, threatening behavior.

'I think we can lay a trap for him,' said Georges. Though still groggy, Pierre had recovered well enough for an interrogation. In brief, he claimed that the count had killed Bouchard. Gillet had simply stumbled into the river while drunk. The count had also poisoned the tea for the guard in the château's basement, freed Pierre, and slit Rivard's throat.

'I think his story is plausible,' Georges concluded. 'Though perhaps he gave Gillet a push. In any case, the count is the chief villain. Pierre might help us prove it.'

As a dangerous, if wounded felon suspected of murder, Pierre had been taken to one of the hospital's few isolated strong rooms. Peepholes were hidden in the walls, through which the patient could be observed. Pierre's room was furnished with a bed, a table, and two chairs. Its single window was barred. The walls were irregular, the plaster gray and crumbling. The door was stout, the lock secure.

When Georges and Anne entered the room, the patient's eyes were closed. He awoke with a start, grimaced as if they were coming for his execution. 'I was dreaming of you,' he said to Georges. His eyes shifted to Anne, still in disguise. He blinked, shook confusion from his mind. 'And I know *you*, the colonel's wife.'

Anne nodded. The man seemed weak, vulnerable, almost childlike. The crafty look had diminished.

'Let's be quick,' said Georges. 'We're giving you a chance to prove your innocence, or at least point to the principal villain. The Comte de Serre, your father, is coming here—to poison you.'

Pierre stared at Georges with disbelief.

'Yes, we know he's your father. And, believe me, he's in Paris, probably entering the hospital at this moment, and carrying a small bag of rat poison.' Georges leaned close to Pierre, locked eyes, and said slowly, 'This is what you must do . . .'

Pierre thought his heart would burst, it was pounding so hard. His shoulder hurt, stabbing him with pain whenever he moved. The laudanum they gave him barely eased the torture but dulled

225

his mind as well. And now, if ever, he needed to think clearly. His intricate web of patrons and clients had served him over many years, and had made him rich and feared. But it had suddenly fallen apart. Now he lay wounded, helpless, threatened by the police and by his own father.

He heard voices just outside the door—must be his father talking to the guard. A key turned in the lock, and the door swung open. His father walked in, the door closed behind him.

'How are you, Pierre?' the old man asked. He seemed to have aged years in a few days. His cheeks were pale and sunken, his eyes glistening. He took a few uncertain steps toward the bed.

'As well as can be expected, Father.' This was the first time in his life that Pierre had ever addressed him thus. It felt strange on the tongue.

The old man appeared not to notice Pierre's new familiarity. He seemed fatigued and sat down near the bed. 'Have the police questioned you?'

'Yes, but don't worry. I didn't tell them that you ordered me to kill the countess. But I've since wondered why you did it. Was it because I told you that she made love to Moretti?'

'I observed them for myself. Yes, though she was my dearest possession, I killed her. Whenever I gaze at her portrait, I still grieve for her. But it can't be helped, she had cuckolded me. I will not tolerate an insult to my honor. That's also why I killed the painter Bouchard without regret. He was a mere insect. And I have waited for the right occasion to kill Moretti.' Serre paused for breath. 'Earlier would have aroused suspicion. And until now, I needed his help with my art collection. But no longer. I shall kill him within the hour.'

The count rose to his feet, an exalted expression on his face. His usual pallor had now given way to feverish, flushed cheeks. He rocked back and forth on his heels. Pierre felt the grip of fear. His father appeared on the verge of madness.

'Son, there's nothing worthwhile left in life for either of us. The police believe that you are the strong, clever, right arm of my will. They will condemn you in the same verdict as me and sentence you to a painful, degrading death. You must anticipate their scheme, just as I shall.' He drew a small package from his pocket and handed it to Pierre. 'Hide this powder. Take it when you have heard of my death.'

Pierre was stunned, at a loss for what to say. Conflicting emotions churned in his breast as he stared at the sick old man gazing down at him. Fear and revulsion gradually yielded to pity and a deep sadness. For decades, a cruel fate had linked them together, father and son, in an inexorable journey to this present disaster. Only now, almost at the last minute, did his father acknowledge him.

'Adieu, Pierre.' Serre squared his shoulders, turned, and strode to the door. He rapped for the guard. The door opened. For a moment, Serre hesitated, then he stepped out. The door closed behind him.

Thirty-Three

Resolution

September 20–21

The Comte de Serre paused, staring at the closed door, then strode down the hall toward an exit. Georges and Anne rushed out from the next room. 'Hold that man!' they shouted in unison. The guard raised an arm to stop him. Serre brushed it aside and marched on. The guard seemed paralyzed. His eyes shifted back and forth between the count and Georges.

Georges broke into a run, Anne close behind. They caught up with the count at the exit. Suddenly, he whirled around and pointed a small cocked pistol at Anne's head.

'Stand back,' he commanded Georges. 'Madame Cartier must come with me. If you do as I say, I shall not harm her. I have a score to settle with Monsieur Moretti. Do not interfere, or I will kill her.'

Georges was coiled to leap, his fists clenched, his eyes bulging with cold fury.

'I'll be all right, Georges,' Anne assured him. 'Do as he says.' She sensed that the count had drawn deeply from his scant reserves of emotional and physical strength. He looked twenty years younger, but he would soon fade. Then it would be easier and safer to disarm him. 'I'll be all right,' she repeated, reinforcing her words with a confident, determined smile.

Georges appeared to grasp her plan and took a step back.

The count bowed to Anne. 'I'll hail a cabriolet outside for us. Go ahead of me.' As she walked through the exit, the gun barrel jabbed into the small of her back.

The ride to Place Dauphine along the Seine was brief, tense. The count's pistol, concealed beneath a kerchief, prodded her ribs as the vehicle rocked and jolted over uneven paving stones. The count, she feared, could accidentally discharge the weapon. He seemed alternately absorbed in his own thoughts and keenly aware of her.

She ventured a question, in a low voice so as not to startle the coachman. 'Why have you waited so long for revenge?'

Serre didn't reply at first, didn't even look at her. Then he, too, spoke in a low voice. He repeated the reasons he had given to Pierre, and added, 'I didn't wish to spend the last years of my life in prison or in exile. Recently, my doctors have told me that I have only weeks, perhaps months to live. My mind and body will soon decline. I must reckon with Moretti while I'm still able.'

The cabriolet halted in Place Dauphine in front of Moretti's gallery. The count descended first, then offered Anne his left arm, while pointing the concealed weapon at her heart. In the gallery, three men and a woman were speaking with Moretti in front of a painting. Anne recognized it as from the count's collection, one of those being offered for sale.

'Leave the gallery immediately,' the count ordered the visitors.

They stared at him, wide-eyed with disbelief.

'Get out!' He pointed the pistol at them.

Fear flashed on their faces and they hastened toward the door.

Meanwhile, Anne watched Moretti. For a moment, he was taken by surprise, but he quickly realized his danger. He inched sideways until he stood in front of a rack of walking sticks and canes. His right hand reached among them.

The count seemed to have forgotten Anne, cowering quietly beside him. He shoved the pistol into his pocket. 'I'm saving it for myself,' he told Moretti. Then he reached for his sword. 'This is for you, dog.'

The weapon seemed to leap from the scabbard and hovered in the air, poised to thrust. But in that same moment, Moretti whipped a long, slender blade from the gold-headed cane and pierced the count's throat.

What happened next was a blur in Anne's mind. The count's body had scarcely hit the floor when Georges burst open the door.

'Thank God, you're safe!' he cried, embracing Anne.

She felt strangely calm. The shock, she knew, would come later. 'He's dead,' she said quietly.

Georges stepped back and stared at the count lying crumpled in a pool of blood, at Moretti cleaning his blade, then at Anne. 'I've sent for Quidor. This is his job. Should be here in minutes.'

As predicted, the burly inspector walked in with a pair of his agents. Anne and Georges explained briefly what had happened.

'I'll take statements from you later.' He shook his head. 'There's a crowd already gathered outside. Rumors are flying like sparks from an anvil. In an hour, the whole city will know the story.'

A bell rang in Anne's head. She turned to Georges. 'The count told Pierre to take the poison at the news of his death. That may reach him quickly.'

They ran from the gallery, pressed through the crowd, and jumped into the count's cabriolet still standing idle. In a few minutes, they were back in the hospital and racing to Pierre's room. Georges fell short of breath. 'Go ahead,' he said. 'I'll catch up.'

'Open!' Anne commanded the guard. He looked bewildered, but he thrust the key into the lock, turned it, and pulled on the door. Anne darted in.

229

Pierre was sitting up in bed, his face a mask of pain. In his left hand he held a cup. A little bag lay open on the bedside table. As he raised the cup to his lips, Anne dashed forward and knocked it from his hand. The cup flew across the room and shattered against the wall, water splashed on the floor. She seized the bag, pulled the drawstrings tight, and put it into her pocket.

'The guard just told me that Serre's been stabbed. Is he dead?'

'Yes.' Anne studied the man's face, noticed perhaps a flicker of feeling.

Georges joined her, glanced at Pierre, then at Anne. 'Did you get here in time?'

Anne nodded.

'The cup held only water, madame. Thank you, anyway. I opened the little bag, then decided I'd rather trust the King's justice, and my own wits.'

An hour later, Anne met Paul in front of Moretti's gallery. News of Serre's confession and subsequent eruption into violence had not yet reached him.

He surveyed the agitated crowd of curious onlookers staring at the building. 'What's happened here?'

'Moretti has killed Serre.' Anne briefly described the count's visit with Pierre at the Hôtel-Dieu and his failed assault on Moretti in the gallery. At that moment, the door opened and the count's body was carried without ceremony to a common cart hitched to a donkey.

Paul's expression had become somber. 'I'm grateful you weren't harmed.' He embraced her tenderly. As the donkey began to pull the cart away, Paul added, 'Serre had no friends or relatives to care for his body or to mourn. I'll make the final arrangements.'

A fitting gesture, Anne thought, one of the King's officers honoring another. After all, Serre had served in war alongside Paul's father. 'Where have you been?' Anne asked.

'With Thérèse Fauve.' He patted the portfolio under his arm. 'Quidor's agents threatened to tear her brothel apart and arrest all its occupants. With a promise of consideration from

230

the magistrate who would hear her case, I persuaded Thérèse to give up the countess's diary and letters, together with her brother's hoard of extortion materials. We must decide what to do with them.'

'There's other unfinished business we should attend to,' Anne remarked.

Paul glanced quizzically at her. 'And what's that?'

'The damaged portrait of the Comtesse de Serre.' Anne was thinking as much of her friend Michou's personal advantage as of the finished painting's intrinsic worth.

'Yes,' said Paul. 'Now that the count is dead, who shall pay for it? Possibly the Crown. If not, Hamel might abandon the project.'

'I know a better solution right here at Place Dauphine.'

Monsieur Moretti had closed his gallery and was upstairs resting by a glowing fireplace in his parlor. He welcomed his visitors, sat them comfortably facing him, and served them cider. His cane leaned against his chair. Anne wondered why.

He read her thoughts. 'It's my talisman.' He rubbed its golden head.

'Were you at all surprised that the count attacked you?' asked Paul.

'Not really. It was only a question of when. That's why I adopted the habit of carrying the cane or having it near me.'

'How has the count's death affected you?' Anne asked. The shocking violence of a few hours ago had left his cheeks rather pale and drawn. His customary self-control concealed any deeper anxiety he might have experienced.

'I have no regrets. He deserved death for killing Virginie. The sale of the goods he entrusted to me has become more complicated. But I'm relieved to be free of suspicion for the crimes he committed.'

Paul opened his portfolio and glanced at Anne. She nodded. He turned to Moretti. 'I have retrieved these items from Thérèse Fauve.' He held up the countess's diary and letters for Moretti to see.

For what seemed a long moment, he stared first at the diary, then at the letters. An expression of sorrow came over his face. Anne thought he might be about to weep. But he pointed to the items and addressed Paul in a normal voice. 'How shall you deal with them?'

'My wife and I have read them and have determined that they are not relevant to any judicial proceeding. They contain only the countess's most personal reflections. While she was alive, she hid them from others. We can best respect her wishes now by destroying them. They will no longer pose a threat to you.'

Moretti nodded agreement with Paul's decision, and murmured, 'Yes, that would be best.' But his eyes betrayed his disappointment. Anne felt certain that he wanted to read what the countess had written about him.

To Anne, he was too much of an actor, as well as a lothario toward women. Though she doubted his sincerity, she said nonetheless, 'The nearly finished portrait of the Comtesse de Serre should soon be available for purchase. You might want to contact the painter Hamel.' Anne had Michou's commission chiefly in mind.

Moretti seemed to calculate where his advantage lay. 'I didn't realize he was working on it again. If he's incorporating your little friend's copy, it should be a fine painting. I must ask myself whether I could live with its painful memories.' He paused, reflecting for a moment. '*Amor vincit omnia.* Love overcomes all. I shall tell Hamel that I wish to buy it. Even to think of her now warms my heart.'

Anne was sorely tempted to call him a liar, but she held her tongue.

At the nearby Cathedral of Notre Dame, Anne and Paul rested on a bench facing the great west facade. Paul glanced at her. 'How could you know what the count said to Pierre while they were alone in the hospital room?'

'Through peepholes in the wall I could see the count's full face only a few paces away. He spoke slowly and clearly. From his lips, his expressions, and his gestures, I caught the gist of what he was saying. Afterward, Pierre repeated the conversation with his father. I wrote it down, then compared it with what I remembered. Virtually the same. Pierre signed it before two witnesses.'

'Well done. It should satisfy the magistrates hearing this case.' He put the report into his portfolio.

The sinking sun cast a soft, golden light on the church's west front. Anne's eyes were drawn to the central portal and its majestic sculpture of the Last Judgment. Christ sat there in majesty. Beneath him, demons dragged the damned souls into hell and angels lifted the saved into heaven.

Anne shuddered in spite of herself. 'What do you think will happen to Pierre and his family?'

'Punishments ranging from severe to light,' Paul replied. 'In the eyes of the law, Pierre served as the instrument of the count's murder of his wife and shares the guilt. He also marked Bouchard for death, supplied the poniard, arranged the body to cast suspicion on Moretti or Hamel. He probably pushed a drunken Gillet into the river, though we can't prove it. The engraver apparently had observed the Bouchard murder and had begun to ask for money.'

'On the other hand,' countered Anne, 'Pierre helped us obtain his father's confession.'

'Yes, he is also willing to share his vast knowledge of crime in Paris with the police. Hence, he is likely to escape the hangman's noose and be sentenced to life at hard labor in one of our naval prisons—in the eyes of many, a fate worse than death. As a convicted felon, he will lose his inheritance. The count's property will go to the Crown. But even in prison, Pierre may find a way to make life tolerable for himself. The rest of the Fauve family will receive lesser punishments—a fine, a whipping, a day or two in the pillory, a year or two in a workhouse.'

They rose to their feet as the cathedral's bells began to toll the Angelus, the evening prayer to Mary, the mother of Jesus. All around them, the city's bustle relented a little, its raucous noise dampened. Paul took off his hat and murmured the prayers. Childhood habits died hard, Anne thought. He otherwise made little public display of his religion.

She admitted to loving the sound of church bells, whether in England or in France. They lifted her mind above the squalor and the evil that seemed at times to surround her. At this moment, the bells reminded her of the love she had received from Paul and made her vow to return it.

At noon the next day, Anne heard Paul return to his office. He had left early in the morning for a conference at the lieutenant-general's office on the results of the Bouchard case. Decisions had to be made concerning the Fauve clan and the Comte de Serre's property.

'Do you have any news to share, Paul?'

'Some interesting pieces, Anne.' He beckoned her to a chair, then explained that Baron Breteuil had already sent one of his aides to administer the Serre estate until a permanent arrangement could be put in place. In the meantime, Laure and Vincenzo would remain at their posts. Cécile had returned to her shop.

'What has happened to the scandalous documents recovered from the Fauve brothel?' Anne asked.

'Quidor claimed the most incriminating of them, since they could be used to solve several criminal cases in his district. But I persuaded him to let me have Monsieur Tremblay's papers as steward of the Serre estate. They belong to my jurisdiction.' He pushed a pile of documents across the table to Anne. 'Here they are, the key to Pierre's power over Cécile.'

Anne scanned a bundle of receipts, plus sheets of financial statements. 'It would take me hours to understand them, Paul. Tell me what they mean.'

'Georges and I have determined that Cécile's husband, as steward, embezzled about ten thousand livres during the months prior to leaving Château Serre and spent most of that money on the shop in Paris. Legally, the Crown could force her to restore the money to Serre's estate.'

'But,' Anne countered, 'she doesn't have any left. The shop produces barely enough for her to live on. If she had to sell it to repay the Crown, she would become destitute. That doesn't make sense. Serre paid her poorly and gave her no pension. I think she's entitled to the ten thousand, whatever the law might say.'

'I'm less sure than you where justice lies,' said Paul, 'but

I'll give Cécile the benefit of the doubt.' He pointed to the documents. 'I would like you to return them to her.'

Cécile looked up from a garment as Anne entered the shop. 'Could we speak privately?' Anne asked.

Cécile hesitated. There was much work to catch up. But, she saw that Anne had come on serious business. Cécile left the shop girl in charge and beckoned Anne to follow.

They walked past the flint-eyed concierge and climbed the stairs to Cécile's room on the first floor above the shop. It was pleasant and spacious, decently furnished. Anne inspected it carefully.

'What are you looking for?' Cécile asked, annoyed.

'Peepholes. The concierge spies on you.' Anne pointed out a couple of holes hidden in a wall. She tapped around them. 'The wall here is very thin. She can hear everything you say. Fix these problems later. Let's go to a more private place.'

Within a few minutes, they reached Comtesse de Beaumont's town house on Rue Traversine. Cécile had hardly said a word. Her face was pale, distressed. Anne ordered tea, and they sat down at a table in a parlor.

Cécile began, her eyes wavering. 'You've spoken to the concierge, I gather.' She struggled to maintain a measure of dignity.

'Yes, I have. But now I would like to hear from you. Perhaps I can help.' At that moment the tea arrived. Anne waited while it was poured and the maid withdrew. Then she asked bluntly, 'Why did Monsieur Tremblay steal ten thousand livres from the count?'

Cécile flinched. 'My husband was desperate. His health was poor. He couldn't work as steward much longer. We had no savings, no pension. So, without telling me, he took the money. Told me a cousin had left it to him. I doubted his story, but I didn't object. Soon afterward, the countess died. Pierre came to me with proof of the theft and demanded that I give him her diary and other private papers, or else he would denounce my husband to the count. My husband and I would go to prison; Laure and Vincenzo would lose their jobs. So I did what he asked.'

'But he wasn't satisfied, was he?'

'No, shortly after my husband's death, Pierre demanded money from my shop. Claimed he owned a share. When I couldn't pay, he collected in bed.' Cécile cast down her eyes. 'The concierge has told you, hasn't she?'

'Yes, but without explaining the circumstances. Do you know that the police have arrested Pierre?'

Cécile nodded without enthusiasm, believing perhaps that such a clever man could still elude punishment and continue to tyrannize her.

'He will spend the rest of his life in a naval prison, deprived of his chief weapon against you.' Anne pulled Monsieur Tremblay's papers from her portfolio and handed them to Cécile.

She studied them, speechless. Incredulity spread over her face. 'Is this all of them?'

'Yes,' Anne replied, 'you are free.'

Thirty-Four

Beauty Restored

October 3

The sky had darkened and let loose a torrential rainfall on Paris. Anne, Michou, and Paul shook water from their coats as they climbed the stairs once more to the Salon of 1787. It had reopened in the Louvre a few days earlier. Artists whose work had been poorly displayed had complained bitterly. So the Academy rearranged the exhibition, giving the malcontents better positions on the walls, removing inferior works, adding a few noteworthy new ones.

Among the additions was Bouchard's *Andromeda*, listed under his name, though finished by his wife. She could draw consolation from the Crown's purchase of the painting.

Fortunately, critics took notice of her hand in the work, especially in the sacrificial maiden, rendered with such chaste feeling, technical skill, and dramatic truth. Their praise would help win portrait commissions for her, and sufficient income to open her own studio.

Another addition was Hamel's portrait of the Comtesse de Serre, mounted in its rightful place on the entrance wall. The academician had successfully repainted the damaged portion. Moretti paid 6,000 livres for it. Michou received her ten per cent.

Gathered in front of the portrait, the three friends fell into a reflective mood. Anne felt profoundly moved by the image of the dead countess who stood facing her, life-like in her red riding dress and tricorn hat, riding crop in her right hand. To Anne's eyes, the woman's beauty seemed even more vibrant and complex, since getting to know her better. The sensuality in her lips and mouth, the smoldering fire in her dark brown eyes, revealed an impulsive and passionate nature. A slightly hesitant tilt of her head, the hint of sadness in the smile on her lips, the soft texture of her creamy white skin suggested a tender, yearning, almost child-like spirit.

Michou's version of the portrait had captured all this. Anne simply hadn't noticed. She asked Michou, 'From what you have learned about the countess, would you paint her portrait differently now?'

'No,' she signed thoughtfully, 'When I copied her portrait, I recognized the kind of person that she was.' She pointed to the painting, shook her head. 'How could Bouchard bring himself to destroy such loveliness? An artist is supposed to see beauty in God's world and recreate it for us to enjoy.'

Anne replied, 'He resented losing the commission. Money mattered more to him than art.'

'Then the count killed him,' added Paul, 'for a fancied insult to his honor, and he killed Virginie for the same reason.'

Her murder prompted Anne to wonder aloud, 'Is it possible that Virginie's beauty was somehow at fault, as if it had a peculiar quality that bewitched men, deprived them of common sense?' She paused to weigh the idea. 'The count believed that he owned her, a masterpiece of his collection. Moretti tried to steal her for himself. They fought over her to the death. May we say that her beauty was deadly?'

Paul replied, 'Virginie, like Helen of Troy, aroused passions in men, which they failed to control. They chose to fight each other over who would have her. Rather like our Kings' fight over Canada or Gibraltar.'

Anne agreed with a nod. 'So, a deadly evil hid in the hearts of these men who lusted, then killed, for her beauty.' As she gazed at the portrait, a wave of deep sadness came over her. She sighed, 'What a pity!'

NOTES

The value of French money remained largely unchanged in the sixty years prior to the Revolution. The livre was the basic medium of exchange and equal in value to twenty sous. Twenty-four livres were worth one louis d'or, a gold coin. Three livres equaled one écu, a silver coin. In France, the louis was exchanged for one British guinea.

For a sense of the value of French money, consider that in the 1780s, a typical artisan earned annually about 450 livres. A country priest earned about 750 livres. The Cardinal de Rohan, principal figure in the scandal of the Queen's necklace, enjoyed an annual income of some 500,000 livres. The royal government's annual income was about 500,000,000 livres. Its annual expenditure was about 600,000,000. A convenient, accurate source for prices in the 1780s is Thomas Jefferson's *Memorandum Books* (two volumes, Princeton: Princeton UP, 1997). At the time, he was the American ambassador to the French Court.

The 6,000 livres that the fictitious Monsieur Hamel expected for his portrait of the Comtesse de Serre was typical for prominent members of the Academy. In real life, his colleague in the Academy Elisabeth Vigée Le Brun was paid 2,500 livres for painting the Bailli de Crussol's portrait. Calonne, the Comptroller-General, paid her over 4,000 livres for his portrait. Princess Lubomirski sent her 12,000 livres for a portrait of her nephew. See Vigée Le Brun's *Memoirs* (Bloomington: Indiana UP, 1989).

Then, as now, most artists struggled to earn a living, little better than an artisan's.

Thomas Crow, in *Painters and Public Life in Eighteenth-*

Century Paris (New Haven: Yale UP, 1985), offers a view of life among artists.

In 1787, the Palace of the Louvre was unfinished and about half the size of the present museum. After the Royal Court moved to Versailles at the end of the seventeenth century, construction nearly ceased. The building was turned over to the royal academies, the Royal Printing Office, and other royal institutions. Apartments were granted to artists and to royal favorites, such as the fictitious Comte de Serre. In 1793, the revolutionary republican government transformed the Louvre into a museum, enriched with confiscated royal, noble, and ecclesiastical collections. Napoleon filled the Louvre with art looted from Italy and other lands conquered by French armies.

On the eve of the Revolution, the sewers of Paris were at a primitive stage of development, not yet an interconnected system. For a detailed description, read Victor Hugo's *Les Misérables*, Volume V, Books Two and Three. I used the illustrated edition, translated by Isabel Hapgood (New York: Thomas Crowell, 1887).